STALKS

JENNA MOQUIN

LIQUID MIND PUBLISHING

PROLOGUE

The forest doesn't scare me anymore. The rustling tree branches and bird caws fall into a backbeat behind me and are nowhere near enough to harm me. I'm moving too fast this time.

My nails scrape the lace of the wedding dress as I pull up the skirt and pump my legs as I run. I focus only on getting past the trees in my path, with no sense of direction. I don't care where I'm going as long as it's away from here.

Branches scratch the sleeves and tear the dress, and twigs and rocks jab my bare feet but it doesn't slow me down. I'm used to the pain by now. The forest thickens and dims the sunlight. A growl comes from somewhere distant. I'm short of breath, but I keep running for what feels like hours.

Soon the sunlight brightens and the forest opens to a brief clearing, and the edge of a cliff looms up—I skid into the ground like I'm stealing bases in softball and slide on my hip. A big rock saves me from going over the edge.

I drop down to my knees and peek over the edge. The waves crash against jagged rocks, and the cliff's edge curves inward to a clearing lined with trees.

No one could survive that jump. Least of all me. And what if I hit that clearing instead? I'll be lying there with broken bones and gangrene before anyone finds me.

My throat closes in a knot, and tears fall onto the blood stains in the wedding dress. My stomach churns and I hold back the bile creeping up my throat. Take some deep breaths, close my eyes, and feel the sun on my face.

When I said yes to Jared, despite my misgivings, I'd never imagined something like this would happen. The ring isn't on my finger anymore, but it feels like it is.

Twigs snap behind me. Did he follow me out here? I whip my head around—nothing there. I turn back toward the cliff as a seagull glides down to the water. Right before it reaches the surface, the bird pumps its wings and flies back up in a glorious arc.

I stand up at the edge of the cliff, my legs shaking. The water looks so inviting, as if I can just dive right in, maybe do a cannonball, with no repercussion. Pretend I'm diving off the raft at the pond—no big deal, just a quick dip and then I'll head home. To that final resting place.

I'm waiting for my life to flash before my eyes, but nothing is happening besides the sounds of waves and nature around me. Maybe remembering that base I stole at last week's softball game when I slid into the ground is all I got.

A twig snaps, more loudly than the last one. He must be getting closer. I move along the edge of the cliff with my eyes on my feet. The waves crash against the jagged rocks that I'll probably land on if I go over.

I don't know if that's better or worse than facing what's behind me.

ONE

WHEN YOUR BOYFRIEND tells you it's been arranged for him to marry another woman, that can make you re-evaluate the relationship. I've been dating Jared for almost two years, and while getting married isn't on my to-do list, giving him up for another woman isn't on my agenda either.

We're on our way to his parents' grand house in Brookline to pick up some things for our Sunday afternoon picnic when he decides to drop the bombshell. I guess he hadn't thought to do this at his place, or even mine, or out to dinner. No, he thought it better to casually drop it in the middle of a light-hearted conversation about the weather. Here, along the tree-lined streets of Brookline, while preppy families walk strollers and Labradors around us. *So, my parents are arranging my marriage to this other woman*, as if he's commenting on the fall foliage.

I stare up at Jared—who's an entire foot taller than me—and blink as I ask, "Who is she?"

He stops walking, and I nearly bump into him. He sighs and looks away from me.

"Her name is Abigail Adams."

If that isn't the most blueblood Boston name, I don't know what is.

"We're distant cousins," Jared says as his eyes find their way back to mine.

I can only manage to stare at him. "What?"

"I know...it's creepy. I've always found it creepy, the idea of marrying a blood relation, even a distant one. They do it in other countries, but still, it doesn't sit well with me."

I nod, feigning comprehension. "A relative? Isn't that...illegal, or something?"

"No, not really. I think there are laws against siblings marrying, immediate family, but not distant cousins."

"But...that's still weird. Why do your parents want you to marry her?"

He rubs a hand on the back of his neck, looking away from me again. "It's what they do. They arranged Preston's marriage too. There's no blood relation, but they picked Lacey for him. He didn't just meet her serendipitously."

"But they seem happy."

They really do, too. We went on a double date with his brother Preston a couple of months ago, and he and Lacey were very affectionate. But how can that be if the marriage is forced?

"They are a good match—they just didn't choose each other. It's different. I don't like the idea of someone else choosing who I'm going to spend the rest of my life with. I love my family, and tradition is important, but this one is so out of whack I can't get my head around it."

"Wow." I sigh and wrap my arms around myself. "I just can't believe this."

Warmth spreads in my cheeks and dampness in my armpits as I let this news digest. Is this his roundabout way of saying he's about to break up with me? Then why are we going on a picnic? Prolonging the breakup until the end of the date is just a form of torture if that's his plan.

"Liz." Jared takes my hands and looks into my eyes. "I told them I'm not doing it."

My face lights up and tears sting the corners of my eyes.

"Really? You're not going to marry that Abigail cousin?"

"Are you kidding? The thought of marrying a relative makes my skin crawl. Besides, I love you."

He leans down and kisses me, and all I want to do is wrap my legs around him and have him carry me to the closest available bed. But we can't. We're in the middle of the street, about to walk into his parents' place.

And then it hits me.

He just told his parents he's not marrying the woman they want him to marry.

And he's about to walk in there with the common, lower-tier class woman he's currently dating. His parents probably hate me.

Jared holds my hand as we approach the door. I get this weird sensation that something big has shifted. Something has changed in our relationship. Despite how long we've been dating, the subject of marriage has never come up until now. It had to at some point, but I never expected it to be regarding him marrying a distant cousin.

I take a deep breath as we cross the threshold, while wringing my hands. His parents' house is like a big museum, only missing roped-off barriers to keep visitors from touching portraits and other items on display. And everything in that house is on display, from the artwork to the vintage furniture and wine racks. Whenever I come here it feels exactly like going to a museum, where I need to keep quiet, subdued, and on my best behavior. The first time his mother Katharine showed me around the house, nearly everything had a story behind it, some family heirloom passed down over the years or given to the Galbraiths from another prominent family.

The foyer holds the accomplishments of Jared and Preston on tiered shelves. There are dozens of plaques and ribbons from decathlons, both athletic and academic. Each son has his own little shrine with school photos and their many achievement placards, as well as a bronzed pair of baby shoes next to their diplomas.

The sound of no-nonsense heels clicking against the Spanish tile grows louder in my ears as the room grows colder.

"Hello, Elizabeth."

Everyone calls me Liz, including her son. But Katharine still calls me by my full name. I don't know if it's because she prefers formal names, or if she does it just to annoy me. Boyfriends' mothers have never liked me—I think my well-endowed figure gives them a wanton-woman vibe.

"Hello Mother," Jared says, and lets go of my hand. He takes two big strides over to Katharine and embraces her.

"It's lovely to see you as always, dear," Katharine drawls as she pulls away from her son.

"Did you find the big picnic basket?"

"Yes, I did. I have some other things for your picnic as well. There's food in the fridge, Jared. Elizabeth, come this way—I have something to show you."

She flicks her wrist at me and walks toward the French doors. I shrug at Jared, and he smiles and saunters off to the kitchen.

Katharine leans down toward a hutch and comes back up with a handful of cream-colored napkins.

"These are the monogrammed napkins from my wedding."

She hands me the set and I see they're initialed BKG. For

Bradly and Katharine Galbraith. Or does Jared's father's middle name start with a K?

"They're lovely," I say, fingering the lettering. Silver and gold threads, striking against the cream color of the linen.

"I'm sure you know how my son feels about you," she says, her icy blue eyes staring into mine.

I try not to cower under her gaze and hold my breath as I look back at her, deep into her eyes. I can sense the love for her son, and how much she cares about him. How precious he is to her, how much it means for her to approve of the woman he's dating. And just from the way she's looking at me, I know she does not approve of me. Katharine has never approved of me.

"Yes, I do." I let my breath out. "I feel very strongly about him as well. He's a wonderful man."

I'm gripping the napkins hoping the sweat from my palms won't stain the precious monogrammed linen.

"He is."

"And I think that's a testament to his mother, and how she raised him." Hoping that this little form of flattery makes her relax and stop staring at me like that.

"I agree. Breeding and upbringing are very important traits in how a person will turn out as an adult."

She tilts her head, so she's somewhat looking down her nose at me. I know what she's saying with that look. That I'll never be good enough for her son.

But that's okay because I don't want to get married anyway. To anyone. I'll never say this to her face, but I'm just having fun with Jared, happy being his Marilyn Monroe before he marries his Jackie O. Where the only thing I'm planning for is this Sunday afternoon picnic, and what restaurant we'll try out next Friday night.

Jared bringing up his refusal to marry Abigail Adams was a

jolt, not just from the news itself, but that *I* might be the reason he doesn't want to marry her. The way Katharine is acting toward me, it's making me suspicious of that as well, as if she's begrudgingly accepting me into the family. And that frightens me. I don't want to think about marriage right now, and this whole scenario just dropped into the wonderful bliss of no commitment I've been living in with my tall, handsome, rich boyfriend.

"Well, well, well, if it isn't Elizabeth Martel!" Jared's voice, in a British accent, floats into the room when he walks in from the kitchen.

It makes me smile. I happen to have the same name as a British supermodel. We even look similar with our blonde bobs and pale skin. She did a commercial with a voiceover saying: "Well, well, well, if it isn't Elizabeth Martel!" and then a mention of whatever product she wore for the ad. I think it was some makeup campaign, or maybe perfume.

Jared leans down and kisses me full on the lips, in front of Katharine, which is a bit awkward and uncomfortable. It's like he's trying to prove something.

Katharine clears her throat, and I pull away from Jared.

"Jared, dear." Katharine flicks her hand at him. "I want to show you something."

"What is it?"

"We've framed one of the portraits of your Aunt Jolene. I thought you'd like to see it. It's in the library."

She turns and walks toward the foyer. Jared and I follow.

"Aunt Jolene?" I glance at Jared.

"My aunt who went missing a few years back."

"More than a *few* years!" Katharine looks back at us. "She's been gone for nearly twenty years. She was legally declared dead over a decade ago."

She gestures at the two of us to follow her into the library, where she points toward the mantel. The stone fireplace is enormous, almost big enough to stuff a small person such as myself inside. I look up to see a gold-framed portrait of a blonde woman wearing a yellow dress, with a field of sunflowers behind her. The golden hue overload is jarring. I look up at Jared, and his eyes are downcast, as if he doesn't even want to look at the portrait.

"What side of the family was Jolene on?"

"She was Bradley's older sister," Katharine says. "His only sibling."

"What happened?"

"Jolene battled addiction most of her life. She would sometimes run off for days at a time, and then return home apologetic, and spend another twenty-eight days at a facility trying to clear her head."

"That's so sad."

"And one day, she left and never came home."

"I'm sorry. That's awful."

"Thank you," says a deep voice from behind me.

I turn around to see Jared's father walking into the library. He resembles a much older version of Jared with his tall frame and chiseled chin. I can see how well Jared will age. His dad is a silver fox.

"Bradley," Katharine says, her expression cool and her hands clasped in front of her. "I was just showing Jared the portrait of Jolene."

"It's lovely," Jared says, and I catch him wiping beneath his eyes. I had no idea how much his aunt meant to him—he'd never mentioned her before. Maybe it's too hard on him.

"We never found her," Bradley says, placing a hand on his son's shoulder. "We weren't worried at first, thinking she'd gone on another one of her benders. But after a few weeks passed, we knew it was time to call the police. Searched for her everywhere, hired private detectives...we tried everything."

"Poor Jared was devastated. He was only ten years old at the time. He and Jolene had a special bond."

I reach over and rub his arm. "I'm so sorry."

"The painting's beautiful, Mother." Jared leans down and kisses the top of Katharine's head.

"I thought you'd like it. We're planning to redo the entire library with family portraits—I'll contact you and your brothers to pose for a new one soon."

"Another? Don't you have enough paintings of us?"

"Not nearly enough!" Katharine gives Jared's arm a playful smack and says, "Now, run along you two. Enjoy your Sunday afternoon picnic."

Bradley beams. "Have a good time."

"Thank you, Father."

"But don't forget"—Bradley points a finger at Jared, who seems to grow a bit pale—"we are meeting with Mark Adams first thing in the morning."

"Oh." Jared glances from left to right. "Right. I forgot."

"We have to settle some accounts. Looks like he won't be doing business with our firm anymore."

Bradley sighs, and Katharine reaches out to grasp his hand. Jared won't look me in the eye and he doesn't make a move to leave. Tension tightens the tendons in my neck. What's going on here? And then it hits me—Adams. Mark must be a relative of Abigail, perhaps even her father. Are they taking their business away from the Galbraith firm just because Jared doesn't want to marry their daughter? That's so...petty. But I guess getting turned down for an arranged marriage makes you re-evaluate the relationship you had with the family. Hopefully Jared didn't burn too many blueblood bridges with this.

Jared's eyes darken, his brow furrowing. "Maybe you should've thought of that before you started planning out my life for me."

"Jared!" Katharine snaps. "Lower your voice."

He sighs and rolls his eyes. "Right, we have to pretend we don't have emotions in this family."

I keep my mouth shut, my eyes on Jared. I've only seen this temper of his on occasion, and only in small doses. Like the time he threw a corkscrew at the wall after it'd broken the cork in half, and sent it into the bottle of wine. Or the time we tried to see a show that was sold out, and bribing the ticket guy didn't work. I remember how he'd kicked the door of his car and I'd backed away from him, and then his face softened and he smiled, apologizing for losing his temper. We had a good night at a restaurant after that.

His anger comes out in short bursts, but when it does it's always unsettling. And now it's happening during his family squabble, and I'm right in the middle. All I want to do is disappear and pretend I didn't witness any of this.

Bradley and Katharine glance awkwardly at me, as if they'd forgotten I was here.

"We'll talk about this tomorrow, son," Bradley says, giving Jared a stern look.

"Fine. Whatever."

Katherine's face turns around with a smile that doesn't quite reach her eyes. "Enjoy your picnic, you two. Looks like a beautiful day out there!"

As we start to leave the room, Jared turns back to his mother. "You should go out and get some sun," he says. "I think you stay indoors too much."

Katharine waves a hand at him. "I just have so much to do, dear, you know that. Being the wife of a Galbraith is a full-time job."

With that, Katharine turns her ice-blue eyes on me. Does she really think that just because Jared doesn't want to marry Abigail that I'm next in line?

No way am I marrying into this ultra-rich museum family.

As we walk down the tree-lined streets back to Jared's car, the air between us is silent. A few leaves have fallen onto the windshield of his Bentley SUV and he brushes them off with a sigh.

"Sorry if my mother was making you uncomfortable back there," Jared says as we climb into his car.

"It's okay, she was fine. No worries." I feel like I'm trying to convince myself more than him.

He doesn't press the subject further. "Let's stop at the cheese shop. She forgot the brie for the picnic basket."

"Can we pick up some wine too?"

"Sure, I won't drink too much though. We've got a long drive there and back."

I raise an eyebrow at him. "Where are we going for the picnic anyway?"

He winks at me. "It's a surprise."

"Well, Jared, unless you're blindfolding me, I'm pretty sure I'll guess where we're going on the drive."

He chuckles as my phone dings with a text. I glance down and see my sister Courteney's name light up my screen.

. . .

ARE YOU FREE TODAY? Chet's at a Sox game
   Want to grab lunch?

MY HEART TWINGES. Courteney and I used to go out to lunch practically every Sunday, back when we were both single. Lunch and window shopping, which would typically turn into shoe shopping. We haven't done that in a while—hell, we haven't spoken in months. Why is she texting me now, as though nothing has changed?

"Who is that?" Jared asks.

"Um...it's just Matt from work. Wants to know when the next company softball game is scheduled."

I glance at Jared. His eyes are on the road as he nods in acknowledgment. I tap out a reply to Courteney.

SORRY COURT but I can't—already made plans

SHE TEXTS BACK: With Jared?

I TURN off my phone and put it in my pocket. Jared turns the radio to a jazz station, and I lean back in my seat. Things have been a bit tense between me and my sister since I started dating Jared, because he dated Courteney first. And broke up with her the same day he met me.

Courteney brought Jared to our parents' thirtieth wedding anniversary for their third date. They hadn't even slept together, and already she was introducing him to our parents. But that's Courteney. She and her now-husband Chet had a whirlwind courtship and eloped, about two months after they met. I wouldn't be surprised to learn she had already been writing "Courteney Galbraith" on notepads at the time she introduced Jared to our family.

When Jared and I met at the anniversary party, a little spark of electricity passed between us when we shook hands. Jared made eyes at me during the whole evening, and I watched him as he danced with my mother to her favorite Frank Sinatra song. I found out later that he'd broken up with Courteney at the end of their date. He told her he didn't think they were the right people for each other, but that he wanted to stay friends.

A couple of weeks later, Jared called me, sounding completely casual. He asked about Courteney and how she was doing. Then he started asking about me, my job, what kind of food I liked.

When he said, "So what are you doing for dinner tonight?" I got tingles, in every spot that mattered. I'm not proud to admit this, since he dumped my sister, but that did wonders for my ego. He broke up with her just so he could ask me out. It made me feel like the most beautiful woman in the world.

I didn't agree to the date right away, though. I had to talk to Courteney. I couldn't see him unless she was okay with it, no matter how much I wanted to. Even though I'd probably date him regardless.

I told Jared it was appropriate for me to run it by my sister. He completely understood, and said he liked that about me. That made me smile. And when I brought it up with Courteney, she didn't care in the slightest since she'd already started dating someone new by then.

A few weeks later, Courteney's new boyfriend broke up with her. She started mooning over Jared, saying he was the one who got away, kicking herself for telling me it was okay to date him because she didn't really want me to. This all came out in a late-night drunken phone call, and it wasn't the last drunken phone call I'd get from her.

There was a particularly tense night at our parents' house one Christmas Eve. It was the first time I'd brought Jared to a family event. The last time everyone had seen him he'd been dating Courteney. She walked up, stumbling a bit, took our coats and brought Jared over to meet Aunt Rose and Uncle Jack.

"This is Jared Galbraith," Courteney said, her words slurring as she swayed from side to side.

"Nice to meet you," Aunt Rose said, smiling and shaking his hand. "You look awfully familiar."

"You do!" Uncle Jack smiled.

"Oh," Courteney said. "That's right you did meet, at Mom and Dad's anniversary party last summer. Back when Jared was still dating me. He dumped me for Liz the same night!"

Courteney laughed and slapped her knee. Wine sloshed out of her glass and onto the carpet.

"Oops! Looks like I need another drink!"

Jared gave Aunt Rose a tight-lipped smile, and Uncle Jack struck up a conversation about the Bruins.

My cheeks burning, I stared at the wooden clock on the wall, one of the models my dad makes and sells. His trademark shamrocks were painted along the edge. I concentrated on the shamrocks while Jared looked uncomfortable and cleared his throat several times. Courteney stared at him with glassy eyes in a seductive manner while he avoided her gaze.

My mother stepped in, took Courteney's wineglass from her, and told her she'd had enough.

"Though you can't blame her for being upset." My mother turned to Jared. "Considering how cruel and heartless some people are."

She clucked her tongue and stalked off, and then my

father began yelling about the cable going out and she put down the wineglass to calm him down. She has this way of rubbing his upper arm and speaking to him in a soft voice that always does the trick, at least most of the time. I wonder if it took her a long time to learn that trick, or if it just came naturally the first time Dad had a fit.

While Mom was busy placating Dad, Courteney picked her wineglass back up and refreshed her drink. I think she passed out in her bedroom that night.

I try not to bring up Jared's name whenever we speak, and we've been taking turns going to family events. She didn't attend our cousin's sweet sixteen party, and I didn't go to the Fourth of July barbecue. But the estrangement in my family due to Jared isn't the only issue in my family. It's just the latest case.

CHAPTER

THREE

WE STOP AT A SMALL, corner liquor store on Boylston Street before we reach the highway, and I'm amazed there's a spot right in front.

"Guess it's our lucky day!" Jared says. "I want to get going, so if you're okay with no brie for the crackers, let's just grab the wine and head out."

"I'm fine without brie. You're the one who's so picky about it anyway."

Jared grins and winks at me. I step out of the car into the warm September sunshine. Now that I'm no longer in school, I love the month of September. The stifling summer heat has passed, but it's still warm enough to wear sundresses and sandals and have cocktails on patios. Soon the holidays will arrive, and I can't wait to see what Jared has planned for Christmas this year. Last year he planned a trip to Aspen to get away from both of our families, and it was the best Christmas I've ever had. We went skiing and drank hot toddies by the grand fireplace in the hotel, then champagne and chocolate-covered strawberries in the jacuzzi in our suite, along with other sensual pleasures.

Jared holds the door open for me, the little bell above it chiming. The clerk behind the counter waves at us.

"Good morning!" the clerk says. "Welcome."

I smile and thank him, admiring the autumn leaf tinsel wound around the display tables and countertop.

I see my favorite wine on display.

"Yes!" I snatch up the bottle of pinot grigio.

"Make sure it's a screw-top," Jared says, then he lowers his voice, turning away from the clerk. "I didn't bring a corkscrew and the ones they sell here are kind of cheap."

I grimace, thinking about the corkscrew incident. Maybe screw-top wine bottles will just be a must in our relationship.

"Do you see any chardonnay?" Jared asks.

I glance around the small aisle, spotting riesling and sauvignon blanc—but no chardonnay.

"There's sauvignon blanc—want to get that instead, Jared?"

"Jared?"

An unfamiliar voice says his name a few feet away. I turn and see the most beautiful brunette I've ever laid eyes on. She has one of those sleek manes of hair that looks naturally thick and shiny, bright blue eyes, cream-colored skin, and pouty lips. She is also about seven or eight inches taller than me, putting her around 5'7". She's even taller in the three-inch heels she's wearing.

"H-hello," Jared stammers and runs his hand through his hair.

"Fancy running into you here," the brunette says, glancing my way.

"Just picking up some wine for a picnic." Jared slides his arm around me with a squeeze so tight there's a slight pain in my side. It's like he's trying to prove something, just like that inappropriate kiss in front of Katharine earlier.

There's a moment of silence as she glances back and forth

between us. We each stare at her. She clears her throat. "You must be Elizabeth."

"Sorry, have we met?" We've never met, but how the hell does this woman know my name?

"Yes, this is my girlfriend, Liz," Jared says. "Uh, Liz. This is Abigail."

My cheeks grow warm. *This* is Abigail Adams? The woman he didn't want to marry? My mouth hangs open for a second before I realize it and clamp my lips together.

"It's lovely to meet you." I shoot out my hand toward her, and she gingerly shakes it with a stiff smile.

"You too. I should be heading out. It was nice to see you, Jared. Hopefully we'll see each other again soon."

"I'm sure we will, at the next family gathering most likely."

I could've sworn Jared made a slight emphasis on the word "family" just then, and I also could've sworn I saw Abigail flinch.

"I'll go pay for this," Jared says, taking the wine from my hand. He turns toward the counter, and I hear him asking the clerk if they have any chardonnay from France. Then he follows the clerk toward another part of the store, leaving me and Abigail alone.

Why is she still standing here, looking at me? I thought she said she was leaving and now she's what, sizing me up? The woman Jared chose over her? Believe me, I have the same questions.

"So, uh," I stammer, not sure what else to say. "I really like your cardigan."

It's a nice shade of burgundy and flatters her slim figure. But instead of thanking me for the compliment, like a polite person would, Abigail gives me a small smile, and a head tilt.

"How quaint. I suppose I can see the appeal, you have all

of the qualities a typical red-blooded male desires. But that sort of desire doesn't last. So I doubt *you* will."

"Excuse me?" My entire body goes hot. I'm perplexed she would have the gall to say that to my face.

"I just don't think you'll be able to live up to his standards, Elizabeth."

Abigail took a step closer to me while she spoke, now just a couple inches away from me. I have to strain my neck to look into her eyes. They're so wide I can see the sclera all around her irises—it feels like I'm looking into the eyes of a madwoman. Her lips curl into a sneer as she leans toward me. I flinch, taking a step backward.

"The Galbraiths are a very special family. Just like mine. Inner circles always work best, and birds of a feather should always flock together. It just makes things work better, wouldn't you agree?"

"Listen, I know about...the arrangement, and I'm sorry it didn't turn out as planned. Jared only just told me about it this morning. It's still a bit of a shock."

She's still looking down at me with that creepy head tilt. Like I'm a bug she's about to squish. "Why is that?"

"Why? Because..." *Because he's her cousin!*

"Because you already have your hooks into him, and didn't realize you might have some competition?"

"N-no. My hooks?"

"You may have Jared now, but nothing is set in stone. All's fair in love and war."

How many more clichés is this woman going to spew out? Abigail leans down, almost touching her nose against mine. Her eyes narrow into thin slits.

"I don't give up easily."

"Jared?" My voice squeaks.

I back up a bit more, only to crash into a display of red wine, making the bottles topple. Two fall over on the shelf and one crashes to the floor—glass and red wine cascading everywhere.

"Shit." I crouch down, not sure what I'm planning to do since I don't have any towels or a trash bin.

"Liz, stop!" Jared rushes over, his voice stern. "Don't touch the glass, you'll cut yourself."

I look up at him, still crouched, and raise my right eyebrow. "I know how to pick up glass, Jared. I'm not a child."

And then it hits me that Abigail is probably still standing there, watching this whole exchange, delighting in our bickering.

I look up to see her towering figure and sly smirk, but she's not there anymore. Guess it's my lucky day. Then I look down at the broken wine bottle.

The store clerk rushes over with a mop and a bucket.

"I'll take care of that, miss. Don't worry about the bottle, we had an overstock on this brand." He smiles warmly at me and gets to work cleaning up the mess I made.

"Are you sure?" Jared says as he takes my hand and pulls me upright.

"Don't worry about it, Mr. Galbraith."

How does the clerk know his name? Just from his credit card, or are the Galbraiths *that* well known around Boston?

"Thank you," Jared says. "Let's get going, I've got the wine."

I glance at the store clerk and apologize, thanking him as we leave. As we get into the car, I keep a lookout for that creepy Abigail Adams, but she's nowhere in sight.

AFTER WE'VE SETTLED into the car, Jared takes my hand and squeezes it. He looks at me and smiles. I can tell he wants to say something but he holds back. I smile back and give a small nod, encouraging him to say whatever it is he's going to say.

A car honks behind us, and I wonder if they saw us leave the store and are waiting for us to leave so they can park there. I clear my throat.

"I'm sorry about that," he says. "I had no idea we'd run into Abigail there."

"Yeah, that was awkward." I want to tell him what she said to me while he was with the clerk looking for chardonnay, but I bite my lip. I don't want to spoil the mood, especially since our picnic hasn't even begun yet. We have the whole day ahead of us.

"She can be a bit...intense sometimes."

I shudder in my seat, thinking about those madwoman eyes. "I'll say."

"Her whole family is a bit like that. It was rumored that her grandfather had an underground compound where he trained a special security team for him and his family. They're like the 'Men in Black' or something, travel with them nearly everywhere."

"Like their own secret service?"

"Yeah and made up of supposedly former mob guys and hitmen."

"Are you serious?"

Jared shrugs, leaning his elbow on the center console. "Like I said, it's just a rumor. I mean, they do have a special bodyguard team that travels with them, but for all I know the guys are just former security guards from strip malls or something."

I laugh, picturing Abigail strolling down Newbury Street with a rent-a-cop on a Segway trailing behind her.

Jared laughs too. "Let's just forget about it and have a great day together. What do you say?"

He leans in and kisses me, and I run my hands through his hair. He has such a nice, thick head of dark hair I can't help myself sometimes. When I get older, whoever I'm with will probably be bald or have thinning hair—I want to enjoy this while I still have it.

Jared pulls away and starts the car. He waves at the jerk idling behind us, leaning on their horn, as we back out of the spot. Why are people so impatient in the city? Where I grew up it can get a bit road ragey, especially during rush hour, but people aren't jerks like this in the suburbs. I met a woman years ago who'd moved here from the Midwest, and she had the best description of Bostonians I've ever heard: "I'm not happy about where I'm going, but I'm in a really big hurry to get there!"

"So, how about that blindfold now?" Jared says and caresses my knee as we drive toward the highway.

"Are you being serious?"

He laughs. "No, not really. Unless you're into that sort of thing."

I take his hand on my knee and squeeze it with a giggle before pushing it back for him to hold the steering wheel. He likes having sex outdoors, but I've never been a huge fan. I'm always worried someone might be watching us. Not only watching us but taking videos and uploading them somewhere before we even finish. The thought of that makes me shudder.

"You cold?" Jared asks. "Want me to turn the heat on?"

"No, no, it's not that. Just had a little chill for a second, that's all."

Part of me wants to tell him the things Abigail said, the way she threatened me. I don't want her to retaliate against him or his family and their social standing. I certainly don't want to be the reason for anything like that.

How am I supposed to deal with this mess? If I really am the reason he doesn't want to marry this woman, and not just because of the family relation, we need to have a serious conversation about what we both want in life. I have a feeling it's not the same things.

I glance over at Jared, his eyes are on the road and his right hand is resting on the console. Looking down at his manicured hands, and the neatly pressed shirt sleeve, I realize that no matter how much I love him, the thought of being a "Galbraith wife" does not appeal to me. I'd rather spend Sunday mornings on my couch with a mimosa wearing flannel pajama bottoms, not at a country club with a smile plastered on my face wearing a Chanel suit.

But I've been looking forward to our picnic for so long, with my handsome, sophisticated, loving boyfriend who takes me on actual dates, and doesn't want to just "Netflix-and-chill" all the time or watch sports or play video games. I don't want to ruin this. He's a dream. It's just his family that seems a bit nutty like mine.

Maybe that's what draws us together. We both come from controlling families. Jared's parents are trying to control who he is going to spend the rest of his life with, and my parents have tried to control everything else. Who I hung out with, who I dated, what clothes I wore, what subjects I studied, books I read, shows I watched, etcetera. I get it when a child is young. Parents do have to dress them, feed them, and make choices for them—but once a child turns into a teenager, it's important to let them figure out who they are.

I remember being grounded for a whole month just for wearing a mini skirt to school when I was fourteen. I wore a peasant skirt over it on the way to school, and then changed when I got there. Courteney was the one who ratted me out.

And then there was the time I got caught sneaking around with an older boy from another school. Another tattle from Courteney. My punishment for that was being locked inside a utility closet for two days. They gave me food and water through a slot my dad built into the door, like a doggie door. It was like being inside a coffin. I've been claustrophobic ever since then. I can't even ride in elevators.

As soon as I hit junior year of high school, I started applying for early college admission, and chose one a five-hour drive away so they couldn't just "pop in" on me. And I rarely came home. Every holiday, school break, and summer vacation I'd find some way to stay on campus, either by taking a job or extra classes for credit. I was able to graduate by the time I was twenty-one, got an apartment with my roommate Andi, and lived with her for years until I was able to afford my own place.

Courteney always did everything my parents wanted and let them control every aspect of her life. She loved it whenever I did something they didn't approve of because then she'd be cast in the spotlight as their perfect child, their good girl. Not the black sheep I am. Things have been worse since I've been dating Jared, after he broke it off with Courteney, so needless to say my parents are not big fans of my boyfriend.

As soon as we cross into New Hampshire, I know Jared's taking me somewhere remote for the picnic. Maybe Maine—but a day trip into Maine sounds like a bit much.

I'm already dozing off soon after we cross the state line. Jared didn't really need a blindfold after all since I'll probably be asleep when we reach his special picnic spot. The soft jazz on the radio combined with the passing cars creates a steady white noise. It soothes me into drifting off, and Courteney appears in my dreams. We're swimming in a lake and end up at Mom and Dad's. We're opening Christmas presents and making dream houses for our Barbie dolls. We fight over a fluffy pink couch we both want to use. We're grown up now, and the pink couch grows along with us, then morphs into Jared. We both tug at him, each of us at an arm. He's letting us do this, completely unfazed.

The sound of a car horn wakes me, and I rub my eyes and yawn. We're driving down a narrow, unpaved road lined with trees. There's a vague whiff of ocean air in the breeze. Ahead of us, the entire road is covered with leaves and forest debris. Behind us, the debris is flattened in the shape of tire treads. We're in the backwoods of somewhere rural and unkempt with lots of forest overgrowth and houses far apart from each other.

Jared stays focused on the road, only taking his eyes away to glance at the map on the dashboard. I wonder why he's using a map instead of GPS, but it's probably because he wants to surprise me.

He slams the brake pedal, stopping the car completely and pushing me forward. He doesn't seem to notice as he shakes his head. His hand grips the gear shift and he puts the car in reverse. The road is so narrow, it takes him a while to turn the car around.

He drives back the way we came, and then he turns onto another road. A gust of wind catches the map and it flutters into the windshield. The car veers to the left. Jared catches the steering wheel and jerks it back, and slams on the brakes again. His eyes darken and a small crease appears between his eyebrows. He slaps the steering wheel so hard it makes me flinch.

Are we lost? I'm afraid to ask it out loud as I watch his temper rise.

Jared sighs and reaches for the map. He steps on the gas, but instead of turning around and heading back toward the main road, he drives forward, faster than before. The road becomes so narrow the side view mirrors nearly hit the tree branches we pass. I don't see any signs for the highway. I haven't seen any houses for a while, either.

The trees around us become denser. It makes everything look darker, and later in the day than it really is. A marshy aroma replaces the saltwater scent in the air. The barest shiver passes through me and gooseflesh ripples across my forearms.

"I can't believe this is taking so long!" Jared says through gritted teeth. "I thought this was the right way."

"Want me to help navigate?"

Jared shakes his head. He pulls over, though the road is so narrow we're still very much on it. But it doesn't seem like any cars are coming by, or that anyone has driven down here in a while.

"This place doesn't have a physical address, it's a spot my father suggested. I thought I had it all mapped out. I know it's around here somewhere!"

He hits the steering wheel again and I cringe. Sometimes

changing the destination of the date helps his mood, and I get an idea.

"Why don't we just picnic on the beach? The ocean must be close by, I can smell it in the air."

"That's too common," he says with a pout, and leans back in his seat. "I wanted this to be...something..." he pauses as his fingers tap the steering wheel.

"What, Jared?"

He shakes his head. "Nothing."

Then he flashes a smile, and that pouty look vanishes. Jared's moods can swing like that, and he isn't always this temperamental. I wonder if the tension in his family right now over the broken arrangement is affecting his mood. He said he would've broken things off regardless of me, but I still feel like this is partly my fault. I shrink back in my seat, my stomach rumbling and thinking of the food in the picnic basket.

He puts his foot on the gas and drives forward, keeping his eyes on the road. Or whatever you could call the terrain we're driving over. Something about this place feels off. Jared doesn't seem to have a clue where we are, despite what he says. I'm getting a subtle sense of foreboding in the pit of my stomach along with the hunger pangs, and I'm about to ask him to just turn the car around and head home when we come upon a clearing.

The road widens and opens to a circular path with less leaves and debris. The trees are thinner and the sun shines over the tops. A bird flies by the car and tweets. To my right, a path is flanked by lush trees in the beginning stages of chlorophyll breakdown for the fall. Jared pulls up to a large rock and parks.

"This is it! I knew this was the way." He folds the map and puts it in the console between the seats.

I smile and keep a snide comment to myself. I hope he

knows where we are, and he isn't just saving face, and potentially leading us to a family of cannibals.

As if he can read my mind, he says, "Come on, you love adventures. Just trust me." He tugs my arm and I follow him out of the car. He opens the trunk and pulls out the picnic basket prepared by Katharine, complete with the monogrammed napkins from her wedding. My underarms begin to sweat even though the air is nice and crispy warm, not hot.

Jared leads me to a path between the trees, and we walk into the forest. I've left my purse behind in the car and tap Jared's arm but he doesn't turn around. I probably won't need it anyway. My phone is in my pocket, as it usually is. I've always been a fan of pockets over purses. It's too easy to leave a purse somewhere.

The air cools and the sweat in my underarms becomes clammy. A misty, woody forest scent permeates the air, and I'm getting that feeling city slickers have whenever they go into the country, like I'm about to step off the face of the earth.

"We're almost there, Liz!" Jared calls over his shoulder.

Since all I can see are trees, I have to believe that we're about to be somewhere where we can sit down and enjoy our picnic.

The trees thin out a bit and everything around us brightens. We step into a clearing that's so bright it's like walking onto a beach without sunglasses at the peak of summer. A large empty field contains a dilapidated red barn at the edge, surrounded by an old, splintery-looking fence. A tire swing hangs from a tree by a rusty chain. Some old, abandoned farm from the looks of it.

The grass is long and sprinkled with dandelions. Although they're weeds, I just love them. The way they grow so wildly and sometimes pop up in the middle of cracks in the pavement in the city. The life force breaking through the man-made concrete, finding a way to survive and flourish.

Across the field, a rusty wheelbarrow and broken white fence peek from behind the barn. It overlooks a steep hill, over which I can only see the sky. There is something so romantic about a rustic old farm. I've been to a couple farms in my life, and have probably only mentioned to Jared once, maybe twice how much I love them. I'm not sure if this is the place he'd originally intended for our picnic spot, but it is perfect.

Jared carries the basket to the middle of the field. He opens it and pulls out a king-size bedsheet and spreads it across the long grass and dandelions. I pick one from the ground, hold my breath, and wish for this moment to last a long time. I blow on the seedhead as hard as I can, open my eyes, and sigh when I see that several pieces of fluff remain on the stem.

I pull out my phone and snap pictures of the farm while Jared unpacks the rest of the basket. It says "No Service" up top, which is weird, but maybe I just need to reboot it. I'll do that later.

I repocket my phone. "Jared, this place is adorable!"

Jared grins at me, and I'm impressed by each item he pulls out from the picnic basket. Aside from the tiny bottles of wine, there are chocolate truffles, cucumber and hummus sandwiches with the crusts cut off, fruit salad, and caviar. For dessert, tiramisu—my favorite.

Jared feeds me grapes from the fruit salad, and I feed him caviar on crackers before we dig into the rest. I let myself get a bit tipsy on the wine, since I have a designated driver. Wine sometimes gives me the munchies, or drunchies as some say, and I'm happy he brought so much food.

"I wish we didn't have to go to work tomorrow," I say with a yawn. "Why do weekends slip by so fast?"

Jared smiles and kisses my forehead. After I gorge myself on bites of everything, he pulls out a basket of dinner rolls. When I notice something black resting on top of them, I nearly jump thinking it's a big bug. But when Jared remains calm and shifts position, I realize it's not.

It's a velvet ring box.

CHAPTER
FIVE

THIS IS EXACTLY what I've been afraid of since his bombshell this morning.

Jared picks up the velvet box and opens it. A princess-cut diamond ring rests inside, sparkling in the sunlight. Time stops completely and I forget how to breathe.

A surprise marriage proposal is a wonderful thing, if you want to get married. If you don't, and the man you're dating gets down on one knee and holds out a ring, you're in a tough spot.

If I say "No," this relationship will end—there's no way he'll stay with me if I turn down his marriage proposal, will he? I definitely don't want that. But if I say "Yes," it means I'm getting married, and I don't want that either. And there's that vital first reaction I have to be mindful of—any sort of hesitation looks like a "No," but it's not as if I have a lot of time to mull it over.

So, I opt to stall for as long as I can. "Jared, the ring is beautiful!"

The diamond shines and sparkles as the sunlight hits it, trying to tempt me into saying yes.

He takes the ring out of the black velvet box. He picks up my left hand and starts to put it on my third finger. I didn't say yes. He didn't even officially ask me yet, but he's already putting the ring on my finger?

My breathing quickens and I make a joke to stall. "Where did you get the ring? Did you go to JARED, Jared?" I let out a giggle.

Jared stares back at me with his eyes narrowed, and they begin to darken. He had that same scary look back in the car when we were lost. That look alone makes me want to turn him down.

But what if I say "No" and he leaves me here, stranded? His temper is so unpredictable. I don't know where we are, or how we got here. I have a feeling I can't just summon a rideshare way out here. I need him to get back home.

"Will you marry me, Liz?"

At least he finally asked the question, but the ring was already on my finger. I still don't know how to answer.

Maybe I should marry him. Will I ever find a better guy than this? Tall, rich, handsome, sophisticated. Sweeps me off my feet with picnics and surprises. Takes me to fun places and expensive restaurants. We have lots in common, too—we both like pistachio ice cream and watching old movies, especially black-and-white flicks. We both love to travel and try out new foods.

Jared clears his throat. "Liz?"

I open my mouth to say something, but I can't get out the words. I need to give him an answer, and the little crinkle between his eyebrows getting bigger by the minute makes me feel bad I'm keeping him in suspense. I wonder how many other marriages began due to the woman feeling pity toward the man kneeling and holding out a ring. Even someone who can look as intimidating as Jared, can appear vulnerable in this position. It's the Florence Nightingale effect: feeling sorry for the poor guy.

I close my eyes, take a deep breath, and say, "Yes."

And hope that I don't regret this. I open my eyes, and Jared's face lights up as he scoops me into his arms and kisses me.

"We're going to be so happy!" Jared says when he pulls away.

I smile but can't help but think those sound like famous last words. Nothing says unhappy quite like a person's consistent need to convince the rest of the world that they're happy.

I nod and stare at the ring. It really is beautiful. And huge. Jared kisses me and traces my bottom lip with his tongue, the usual indication that he wants to have sex. I'm not in the mood, but since I said yes to marriage, I probably should. He'll get suspicious otherwise, and I need time to think about whether I'm going to change my answer, or not.

Is this the life I'm potentially agreeing to, where he gets sex whenever he wants? Sure, he pretty much gets sex whenever he wants now anyway, but that's beside the point.

These kinds of thoughts go through my head while I'm giving him head on the picnic sheet. Sometimes I can't stop thinking about things during foreplay and sex. And men wonder why some of us have trouble achieving orgasms, or why we can be so hesitant about having sex. It's just different for us. Being penetrated is symbolic of being impaled, or stabbed, something violent. And in a sacred part of our bodies. Of course we want to give a lot of thought and mull over exactly who it is we're letting penetrate that sacred part. It's so much easier for men; they're the ones penetrating. Instead of being pierced open, they're doing the piercing.

When he pierces open that sacred orifice, I close my eyes and suck in a breath. It can still sometimes be a little painful on that first thrust, even after years of having sex. Maybe painful is the wrong word. More like a shivering intensity that rushes through, shocking me. But it gets better after that first thrust. Much better.

And while we're having sex, I remember just how much I love him. I guess that's why they call it making love. It makes me feel so close to him, it solidifies the bond, and when I look deep into his eyes while he's inside of me, I have no doubts that I want to be with him.

Jared thrusts deeper inside of me while holding my thighs tight, the usual indication he's about to come, and I get the strangest sensation that someone is watching us. I turn away from Jared, whose eyes are closed as he's in his moment. The field appears empty except for us.

Jared lets out a grunt as he pulls out and promptly puts on his pants. I search for a tissue to wipe myself, but there's only the monogrammed linen napkins. I grimace and pull on my cotton bikini briefs, glad I'm wearing that instead of a thong.

The ring catches my eye and I take a closer look at it. The princess-cut diamond is set in a platinum band. I take it off to see if there's an inscription, and sure enough, there is:

$$J + E$$

Nothing but our initials together. Simple and strong, resembling a company logo. Is this what marriage means to him, an institution? Some people see it that way—his family included. The Abigail Adams family, too. And probably the Cabots, which is where his brother's wife hails from. Preston's arranged bride.

"Do you like the engraving?" Jared smiles. He takes my

hands and pulls me to my knees, and we get up from the ground.

"I do."

"I like hearing you say that." He pulls me in closer. "Say it again."

"I do." I put the ring back on my finger. He kisses the top of my head and embraces me.

My heart is pounding and I know he can feel it. I just hope he thinks it's from the sex, or the wine.

Can I really marry this man? Do I have it in me to marry anyone? The only real goal I've ever had in life is to travel and see the world. Visit every museum to see the portraits and pieces I've only seen in photos. I want to see every natural wonder, and not just from travel videos on YouTube. I want to visit all the major cities like Paris, New York, Montreal, figure out which I like best and settle down there. I've never thought about any sort of career outside of a day job to pay rent and bills. I don't care what I do for a living as long as the job doesn't drive me crazy. I live for weekends, vacations, and holidays, anyway.

Getting married was never on my to-do list, and I'm even less sure about having kids. They don't quite fit in with my plans of traveling the world, but I have time to decide on that since I'm not even thirty yet. Courteney's the one who wants to breed anyway, so she takes the heat off me for supplying our parents with grandchildren. She's talked about having kids since high school.

And then my old roommate Andi's brown freckled face flashes in my head. She used to refer to her high school boyfriend as "the one who got away" with a wistful look on her face. She broke up with him after graduation because she was convinced someone even better was out there. The last time I spoke to Andi, she was still single.

Will Jared end up being the one who gets away if I end

this engagement? I look over at him while he shakes out the bed sheet, and notice we missed some of the linen napkins a few feet away on the grass. I pick them up and take my time folding them, and Jared blows me a kiss.

Maybe I just have to stall and bide my time while I make up my mind. I can ask Jared to wait to announce it so I can tell my parents in person. That gives me until the weekend to drive down to see them. Or, insist on having the wedding at some special venue with a long waiting list, like the Museum of Fine Arts, or one of the big hotels downtown. Take my time picking out a dress, a theme, flowers, and all that. Or just wait on the planning itself, say I'm too busy at work and can't decide on the wedding details, or where to honeymoon.

How am I going to keep up a façade for that long? Without feeling incredibly guilty the whole time? Being introduced as Jared's fiancé, making plans with his family and Katharine, who will probably want to train me on being a "Galbraith wife" and give me family heirlooms like her grandmother's pearls or something. There's no way I'll be able to pull this off for a couple of weeks, let alone a few months.

There will definitely be pressure from his rich, powerful family to plan the wedding, and make announcements. They may even pull strings to have our wedding sooner at one of those places with a long waiting list. I'll have to make my decision before he announces the engagement to his family. But will I even be able to make up my mind by then? Maybe I'll never make up my mind. Maybe I'll marry him and always regret it, or *not* marry him and still regret it.

I have to be honest with him as soon as we get home, if not sooner. Maybe once we cross the state line. At least then I'll be able to get a ride if he flips out and kicks me out of the car.

I put the napkins inside the picnic basket and glance at the ring again.

"Not having second thoughts, are you?"

I laugh and shake my head. "It's just so beautiful...looks good on my finger."

Jared smiles. "I didn't want to say anything, but I actually had to do a lot to get my parents' blessing."

Crap. "What do you mean?"

He opens his mouth to speak up, but then he shakes his head and looks away. "Nothing. It doesn't matter. They thought you and I weren't going to last, so I surprised the hell out of them when I not only refused to marry Abigail Adams but told them I wanted to propose to you."

He chuckles, and then his eyes darken. His mouth opens and then closes, as if he were about to say something and changed his mind. He starts gathering our supplies back into the basket.

"These strange traditions in my family." His voice is so low I can barely hear him.

"What do you mean? The arranged marriages?"

He shakes his head. "Nothing. It all went over fine. They gave me their blessing."

My face is getting warm and I don't think it's from the wine.

"I definitely don't blame you for not wanting to marry that Abigail woman now that I've met her. She seems a little scary."

"You can say that again. She's ruthless. You should see her in court."

"She's a lawyer?"

Jared nods. "I swear she's sold her soul to the devil with the perps she defends."

"Should I be worried she's going to hire a hitman to get rid of me?" I giggle, but I'm also thinking of her thinly veiled threat when we were alone in the liquor store. I remember the rumor about her family hiring some kind of special mob army.

Jared shakes his head. "Of course not. She's ruthless, but not crazy."

She certainly seemed a little crazy earlier. What have I gotten myself into?

I look down at my ring. It's becoming something I can stare at, a distraction, whenever I don't know what to say. Everything Jared said is making me feel even worse about wanting to call off the engagement. How can I do that now, after everything he's gone through to propose to me? He caused a rift within his family's inner circle. And if I break off the engagement, it'll look even worse for him, and the entire Galbraith family.

Do we trudge down those hills, the ones we're supposed to travel down? The paths that are once taken, you can't turn around and try it another way. In the maze of life, some people know which path to take, and which career to choose, but the rest of us are left in the cold, not knowing what to do.

"Let's get going before it gets too late," Jared says. "I don't want to hit traffic. And you have the Monday morning sales meeting—you'll need to relax tonight."

"Right." I sigh and roll my eyes. I hate the Monday morning meetings. The sales reps always fight over the leads and since I'm the office manager, I have to play mediator. As if Mondays aren't annoying enough.

Jared picks up the picnic basket and then drops it. He shakes his leg like a wet dog.

"What's wrong?"

"Damn ants!"

He swats at his trousers and bats the sleeves of his shirt. He's not exactly afraid of bugs—they just bug him. Whenever he happens to be accosted by a bug or several bugs, such as the situation at hand, he seems genuinely disgusted over having to deal with them.

I stifle a laugh, and a noise behind me sounds like a twig snapping. And the leaves nearby rustle. My imagination tells me it's a grizzly bear, about to attack us. Or a serial killer with a gigantic knife.

"Did you hear that?" I ask.

"What?"

"That noise. Sounded like something moving through the trees."

The back of my neck prickles, and I get that same feeling I had when we were having sex. Someone is watching us.

CHAPTER

SIX

I look around the field and the forest beyond, my eyes darting back and forth.

"Jared," I say, wringing my hands. "You don't think someone is out here watching us, do you?"

"Liz, come on!" he says with a chuckle, though he does glance at the trees. "We're all alone out here, don't worry."

With the basket all packed up, we leave our picnic spot and head into the forest. A bird makes a weird caw. I reach for Jared's arm but remind myself there's nothing to worry about, that my real worry is what to do about this engagement. Should I call it off once we get home? Or try it on for a few weeks, like a new pair of shoes? Break in the possibility of being married to a Galbraith for a while, and see how it fits.

We walk by a massive tree with gangly branches that look like limbs, hollows like eyes, and a big, screaming mouth. I almost expect it to start moaning. A squirrel scurries by, and I swat at some bugs buzzing by my head. After a while, Jared stops in his tracks and there's a glimmer of that disgruntled look on his face. Without a word, he gestures and turns down an unfamiliar path, leading our trek toward another part of the forest. I take a deep breath and keep my eyes on his back. He stops again, turns around, and shakes his head. "I'm not sure we're going in the right direction."

"Why don't you check the map?"

"It's a road map, not a map of the forest. Besides, I left it in the car."

He motions for me to follow him in another direction, where the trees are thicker. I rush to keep up with him. He's carrying the picnic basket and it's banging against his legs. I can't see much ahead of me, partly because he's so tall, but mostly because of the trees.

I look up to see how big the trees are, deducing they must be close to a hundred feet tall. There are so many of them. They make me feel small and easily squished. Like the time I stood next to the replica of a Blue Whale at the Natural History Museum in D.C.

The tree cover thickens overhead and the temperature drops a couple of degrees. I rub my arms. I don't know how Jared can tell where we're going, since every path looks the same to me. A twig snaps a few feet to the right of us. I gasp and leap forward, nearly running into him again.

"You okay?" Jared asks.

"Just a little jumpy, that's all."

Tree leaves rustle and a bird caws nearby. The scent of earth and leaves mixed with an unmistakable whiff of animal hide that reminds me of petting zoos and the circus envelops me, and makes me shiver. We are really deep in these woods. What if there's something in the forest never seen before? Like a Yeti or Bigfoot? These roads had no visitors before us, at least for some time. Anything could be lurking in here. I could be heading toward a Fay Wray fate of a giant gorilla's prize. Jared gets an arrow between the eyes and I'm held captive by some tribe.

A coldness nestles into my chest and I wrap my arms

around my waist. I concentrate on Jared's back with each step. I reach out to hold his hand, and the ring catches my eye. I pull my hand back.

By putting our entire future on the table, Jared has erased our immediate future. Where our biggest plans were what restaurant we planned to go to on Friday night, or where our next vacation will be. Tears brim beneath my lids when it hits me that from this moment on, I can never return to my normal life, no matter what decision I make. Gooseflesh ripples down my arms and I rub them, hugging myself and ignoring the oppressive glint of the ring that somehow still shines in the darkening tree cover.

The trees have such fuzzy-looking bark that they seem covered in fur from crown to trunk. I exhale slowly and reach out to see if the bark is as furry as it looks. A fat bug crawls over the bark and I jump back, wincing as a blister on my heel bursts. My feet are in trouble from walking over twigs and rocks in a pair of pointy-toed flats. And the ground isn't as smooth as it was a few minutes ago.

Wait a minute—when did we leave the path?

Jared stops and stares at the ground covered in leaves, twigs, and forest debris.

"When did we lose the path?" His voice is low. He sounds worried. And that worries me even more.

"I have no idea. I just noticed it too."

"I think this is the way." He points at some trees to our left. They look like the same trees we just passed through.

"Want me to carry the picnic basket?" I ask, reaching my hand out.

"No, that's fine. Just stay close to me."

We walk and dodge fallen branches until we come upon another path. Is it the same one we were on before? I'm not sure. But it feels better to walk on a flattened path instead of some uncharted forest terrain.

Forests have ingrained in me an eeriness from witches in fairy tales and killers in campfire stories. Lots of creepy things lurk in the woods. Owls turning their heads all the way around. Bats with their beady eyes and long wings. Possum with giant rat tails.

The trees in the forest have been around for so long, who knows what they've seen? Probably lots of sex and death. Circle of life, right? As the trees thicken, we're completely out of the sun. In almost every fairy tale I've read, the scary stuff happens when the forest gets denser, making everything dark and scary. A shiver passes through my shoulders.

After a few moments on the path, the forest grows quiet. The wind dies down, and the leaves stop rustling, but that animal scent lingers in my nose. I can't shake the feeling that someone, or something, is watching us. Stalking us. Waiting calmly for us to get so lost we'll be at its mercy.

It's starting to get darker out. What if we get stranded out here after dark? I don't want to think about that. But as it edges toward the evening and the sun descends at rapid speed, we *will* have to think about that. I'm so grateful we didn't finish off all the picnic food.

The leaves to our left rustle. The bushes next to them shake. I jump next to Jared, and stumble before getting my balance. He reaches out, and I slip my hand into his and get the strangest sensation it will be the last time I hold hands with him. Either we're breaking up when we get home, or we're going to die out here.

"It's probably nothing," Jared says, keeping his large palm wrapped around my much smaller one. "I think we're headed in the right direction."

My throat is dry and scratchy. I let out a cough when a twig snaps just a couple of feet away. We both freeze. Jared takes a deep breath before nudging me forward along with him.

We quicken our pace when another twig snaps louder than the last. It sounds menacing, like there's anger behind the noise. Maybe it's just some animals fighting, or some creature who's lost its prey. But maybe it's now centered on new prey: the two of us.

The trees to our left shake with a force, as if something large and heavy just breezed through them.

"Keep moving," Jared whispers.

A strange new sound comes through the leaves, like a cross between a pig oinking and a donkey braying. What on earth makes a noise like that?

Jared lets go of my hand and picks up into a run, moving so quickly I can't run fast enough to get in front of him. He needs to lead the way anyway, since I have no idea where we are. But I have a feeling he doesn't know either.

SEVEN

THE PATH we're on begins to narrow. We slow our pace, both of us out of breath. The trees in this part of the forest seem older. They have this haunted look with darkened bark and knotty limbs, scraggly crowns of leaves that block the waning sunlight.

The twigs and dried leaves pile up on the ground, and soon I find myself shuffling through them instead of walking on top of them. We're back to that uncharted forest terrain. We come upon a small clearing, hosting a boulder so big it looks prehistoric.

"How did we get so turned around?" Jared says, walking around in a circle. "I don't remember any of this."

"Me neither."

"You probably don't want to go back the way we came, but I think we have to."

I don't want to admit it to Jared, but I'm so scared and fighting hard to hold back tears. This isn't just my childhood fears of the forest. We are really lost. I wish for something, anything, to let us know which direction to take so we don't go even deeper into the woods.

One large tree we pass has a jagged gash in the bark, as if a big claw scraped it. I try to match the claw marks to the paws of an animal, but none come to mind. The lines are too narrow and close together to be a bear. I suppose it could be from a hunter's bowie knife, carving marks into a tree for a marker, or just for the fun of it.

I bring my hands together to wring them, and the cold hardness of the ring startles me. It's weird how it can feel like nothing is there, as if the ring on my finger is completely natural, and then I'll touch it with my other hand and it becomes heavy and clunky, like it doesn't belong there.

Whatever was stalking us hopefully went on to better prey. Maybe it was a crazed hunter. We scared off a deer and he wanted revenge? I know it's ridiculous but my imagination goes there when I'm nervous and unsure. I wonder what's more frightening: an unstable hunter with guns and knives, or a wild animal with teeth and claws? Both are unpredictable, and hard to escape.

I check my phone. Still no service. I don't want to think about what we'll have to do when it gets dark and we're still lost in the woods. I want to go back to worrying about whether I'll marry Jared. That concern seemed so much worse not that long ago.

We walk back down the path we were on before reaching the boulder, and soon it becomes an actual path with fewer twigs and debris. Faintly, a whiff of that animal-hide scent from before wafts into my nose. I check the trees. Nothing rustling, no movement.

"Maybe we were supposed to make a left up here," Jared says. "That's how we got turned around." He points in a general direction to our upper left, and I'm not sure where he wants us to go. It looks like the same trees we've been walking through.

"Are you sure?"

He doesn't answer and leads us to the spot where he pointed. He looks around for a moment, then leads us in a different direction. Guess he wasn't so sure after all.

Blisters are bursting through my heels and around my big toes. Each step makes me wince. My bare arms are cold and covered in scratches from tree branches. If I'd known we would be walking through the woods, I wouldn't have worn flimsy flats with no socks, and I would've brought a sweater. I cross my arms and rub my elbows.

He looks back at me, his eyes filled with concern. "Don't worry Liz. We'll get there."

But nearly an hour later, we're still lost in the woods. We begin taking short pauses to sit and pick at the remaining food in the picnic basket. We just have wine, no water, but there's some leftover fruit salad to keep us hydrated enough. For the time being, at least. I'm trying to take this one step at a time, one second at a time. But the thought crossing my mind that we should be conserving food scares me.

In the reality shows I've seen, where people try to survive in the wild, they always have things like compasses and water bottles, and better shoes. I've never seen a show about city slickers getting lost with nothing but a picnic basket with fancy food, wine, and a bedsheet.

"Maybe we should start marking the places we've already been by," I suggest.

"What do you mean?"

"Like a mark in a tree, or something. I'm worried we keep going down the same wrong path. All these trees look the same!" I stand up and splay out my arms toward the trees.

"We haven't been going down the same paths, don't worry." He doesn't sound very sure of himself, though.

My arms fall back to my sides. "You don't happen to have a Swiss army knife, do you?"

"No, I don't. Just stop worrying, we're not going to get

stuck out here!"

He stands and kicks the tree next to us. A bird flies out from the crown. Jared looks at me while I'm shivering. He offers me the sheet from the picnic basket.

I shake my head and look away from him. "I'm okay. For now."

I hope that sheet will be enough to keep both of us warm once the sun goes down.

Something in the burrows of my mind rustles along with the leaves and gnaws at me. I can't shake the feeling that something dark and powerful is lurking in these woods with us.

I shiver and cup my hands under my elbows for warmth, but my hands are shaking and cold. My feet are sore with a numbness that makes the blisters somewhat bearable. Maybe I'm just getting used to the pain.

"Should we stay put and make camp, or keep trying to find the car?" It blurts out of me before I can stop it.

Jared continues walking away from me, his head hanging down. When he doesn't stop, I take my cue and trail after him. We walk by some trees that look ancient. Jared tries to mark one with a rock, but it doesn't make much of a dent.

"Why don't we try tearing off a piece of the sheet, and tying it around a tree limb, or something?"

Jared's face brightens, and he takes out the sheet.

"Don't rip off too much though. We'll need it when it gets dark."

Jared pauses, and the crinkle between his eyebrows appears. Then he sighs and rips off a small strip from the sheet. He ties it high on a tree. It looks like a little bandage on the limb.

I stay a few paces behind him as we walk, hugging myself. There's a sense of finality to it all, that nothing will ever be the same after this. I can feel it so strongly, that a chill passes through me. Something has changed, shifted. Something is ending.

No matter what, there is no going back to what Jared and I were before this. Who *I* was before this. Tears form in the corners of my eyes, and I blink them back and take deep breaths. I figure I'll save the crying for later, while I'm trying to sleep underneath a flimsy sheet with forest debris as my bedding.

The sky grows darker by the second. We reach a path that looks faintly familiar, but I don't want to get my hopes up.

"I think this is the path we came down when we first got here," Jared says, pointing upward. "I remember the way that tree limb jutted out."

I look up to where he's pointing and have no idea what he's talking about. The tree limbs all look the same to me. In fact, the trees look scarier than ever. The limbs look like they're growing longer, trying to wrap around me and Jared, and trap us here.

"Liz, come on!" Jared shouts, his eyes flashing as he glances back at me. "This is the path!"

"Really? Are you sure?"

He nods with a big grin and picks up his pace. I wince with each step to keep up with him. The more we rush, the closer we get to familiar territory. I can feel it—we've been down this path before.

"We're almost there!"

The waning sunlight shines through, and the trees thin out to reveal the path we first came down, that leads to the car. I take a deep breath, and a wonderful feeling of relief settles into my stomach. That warm, joyous feeling I get when I'm finally under the covers in bed after rushing back from the cold, dark bathroom in the middle of the night, safe from the ghosts and goblins lurking behind the shower curtain or under the bed.

Was something really stalking us out there in the woods, or was it just my imagination? I'll have to ask Jared later if he heard the strange growls too. All I want is to get back home and rest.

I rush up to Jared only for him to stop in his tracks. Was this the wrong path, after all? Did we go in circles again? But no, I remember seeing this circular clearing right after we parked the car.

I take a few steps forward, and now I'm standing next to Jared, looking at where he parked the car.

Only the car isn't there.

"Where the hell is my Bentley?" Jared screams. He drops the picnic basket and his arms fly into the air. It falls onto its side but the lid stays closed.

"Maybe this is the wrong spot?" The words escaped my mouth before thinking about them. It's such a stupid thing to say—it's not like we parked at a shopping center separating rows with red, yellow, and orange—but it's a knee-jerk response when the car isn't where you thought it would be.

On a closer look, there are tire tracks in the dirt and mud, impressions where it was not that long ago. Are they Jared's tracks, or someone else's?

"Did you lock it?"

Jared sighs. "I honestly don't remember, we're in the middle of nowhere—why would I even need to lock it!" He smacks himself on his forehead.

"Don't beat yourself up, Jared, it's not like this is a high-traffic area."

"Exactly, who the fuck would've stolen it?"

Jared doesn't drop f-bombs very often, so I know he's really pissed off and tense. But I can't blame him. How the hell are we getting back home now? I pull out my phone. It still says "No Service" up top.

"Is your phone getting service?" I ask.

"No, I just checked."

"Maybe if we keep walking we'll get some bars?"

Jared turns and kicks a tree, so hard that a piece of bark flies off.

"Fuck!" he screams and kicks the tree again.

"Jared, calm down—we'll figure something out. Either we'll find a signal from a cell phone tower soon, or we'll hitch a ride with someone down on the main road."

Jared nods and runs his hands through his hair, taking deep breaths through his nose. I put my phone away, and reach down to grab the picnic basket.

"Just leave it!" Jared barks at me.

I flinch and cross my arms over my chest. "But what if we need the food later? And your parents' monogrammed linen napkins are in there."

"Fine. I'll carry it—it's heavy."

Jared storms over to me and I back up when he leans down to pick up the basket. I glance at his eyes and see the darkness in them.

I've never seen him this angry before, but then again, he did have his car stolen in the middle of nowhere. And we don't know how we're going to get back home. Can't say I blame him for being like this. But it's still making me uneasy.

"Let's start walking," Jared says, his voice hoarse. He gestures toward the road and I walk in front of him.

I don't realize I'm trembling all over until I start to move. I keep my arms wrapped around myself and my shoulders hunched while we walk toward the main road.

I can feel Jared's eyes boring into the back of my head. It makes me feel cold all over. When the man you love looks at you, it's supposed to make you feel warm all over, not cold. And I don't like him walking behind me like that, as if he's stalking me.

CHAPTER

EIGHT

WE REACH THE MAIN ROAD, and it's just as deserted now as it was when we drove in. I keep my phone in my hand, praying for bars to appear, but nothing yet. I glance at Jared. His eyes aren't as dark as they were before, but they're still not back to normal.

A cool breeze moves through and chills me to my bones. A slight mist covers the grass, and everything grows darker by the second as the sun goes down. It almost feels like déjà vu, scary but familiar at the same time. I rub my upper arms when the chills come through. It's like something in the atmosphere has shifted. Being in the forest reminded me of spooky scenes in fairy tales, and this reminds me of a horror movie.

As frightened as I was being lost in the woods, I'm even more terrified of the way Jared keeps glaring at me. Why is he looking at me this way? Does he think I had someone steal his car? Or maybe he's pissed off that I'm not as pissed as he is about it? If he were a poor man I'd be much more concerned, but his Bentley SUV is only *one* of his cars. I turn my back on him, his eyes still on me.

Something between us has shifted along with the atmosphere, like we crossed a line and won't ever go back. Not just the proposal, not just his refusal to marry Abigail— it's what happened in the woods.

Neither of us says anything while we walk in semi-circles away from each other trying to get signals on our phones. We somewhat resemble two jungle cats sizing each other up, on the verge of either brawling or mating.

I'm afraid we're going to jump into bed and mate the second we get back, like we usually do after making up from a fight, and that I'll forget all about that dark-eyed look once we're safe at home. I want to call off this engagement right now, but I don't think that's a good idea considering we're in the middle of who knows where.

When you're not just a woman, but a *tiny* woman such as myself, you don't want to find yourself lost in parts unknown, with no signals on your phone, approaching nighttime. I don't think Jared will go off to find help and leave me here, but he's already done a couple of things today I never thought he'd do: ask me to marry him, and look as if he wanted to kill me. All within the span of an afternoon.

An owl hoots in the distance. Crickets chirp in the grass. These are the only sounds, and they remind me of how far we are from the city. I check my phone for bars. Messages are probably piling up, and I'll hear notification dings as soon as we get within range of a cell tower, but I feel so helpless just walking around waiting for a car to come by. I need to do something right now, and checking my phone for service is the easiest option. The only option.

I blow into my cupped hands for warmth. After everything that's happened, I'm wishing like mad I'd canceled this date with Jared and gone to lunch with Courteney. He wouldn't have proposed today, his car wouldn't have been stolen, we never would've gotten lost in the woods, and I'd have no blisters on my feet unless it was from walking around Boston in bad shoes. I want to sit on the ground and cry my eyes out over not having made that simple choice. Just curl up in the fetal position and bawl like a baby for a while.

Twilight is creeping in, and the temperature drops rapidly. I'm about to ask Jared to take out the sheet from the picnic basket when something starts heading our way down the road. Headlights of a car.

We both step toward the middle of the road, waving our arms. I can't tell what kind of car it is, but it's red and not an SUV. Maybe a sports car. Definitely a sports car and driving too fast. As soon as it gets close I jump back.

The car zooms by so fast dirt flies up in its wake. If I hadn't jumped when I did, it would've hit me. Jared coughs and waves at the air in front of him.

"Are you okay?" I ask.

"Yeah," he says through ragged breathing. "I think so."

I can't believe that car didn't stop for us. What a jerk. If I saw people stranded in the middle of the road, waving their arms, I would stop to see if they needed help. But I feel better knowing there are at least some cars coming by, that it's not as deserted out here as I thought.

"Can I have the sheet?" I make my way over toward the picnic basket, resting at Jared's feet.

"Sure." He pulls out the sheet and wraps it around my shoulders.

"Thanks."

He stuffs his hands into his pockets. He's wearing a long-sleeved shirt, and knowing him, a t-shirt underneath it. He turns away from me, and as soon as he does another set of headlights starts heading toward us. Jared moves closer to the road.

This car is coming down the road much slower than the last car. I still step back a few paces, though. The headlights grow brighter as they get closer. It's a pickup truck, and it slows down as it approaches us.

The hubcaps are covered in muck and soot and there's so much dirt on the license plate I can't read it. In the front seat are two pale-skinned men with pockmarks on their faces. Both are on the larger side and wearing coveralls that look like they haven't been washed in a long time. The one behind the wheel looks like an older version of the man sitting next to him in the passenger seat. A hound sits in the back, drool dangling from its mouth.

"Evenin' folks," the man behind the wheel says. "Havin' a little car trouble?"

"Yes, we are," Jared says. "My car has been stolen. And our phones don't seem to be working, either."

The man in the passenger seat stares at me. His eyes run up and down my body, lingering on my breasts, and then up to my face. He never looks directly into my eyes. He just stares at my mouth.

His eyes have a slouchy look to them that I occasionally see in guys when they stare at me, especially at my breasts. It's more than just undressing me with their eyes. It's more than just storing a mental image of me. It's a look that makes me want to run home, lock the doors and windows, and sleep with a baseball bat next to my bed.

I look away from him and fold my arms around myself, in an attempt to get him to look away.

"Cell phones don't work much 'round here," the driver says.

"Would you mind giving us a ride to the nearest police station?"

"You mean Charlie? He's the sheriff, and I know for a fact that he don't work on Sundays."

"What do you mean? Isn't there anyone else?"

"There's 911 if there's an emergency, but that'll just get the paramedics and fire department out and about. Charlie, our local law, won't be around right now."

I bite my lip. Pretty sure the fire department isn't going to come out for a stolen car.

"Do you know where we can find a landline to call for a ride back to Boston? I'll be more than happy to pay you for your trouble."

Jared reaches into his back pocket and takes out his wallet. He flashes a few twenty-dollar bills. The two men look at each other. The one in the driver's seat nods, and then looks back at us with a crooked grin.

"Sure, why don't you come along to our place, it's close by —you can use our phone."

"You sure you don't mind?"

"Not at all, get in the back! I'm Herschel, and this is m'boy Sonny."

The man next to him snickers. The repugnant sound is gravelly and hollow and grates into me like fingernails on a chalkboard.

"Jared, I don't know," I whisper, and nudge him.

"Do you see anyone else coming by?" he whispers back.

I shrug, not really feeling like nodding. But he's got a point—what if these two are our only shot at getting home tonight?

We climb into the dirty pickup truck. The hound jumps at Jared and scrapes his legs with its paws, getting mud on his trousers. The dog comes at me, its brown and white coat matted, filthy, stinky. But its eyes are big and round, almost pleading for attention. I let it lick my hand despite the smell.

The entire truck smells like wet dog. And celery, for some reason. It's so strong there must be a bag of it somewhere in the truck. I've met people who say they don't think celery has a smell, but I'm very sensitive to it. I open my mouth so I don't have to breathe through my nose. I smile at Jared and raise my eyebrows. He shakes his head and doesn't return the smile. But he clutches my hand and traces the engagement ring on my finger with his thumb.

The hound opens its mouth in a yawn and the wind makes the drool fly onto my arm. I wipe it off and glare at the dog. It's almost completely dark. I'm thinking about what excuse to use for calling out sick tomorrow. A stomach bug is the easiest, since a cold will require me to sound stuffed up.

Maybe I don't even have to play sick if I let the office know about getting lost in the woods, and the stolen car. I'm not planning to tell Jared that I'm calling out sick. I just need some time to myself to think, regroup, and unwind from today. A clear head will help me make my decision. That's the plan, at least.

I look at my phone and my thumb grazes the Photos tab, and the first picture under the Favorites folder is an old one of my parents from the 1980s before Courteney and I were born. They have their arms around each other while they lean against Dad's old El Camino. I snapped a picture of that photograph when I was helping Mom sort through the attic. It fell out of a dusty photo album, and Mom smiled when she picked up the photo. It seemed to give her some good memories, though she didn't share them with me.

I go back into the main folder and find a more recent photo from their anniversary party. They're standing in front of the big sign Courteney made: "Harold and Jude, 30 Years and Counting!" Dad's wooden clocks trimmed with his trademark painted shamrocks lined up on the wall behind them, with forced smiles on their faces.

It's amazing how different they look in the two photos. Past and present. Maybe that happens to everyone with age. It's not just the extra weight and the wrinkles. They're smiling in both pictures, but in the older one, they look so much happier. It's in their eyes—they're shining brightly, full of love. In the one from the anniversary party, their eyes are darker. Sadder. Maybe that's just a natural part of aging, or maybe something changed after they got married. It makes me worry about what happens to that shining love once the shiny rings come into play.

One night when I was seventeen, I was up late reading in my bedroom when I heard my parents' car in the driveway, pulling in so fast the tires squealed. I heard them arguing the second they came into the house.

When I heard my mother shout, "You don't have to *choke* me, Harold!" I ran downstairs to their bedroom.

"What's going on?" I glared at my father. "Did you just try to choke her?"

He let out an exasperated sigh. "Your mother's exaggerating. We were just arguing."

"Mom?"

She hung her head and didn't say anything.

"It's late, Liz," Dad said, his voice raised. "Go to bed!"

"I'll wait to hear from Mom that she was just exaggerating."

I stared at Dad, my eyes narrowed.

"I'm fine, Liz," Mom said, not hiding the defeat in her voice. "Do as your father said, and go to bed. We'll talk in the morning."

I looked at my mother and waited for her to make eye contact with me. But she didn't. She just stood there with her back against the wall and her head hung low. I didn't know what else to do but go to my room. Courteney was away at college at the time.

The next morning, I went into the kitchen and waited for Mom, who always got breakfast ready before Dad woke up.

"What happened last night?" I asked her.

"He didn't really choke me," she said. "He just put his hands around my neck for a second."

"What?"

"Your father has never really gotten violent with me, he just threatens. That's all."

"That's *all?* Mom—"

"Your father is a good man, Liz." Her voice trembled with emotion. She couldn't look me in the eye when she said, "He just has a bit of a temper."

I knew he had a temper, but I thought he only took it out on inanimate objects, not people. Not his own wife. I wonder if my father had shown that side of himself before they got married, or if he'd kept it hidden and let his true colors come out after the wedding. Maybe he waited until after Courteney was born. My mother would've been officially trapped by then. I don't want something like that to happen to me.

Jared clears his throat, and I look at him. My potential future husband. Who is a good man, with a bit of a temper. I bite my lip and go back to looking at my phone.

The driver opens the window that separates us.

"Almost there, folks, just hang tight!"

He closes the window as his son snickers. I shudder and suck in a shaky breath.

"I'm getting a bad feeling about this," I say to Jared. "I don't like how the son keeps laughing."

"I don't think he's with it or something, he just seems off."

"Maybe. I don't know."

I also don't like the way he was looking at me, though Jared always says I overreact about the way guys look at me. But there's a difference between looking, and leering.

Jared stares at the sky and I watch the trees as we drive down the road. It hits me that we haven't passed any houses or anything else besides trees for a while. I cringe as I wonder how deep into the woods these guys live. It's going to take forever to get back home, to my comfortable bed. I'm really looking forward to taking a sick day tomorrow. A whole day to rest and decide whether to celebrate my engagement, or mourn the end of my relationship.

Jared holds my hand with the ring and the dog licks my other hand. It's getting so dark I can barely see the road.

"Just think about what a great engagement story this will make," Jared says. "We'll be laughing about this for years!"

I give him a tight-lipped smile. We turn onto another road lined with lots of trees, bushes, and not much else. This road is a bumpy one, and the beginnings of a headache are coming on, and each bump we hit makes the pounding in my head stronger.

Up ahead is a dilapidated house. I try to look around the unkempt lawn, but everything is so damn dark now. It's not even that late yet, but for some reason, this part of wherever we are seems darker. Maybe we're so deep into the woods it makes everything look dark and ominous. I really don't like that. What if we're stranded out here overnight? What sorts of eerie things lurk in these woods?

We pull up to the house, and there aren't any lights on. Maybe no one else lives here, or perhaps they're trying to save electricity. The dog whimpers when the truck stops. I pat its matted head and breathe through my mouth. My hand is slimy from the fur, and I wipe it on the floor of the truck.

"Here we are," the driver says. "Come on, Sonny-boy!"

He claps his son's shoulder and they both get out of the truck. Jared and I jump down from the back. The dog follows us and then trots away.

Except for a couple of hens clucking in a coop, there aren't any other farm animals I can see. Just faint scents of manure and hay. Maybe they have a horse or a cow in the barn.

As we get closer to the house, an old celery odor that's

much stronger than the one from the truck hits my nose. I follow the scent to see a skinny scarecrow perched on the fence. I take a step closer to it.

"Is that...a scarecrow made out of celery stalks?"

CHAPTER

NINE

STALKS OF CELERY, tied together with twine to make limbs and a torso. The arms jut out lopsided like a botched crucifixion pose. Bugs crawl along the stalks with many of the edges nibbled from insect feasts. The top of it, the head, has yellow corn husks for hair.

Herschel nods. "My boy Sonny here made that! He loves to make his celery people when we have a surplus. Now that Halloween is coming up, he'll start making some with pumpkins."

I glance over at Sonny, who shrugs and shoves his hands into his pockets. He looks at the ground and shakes his head from left to right. I look back at the celery scarecrow.

"He don't talk much," Hershel says. "But he's real talented."

Celery people? The corn husks for hair make the scarecrow blonde, like me. It makes my stomach churn with an uneasy feeling in my legs. My cheeks fill up with saliva as I move away from the thing.

"Is this a celery farm, or something?" Jared asks him.

"Yup, no somethings about it. Best damn celery farm

around! And maybe if Sonny-boy was feeling up to it, he could show you his other artwork."

Sonny shrugs and keeps staring at the ground.

"And this is our home." Herschel points at the house. "Pretty, ain't it?"

The house doesn't look as bad as I thought it would, compared to the filthy pickup truck. It looks like a normal farmhouse that's just in dire need of a paint job.

"Want a tour of the estate?" He laughs and claps his son on the back. Then he gestures for us to follow them to the house.

Jared takes my hand and squeezes it, and I feel the ring bite into my skin. It's starting to feel like it belongs there. As if it's molding itself to my body. It sort of feels nice though, especially with Jared's hand squeezing it. I'm thinking about what he'd said earlier, how this will make a great engagement story.

We walk up the rickety front steps to a creaking porch. There's a crooked swing hanging by a chain too long on one side. They open the door and switch on a light to lead us inside the kitchen.

The first thing I notice is the smell, a mix of dirt and rotten meat. I have to breathe through my mouth again to keep my nostrils safe. Inhaling the pungent odor through my nose will surely make me vomit. I cough, as does Jared.

The second thing I notice is how bright the kitchen is, and not just from the overhead light. Everything is a glaring yellow color from the wallpaper to the vinyl on the chairs, to a plush Tweety Bird doll in a plastic cage hanging from the ceiling.

The refrigerator is yellow too, an old Frigidaire model that hums so loudly the floor vibrates. I stare at Jared, the amateur interior decorator who's criticized my navy blue curtains, expecting a disgusted grimace. He doesn't seem fazed at all. He almost looks comfortable in this room, like it's familiar to him in some way.

"Tonight's dinner has already been prepared, so why don't you folks have a seat in the dining room," Herschel says, smacking his lips. Sonny stares at me with a big Cheshire cat grin on his face.

Jared and I glance at each other. There's no way we're eating whatever that smell in the kitchen is. It's like they left out a pot roast for days. A couple of flies are buzzing around the room.

Jared's eyebrows shoot upward and he plasters on a polite smile. "Thank you, but we're hoping if we call roadside assistance they'll be here within the hour. No need to set places for us."

"Why don't we call for an Uber?" I suggest.

"All the way out here? How will they find us without GPS?"

"You ain't hungry?" Hershel asks.

"No," Jared says. "Thanks. We'd just like to use your phone."

"Tell you what—I'll call a buddy of mine who has a girlfriend in Boston, he'll be happy to give you a ride back. It'll take him 'bout twenty minutes to get here, plenty of time to eat. And much quicker than roadside assistance! I'm guestimatin' that'll take 'bout nearly an hour and a half, maybe two."

Jared looks at me with his eyebrows raised.

"Been a while since we had company for dinner," Herschel says with a sigh. "It's just been the two of us since my wife passed away."

That makes me feel bad for the poor guy. He seems lonely missing his wife.

"All right, thank you." I glance at Jared with a shrug. He's staring daggers at me. I mouth, "I'm sorry" to him. We don't want to be rude after they helped us.

"It'll be nice for us to have some company for a change. Show 'em to the dining room, boy."

Sonny leads us down the hall. A filmy layer of dust covers the walls. Stains and burn marks on the carpet. A fly buzzes by my face and I swat at it. The smell makes me want to breathe through my mouth, but then I'll be worried a fly might find its way in there.

"Do you think I could use the restroom?"

Sonny points at a door at the end of the hall, and Jared says he'll wait for me just outside the door. I hold my breath while walking in, but the smell in there isn't that bad. I still squat over the toilet seat.

There isn't any soap to wash my hands. There's a shower but no curtain, and no shampoo in there either. I run my fingers under the hot water, which comes out of a separate faucet from the cold water. This place really is rustic.

I come out and take Jared's hand, and Sonny leads us to the dining room. The rancid smell is so strong in there, worse than in the kitchen. I pinch my nose to keep myself from gagging. Jared looks at me and sighs, and I shrug and smile at him. I figure we can just pretend to eat whatever they serve for dinner.

A few more flies buzz around the dining room, and there is a strip of flypaper in the corner. It has a few flies stuck to it, and one appears to still be moving, but maybe my eyes are just playing tricks on me.

The dining table is long with a lacy, dingy-looking runner. Nicks in the wood in the corners, and one of the chairs has a book wedged under a leg to straighten it. Another chair is missing its back.

Four places have been set with two stubby candles in glass

holders in the middle of the table, the flickering flames giving me goosebumps.

"You didn't have to go to all this trouble," I say.

Sonny stares at me. Then he smiles and nods. The hound comes in, sniffing and panting, and licks my hand as it passes by. One of the flies comes at me and I swat it away. Sonny shoos the dog out, pulls out a chair, and gestures for me to sit in it. I sit down as gingerly as possible, scared that if I plop it'll break the chair. He stands there and stares down at me with his slouchy eyes, his mouth gaping open.

I look away from him and stare at the flypaper in the corner, hoping all of the flies find their way to it. Jared sits down next to me, and then Sonny slinks out of the room. His father follows.

Something is so surreal about this. Like it's a set for a play, or a reality show. I half-heartedly glance around looking for hidden cameras. But I'm sure it's just the fatigue from the day making me feel that way.

"What do you think?" I whisper to Jared.

"I think we stepped into the *Twilight Zone*," he whispers back. I giggle just as Sonny comes back. I bite my lip to make myself stop. But then I accidentally take a breath through my nose and cough, so I keep my mouth open. When a fly almost buzzes into my mouth, I snap it closed and try to get used to the smell.

Sonny holds a basket of dinner rolls in one hand, some of which have spots of mold. Herschel walks in holding a large bowl.

"I got the meat roasting. Here's some salad to tide you folks over 'til it's ready."

He serves salad on our plates. The lettuce is extremely wilted, and the only other vegetable in the salad is celery. I see a flash of red that may have been a sliver of pepper, or a tomato, but just one.

After he sets the bowl down, I notice something moving inside of it. I sit up in my chair with a start and lean over to see an ant crawling over a lettuce leaf. I have to cover my mouth to keep from retching. I nudge Jared and nod at the salad bowl, but the ant already crawled out of sight. Jared shrugs and I pantomime something crawling with my fingers. I think he gets it because he pushes his plate away with a grimace.

"Go get somma that wine I put out," Herschel says to his son, who leaves the room clapping. I raise my eyebrows and Jared shifts in his seat.

Jared looks down at his salad with a frown. I spear a piece of lettuce with my fork, and check for ants. There's no way I am going to eat this, but I can pretend to.

Herschel slams his hand on the table so hard the silverware bounces. The hound, who crept back into the room, whimpers.

"Don't you got no manners missy? Who told you to eat?"

Jared puts his arm around me and glares at him.

"I'll ask you politely to not speak to my girl—fiancé—in that manner."

The father raises his palms and shakes his head.

"I apologize to you, sir, but in this house, we don't eat 'til we say grace. Put down that fork, young lady. Pretty please."

I stare at him and give him the same look I gave my father the night he choked my mother. But since I don't want to eat anything anyway, I have no problem putting my fork down. I also no longer care about being rude. I won't even pretend to eat. I'm on the verge of telling Jared I'll wait outside for our ride. Or ask him to call roadside assistance anyway since I'm not so sure I want to get into a car with any friend of Herschel's.

Sonny comes back with the wine and pours some for me

first. Then he pours wine into everyone else's glasses and sits down.

"Now I'll say grace"—Herschel looks at me pointedly—"and then we can eat."

He lowers his head and places his hands in his lap.

"Lord!" he bellows. Jared and I jump in our seats.

"We give thanks," he continues in a much softer voice. "To what you've provided us. Although you took it upon yourself to take away my dear wife, I forgive you."

Sonny sniffles, and I glance over to see him wiping his eyes. The hound is by his side, and while he sobs the dog rests its head on his knees. Herschel seems like a jerk, but I feel a little sorry for his son.

"We forgive you, Lord." He glares at Sonny, who stops crying. "We forgive you and give thanks for everything else you do."

He picks up his glass and raises it. The dog makes an odd, loud whimper that sounds like it has a yawn in the middle of it. Herschel slaps his hand on the table and the hound trots out of the room.

"And now I'd like to make a toast, to our guests," he says. "On their engagement. May they live the rest of their lives happily."

Jared and I hold up our glasses along with them and we each take a sip. The warmth of the wine hits my stomach as soon as I swallow. I'm ready to down the entire glass to settle my nerves.

I take another sip and look around the room. The wine is going straight to my head, probably because I'm drinking on an empty stomach. I notice Herschel isn't drinking the wine, and neither is Sonny. They're both eyeing me and Jared.

Sonny makes a noise that isn't quite a laugh. A guffawed hee-haw noise with a bit of a squeal to it, like a cross between a pig and a donkey. There's something familiar about his laugh.

I remember the sound in the forest that I thought I had imagined. Sonny stops making that noise, and then he hiccoughs. I take a deep breath and my pulse races. My head is fuzzy. The whole room is fuzzy.

I turn toward Jared, but he's not there. Where is he? Did he get up to go to the bathroom?

"Where's Jared?" My voice sounds funny. I start to get up from the chair, but the room is spinning.

"Don't worry, it'll all be over soon," Herschel says, his voice forming the words in a bubble coming out of his mouth, like in a comic book.

Something terrible is happening.

My head is so fuzzy I can't seem to react to or realize what's going on around me, like I have to repeat to myself what I'm seeing.

Jared is gone.

I'm having trouble functioning.

They're acting strange.

A couple beats later it hits me—I need to get the hell out of here.

With all my strength I get up from the table, and Sonny gets up too, coming toward me. I tear away from them and run into the hall, no sign of Jared anywhere. It's like he vaporized.

Stumbling through the hallway, flies buzzing around my face, everything growing hazier by the second. I rush toward the bright light of the kitchen ahead, fast as I can but it doesn't feel like I'm moving quickly at all.

The door we came through is in front of me, it's right there—I can reach it. I'm going to get out of here! I run through the door and onto the creaky porch.

"Help!" I manage to scream, only it doesn't come out as a scream but a mumbled groan that probably no one will hear.

I reach the steps and stumble. Sonny has his arms around my waist. I kick and struggle with all my might, but he's got me. He's four times my size. I'm not going anywhere.

I try to scream again, only for groans to escape my lips. His palm covers my mouth, and he pulls me back into the farmhouse.

"Jared!" My syllables slur out his name slowly, muffled beneath Sonny's hand. He tightens his arm around me, and the hound starts to bark.

"Bring her inside son." Herschel's voice booms into my ears. "No need to let the neighbors hear any racket."

I'm still struggling but my muscles are getting weaker. Pins and needles run down my hands. Everything around me is getting hazier and hazier, blurred and blackening, and soon I'm going to pass out. Whatever they put into that wine is going to knock me out. I try to take in as much as possible before that happens.

Yellow refrigerator.

Flypaper on walls.

Tweety Bird in a plastic cage.

Framed pictures of Herschel with a blonde woman holding a baby I assume is Sonny.

My eyelids droop as I focus on the photograph. And there's another picture of her holding a plush Tweety Bird doll, but maybe I'm imagining that since everything is blurring together.

"Put her in the room," Herschel says, his voice eerily calm, and Sonny heaves me forward. I'm trying so hard to kick at him but my legs are too sluggish, like I'm moving through gelatin.

A door opens and reveals a dank room with a stained mattress on top of a bedframe.

My eyes are threatening to shut for good. The last thing I'm able to focus on as Sonny drags me—not quite kicking and screaming since I can't seem to do either—are the wrist cuffs attached to the headboard.

"Tie her up there, boy." Herschel's voice is muffled and far away. My eyes are glued shut now, my senses getting duller by the second. Blackness seeping in to make me disappear.

"She ain't goin' nowhere for a while."

It's the last thing I hear before everything turns black.

CHAPTER

TEN

THE SCENT of fresh-brewed coffee wafts into my nose, and I silently thank Jared for remembering to set up the timer the night before. There is nothing like waking up to the smell of coffee already brewing. That's one thing I love about staying at his place, the fancy coffeemaker. At my place, there is nothing but an old Mr. Coffee machine in desperate need of a cleaning.

I put my arm around Jared and kiss the back of his neck. He moans softly and moves closer to me. After he stretches, he rolls over and spoons me.

"Morning, Liz," he says with a yawn.

"Morning, handsome."

"Coffee should be ready soon."

"Mmm, sounds good."

This is my favorite part of the day, right after waking up, when I'm still comfortable in bed and the day hasn't really begun yet. Before I have to deal with the coldness outside of the blankets, and the stress of commuting to the office.

Jared kisses my forehead, and a hazy gray fog washes over him. The fog covers everything, even the scent of coffee.

Jared disappears.

The gray fog starts to cover me and turns into this black cloud. I can't see anything anymore.

The aching starts in my shoulders; a bout of dry heaves that hasn't happened yet, but they're coming. I've had this feeling before. Mostly on benders in college and a few since then, but not that many more. It's that morning-after type of density that manifests inside of my mind. It's strange yet familiar, and unkind, sizzling the thoughts that don't want to escape but I know, in a sinking feeling of reality, that I have to wake up and deal with whatever type of hangover this is.

It's heaving…it's dense…it's weighted and surreal, like when I finally woke up from surgery after having my wisdom teeth removed. The effects of anesthesia weren't wearing off like they were supposed to, and I was in a certain la-la land I do not remember, only that it was wonderful, and I was at peace, and I was so sad to wake up from it, having to settle into reality.

This sort of feels like that, but not as much. It feels…real but not. Like an in-between dream, where you sort of know it's a dream, and you sort of know it's not. A simultaneous split of existence.

My thoughts aren't making sense. My mouth feels dry. My eyes feel like they're glued shut. All I can see behind my lids is this dense gray fog twitching and flickering like dull candlelight.

Where am I? Not in my own bed, not Jared's bed…I don't remember drinking that much last night. What the hell is going on? Something is…something is not…right.

The fog starts to dissipate behind my eyes, and the lids begin to loosen as my mind finally wakes up. There's a haze, then a too-bright light. My lashes crackle with dried gunk as I tear them apart and blink. Everything is blurry, and slowly coming into focus.

I'm lying on a bed, facing a wall with flypaper hanging in the corner and a bunch of dead flies stuck to it. I start to cough, and something is inside of my mouth. Something thick and wet with a coppery taste. I try to move my arms to grab whatever is stuffed into my mouth, but they're stuck. I can't move. My arms are stiff, frozen above my head.

I blink a few more times, my eyes watering, trickles of tears dripping from the corners. Sleepy seeds in my lashes. Can't blink them out. Can't get my hands there to rake them out.

On the wall is a plastic pinwheel, stabbed there with a thumbtack. The pinwheel is red, white, and blue, and not spinning. The air in this room is too thick and stifling.

This room...what is it? Where am I?

As my mind fully comes into a conscious state, memories of what happened come swarming at me. Jared's giant picnic basket...diamond ring in a velvet box...trees everywhere...the woods...the pickup truck...the wilted dinner and wine. Sonny grabbing me and carrying me into a room with wrist cuffs on a stained mattress.

None of that was a dream, was it?

My mind falls into a tailspin as reality blankets me. I writhe around and scream, but all that comes out are muffled groans, then a raw buzzing feeling in my throat. I gag and my eyes water. A taste of blood in my mouth. I don't know if the blood is from my mouth or the rag stuffed into it. I'm disgusted either way and start to heave, but I keep it down.

My arms are numb all the way through my hands. Whenever my arm falls asleep and goes numb, I can shake my hand out to get it back to normal.

But this time I can't.

I twist my head up to confirm what I already know—I'm strapped to the bed. I turn my head downward to see what they bound my feet with, and a thick cord is wrapped around my ankles. It's some sort of bungee cord or those ropes used in rock climbing. I try to move my feet and twist around in them, but no luck.

I need to get the hell out of here! Where is Jared?

"Help!" I try to scream through the gag. Nothing but mumbles can be heard. No one will hear that. I guess that's the point of the muzzle, right?

Thank God my clothes are still on. My shoes are missing, though, and the more I move the more I can feel the blisters on my ankles pressing against the cords wrapped around them.

My blouse isn't tucked into my pants. Maybe I forgot to tuck it in after Jared and I had sex? I can't remember. Everything happened so quickly after that, we got lost and then the car was gone. I really hope that's why it's untucked. The thought of those two molesting me while I was unconscious makes me sick. I have to stop thinking about the even worse things that can happen with me tied to this bed.

My body trembles from shoulders to feet and my breathing comes in short, quick gasps. I start to cry, but then stop myself because my nose is the only method of getting air that I have. It always gets stuffed up when I cry, and I can't have that happen now. My face is hot and my ears are ringing from how fast my heart is beating. There is only so much air I can pull in through my nose. Especially when my lungs are trying to take in more air than usual in that quick, halting manner of hyperventilating. There are bright spots in front of my eyes and then everything around me fades. I'm drifting in and out just like that time I had my wisdom teeth pulled. The place I'm falling into is so much nicer and more pleasant than the room I'm in, with fields of flowers and the bluest sky above. So easy to just succumb to this other world of unconsciousness.

I shake my head to stop the fog. I need to focus and be as

alert as possible. As much as I want to scream into the gag, it will only make me hyperventilate, and probably pass out. So I hold it back. I need to conserve my energy to get out of this.

Maybe whatever they drugged me with at dinner is still in my system. Roofies I'm assuming. Whatever this stuff is, it's messing with my head. I'm having trouble remembering everything that happened. Being tied down isn't helping since it's such an unnatural feeling. My mind isn't focusing right. I'm like a scarecrow, tied to a fence with no brains.

I twist my hands in the restraints, and they barely move. Even through the pins and needles of numbness, I can feel the pressure of them around my wrists, and the rope burns from trying to get out of them. I wish they'd used something softer to bind my wrists, like the cloth they'd used to gag my mouth with. That feels like a handkerchief. My tongue presses against the gag and I try to ignore the flypaper and musty, disgusting scent in the air.

I'm getting good at breathing over the scent as I take in oxygen. The scent lies at the bottom of my nose, and when I need air, I intake it over the odor while it rests there, like climbing over a little hill. I'm not sure how or why that works, but it does. Maybe it's just in my head.

Maybe all of this is in my head. Wouldn't that be awesome? In a way, I guess, since it would also mean I'm mentally ill. Would that be better or worse than this being real?

This room's stench reminds me of places near a body of water, like a pond or a lake, not so much the ocean. The scent of mold mixes with an earthy aroma that brings to mind worms and other creepy crawlers. The bed has no sheets on it, and the mattress has yellow blotch stains and some springs are poking out. I check out my foot straps—tied to the metal footboard.

I strain my neck to see how tightly my arms are tied to

the headboard. Maybe, if I can get the bed raised, I can loosen the cords. It's something, right?

I thrust my body to make the bed jump up from the floor, but it doesn't even budge. Jerking around in the restraints doesn't seem to do much either, but I keep doing it, hoping it'll loosen the straps. I can't just lie here doing nothing, even though I can't seem to do much else besides squirm in the straps and blink back tears. I can't accept this helplessness and it's fucking infuriating.

At least when my parents had me locked inside that closet when I was a teenager, I wasn't tied up and could move around—albeit in a tiny space that was very much like a coffin.

This feels even more like being in a coffin. Tied to a bed just waiting for my death, by two crazy men who are most likely going to rape and kill me, or Jared, or both of us.

A fate worse than death. What if they're cannibals or necrophiliacs? What if they have something even more sickening in mind that I can't even fathom, some kind of Jeffrey Dahmer or Norman Bates psycho fetish?

Where is Jared? What if he's tied up in the next room? Maybe he's strong enough to escape the restraints and come rescue me. I have to keep making myself believe that. I want to keep telling myself this is just a dream. A vivid, horrifying dream. Where I was a few minutes ago, in Jared's bed smelling coffee—that was real. Any minute now I'll get back to it. All I have to do is close my eyes, go back to sleep for a little while, and I'll wake up in Jared's warm bed with his arms around me, with coffee and a morning quickie coming right up.

The room wavers in and out of focus and the hazy gray fog comes back, though it's not as heavy. And now I'm sitting on my white couch with Jared. We're getting ready to watch a movie. He spoons me and feeds me a grape from the fruit salad from our picnic. Then he places the diamond ring on my finger. I tear it off and glare at him. My eyes snap open, and I'm back in the hell house.

Tears streak my cheeks as my chest heaves with sobs. The dankness of the room is almost unbearable to breathe in through my nose. During the picnic, I wished I could simply lie down for a while and think about my decision to marry Jared, and now I have my wish. It just would've been nicer to have had that time in my apartment, in my own bed. With the freedom to move around and go to the bathroom, a creature comfort that's becoming more and more needed by the minute. And I'm not sure what to do about that.

The pressure in my bladder is growing harder to ignore. I'm not going to pee into the mattress and lie there in my own urine. But I really can't hold it much longer. Perhaps it's a good thing they haven't brought me anything to drink.

I don't know how much time I have before one or both of them come in here and do whatever they're planning to do. I have to come up with an escape plan, but until I'm out of the restraints, my options are rather limited.

I keep thinking about those horror movies like *The Texas Chainsaw Massacre*. That also took place in the middle of nowhere. For all I know, these two are serial killers on the FBI's most-wanted list, and they're already being monitored. But probably not. Wishful thinking on my part.

I'm so happy we scheduled this picnic on a Sunday, not a Saturday, because it means we'll be missed at work soon. Calls to our emergency contacts will get people suspicious of our whereabouts, and unanswered calls to our mobile phones will get them searching. And someone in Jared's family who went to that big reunion picnic will lead the police in the right direction.

As long as we're not too far from that spot. Hopefully they didn't bring me somewhere even more remote. Holy crap—what if we're in Canada? Or an island off the coast of it?

But the faint scent of celery convinces me I'm still in the farmhouse with the celery scarecrow on the fence. They said it was a celery farm, but maybe they just make scarecrows out of celery for no reason other than the fact that they're crazy.

We will be found soon. I know we will. We didn't drive that far away from Boston, and everyone in his family knew where we were going. At least his parents did—Jared mentioned that his father was the one who suggested taking me to the same spot from their family picnic.

They say when you're lost, it's usually best to stay put until a rescue party finds you. I heard that on the news once, about people stranded in some remote place in the woods, just like us. We just have to hold on a bit longer, and they'll find us. They'll find us soon and we'll be rescued. All I have to do is wait and keep telling myself that. Because it's the only way I can keep myself from losing my sanity.

I wonder how long I've been tied up. It was evening when they picked us up, and it's now the next day. I think I've been out for over twelve hours. There's enough light in the room to make it mid-morning. That means it's time for the Monday morning sales meeting! They will already be looking for me at work. We'll be rescued sooner than I thought.

That gives me a slight tremor of hope, but it doesn't last long. Heavy footsteps approach from outside the room, getting louder by the second.

CHAPTER

ELEVEN

I STARE at the door and wait for it to open. Hold my breath with my heart pounding. Tighten my muscles though there isn't much I can do in these restraints.

The footsteps go past the door, and the sound fades. But it sobers me up from my semi-conscious state. Whichever one it was, I'm sure he'll be back. I have to be alert and stop waiting for a rescue team to save me.

I scope out the room some more. There are yellow stains on the walls and ceiling, most likely from water damage, and mold in the corners. So I'm breathing that in too. Great. But really, that's the least of my concerns.

My limbs are so taut in the restraints I can stretch just enough to see the floor. But even through the numbness, I can still feel the ring on my finger, the cold hardness of it pressing between my middle and pinky fingers.

Dark splotches on the bit of carpet I can see, and piles of dirty clothes in the corner. This place must've gone to hell after Herschel's wife died. Or maybe she was also a slob. I can certainly see that, with these two to deal with. I'd probably just give up too.

In another corner, a couple of garbage bags filled to nearly bursting. I wonder if that's the dank scent I can't stand breathing in. Why don't they just throw them out? Why keep garbage in a bedroom? Nothing about these two makes any sense.

There are two other doors in the room besides the one the footsteps went past. One is probably a closet, and maybe the other one opens to an adjoining room. These old farmhouses tend to have nooks and crannies and extra passageways. They may even have one of those old-fashioned dumbwaiters somewhere.

Across from the bed is a mirror with a big scratch down the middle, and a three-tiered stand with a pair of bronzed baby shoes that probably belonged to Sonny. Next to the mirror is a portrait of a beautiful broad-shouldered woman with hair the same color blonde as mine, only hers is long and flowing behind her. She looks like she's wearing a wedding dress, a white lacy frock, but no veil or flowers in her hand. Nothing in the background of the portrait indicates a wedding, either. Just dark skies with fields of celery poking up from the ground behind her.

Something about the woman's face, I can't quite pinpoint it, but the curve of her chin and high cheekbones feels familiar to me.

There's a window behind me, making a shaded square on the wall. I can see the corners of the window whenever I twist my head upward. It's got threadbare plaid curtains and a shade with cracks. When a gust of wind blows through there's movement around the edges of the square on the wall from dancing tree branches.

If I get out of these cords, I can escape through that window. I've already got ropes to climb down with. Taking a deep breath, I throttle myself around, trying to loosen the restraints. My hands and feet barely twist. The cords are too tight. Yanking on them, I'm about to let a muffled scream out when I hear a heavy noise on repeat.

Footsteps outside the room, getting closer. Louder. When they're just outside the door to this room, they stop.

I hold my breath and keep my eyes on the door. There's a brief knock, which I find odd since I'm tied up and gagged. The door creaks open and Herschel walks in, carrying something that looks like an old curtain.

"Mornin' there!" He smiles at me.

He unfolds the curtain and shakes it much like a matador would at a bull. Only it's not a curtain, but a dress with a full skirt and sweetheart bodice, and long sleeves. Covered in lace.

It's a wedding dress. An old-fashioned, tacky frock so aged and filled with dust that the color is yellow, not white.

"This belonged to my dear departed wife, and my mother before her. Ain't it beautiful?"

He strokes the dress and smiles, then he hangs it on a hook in the wall directly in front of me.

"Where's Jared?" I try to speak through the gag, but only mumbles come out.

"Hush now, no use trying to speak. I'm sure you'll look just as beautiful in it!"

I shake my head and writhe around in the straps. He reaches down and pets my foot. I try to jerk away, but the straps restrain me.

"I have to pee!" Nothing but mumbles. I stare up at him, pleading with my eyes.

"Don't worry! You'll be able to talk on the wedding night."

Herschel chuckles as he turns away, but then glances back. His grin is full of pride.

"As soon as I saw you two on the blanket, I knew you was just right for my son."

He winks and leaves the room, shutting the door behind him.

What. The actual fuck. Wedding night?

THERE'S A SINKING feeling in the pit of my stomach.

When Jared and I were having sex on the picnic blanket, I remember having a strong feeling that someone out there was watching us.

It was them.

Sonny's laugh when I drank that drugged wine reminded me of the weird noise I heard in the woods, what I thought back then was some kind of wild animal. That cross between a pig oinking and a donkey braying.

They were the ones stalking us in the forest.

And they must have stolen Jared's car, then waited for us to come walking down the road.

My body temperature drops a couple degrees as it all comes together slowly, sinking in to such a mind-boggling amount of belief and disbelief. My eyes go to the portrait on the wall of the blonde woman in the wedding dress, a cleaner version of the one he hung on a hook.

They set this whole thing up. Followed us through the woods and then pretended to help us. Just to make me

Sonny's bride. But why me? Are there no other women around up here?

The need to pee is getting so strong I'm ready to release my bladder into the mattress and not give a damn. I thought I was afraid before, back when we were lost in the woods. Hell, I thought I was afraid when Jared asked me to marry him. What the hell did I know? That was nothing.

How long were those two stalking us? Did they happen upon us in the woods while we were going at it, or did they spot our car on the road and then follow us?

I should've made Jared turn the car around the second I got a bad feeling on our way up here. And we never should've gotten into their truck. But what else were we supposed to do? No one else was coming down that road to give us a lift. And they knew no one *would* come down that road.

A knot forms in my stomach and aches. It feels like I got punched in the gut. I want so badly to throw up but I can't with the gag in my mouth—I'll choke on it. Keeping the vomit down is only making the ache in my stomach worse.

All the air rushes out of my lungs and my heart pounds. I'm trembling and sweating all over. I want to scream, and I can't. I want to run away, but I can't.

I can wriggle around in these restraints as much as I want. I won't be able to tear through bungee cords. They're designed to keep two-hundred-pound men from hitting concrete. The only part of my body I can move is my head, which I shake from left to right. I should've known what they had in mind, with the way Sonny kept looking at me. How could I have been so stupid to think it was anything else? The thought of being with Sonny makes my skin crawl...that thing that smells like old celery and giggles so hard saliva drips out from his mouth like a dog.

Those sick, hick assholes. What if they did stuff to me

while I was unconscious and I just don't remember? My shirt's untucked. My shoes are missing.

The gut-punch feeling inside my stomach grows. My face is burning up and even through the numbness in my hands, I can feel a raging heat simmering beneath my skin. The anger festers inside me, settles into my gut, and replaces the fear.

It's stronger than the fear.

Fear isn't going to help, and waiting for help isn't good enough. Anger will get me out of this more than fear will.

I turn and strain my neck as far as it can go upward. Maybe I can get the cords loose from the headboard. Maybe they just need to be shimmied down a bit more, and a nice big jump off the floor will release them from the frame. My hands won't be free from them, but at least they won't be attached to the bed.

I could try moving the bed with force. Somehow get a leg up from the floor and pull the cord free. Bungee cords stretch, don't they?

But it's harder than I think to stretch the cords enough to pull up part of the bed. My legs are stronger than my arms, so I yank my left leg out with all of my might and it barely moves half an inch before it snaps back.

Every muscle in my body flexes and tries to help free my leg. I hold my breath and tug, pull, give it everything I've got —and my leg moves another half inch and snaps back. I let out the air I was holding in and take some deep breaths. Wait a couple of minutes and try again. This time with my left arm.

It won't even budge.

I want to scream. I bang my head against the mattress while I think about those two setting us up, rage bubbling inside of me. It gives me the strength I need to bump and writhe on the bed enough to make it bounce. I throttle myself up and down, and the bed scrapes against the floor.

I got it to move!

I bump and push my pelvis up and down, left and right, until the bed shakes and scrapes against the floor again. I do it once more before the door slams open, and Herschel storms in.

"What in the hell are you doing missy? You're gonna break the floor. Now stop that!"

I scream inside the gag.

"Hush up, now! Don't make me come in here again, got that?"

He wags his finger at me. I shake my head. I say, "Fuck you!" through the gag.

After he leaves, slamming the door behind him, I jostle the bed trying to loosen the cords. The anger and energy inside of me are growing fiercer by the second. The bed shakes and scrapes against the wooden floor. Heavy footsteps pound outside the room.

The door swings open and Herschel walks in. "I told you to stop that!"

I glare at him with my eyes narrowed.

"Don't make me come back in here with the belt!"

The second he leaves, I writhe on the bed, trying not to jump much. Still, the frame scrapes against the floor, loudly. He comes back holding a thick leather belt with a big metal buckle. He raises it into the air and I don't even flinch.

CHAPTER

THIRTEEN

HERSCHEL STARES at me with the belt raised. "I better not hear anything else in here again!"

I stay still. He lowers the belt, wags his finger, and then leaves. His footsteps are heavy as he walks down the stairs.

There's no way I can escape this room without them stopping me. I scream inside of the gag with the dull taste of blood in my mouth and thrash my head on the bed.

After a bout of this, I finally start to calm down. Breathing a little more evenly now. My body cools down. I stare at the portrait of the blonde woman, and then the garish wedding dress hanging on the wall. It looks disgusting, and probably smells about as good as the rest of this place. It looks so much cleaner on the tall, broad-backed woman on the wall. She reminds me a bit of one of my older aunts, I think her name was Mary or Mary-Margaret or something similarly Catholic.

Was this Sonny's mother? Or his grandmother, perhaps? She has this austere, regal look to her, at least in the way she was painted for this picture. Maybe it was done just before her wedding day.

But maybe it can help me escape.

They'll have to untie me so I can put on the dress, and that's when I'll have my chance. I'm in better shape than those two, though they are bigger than me. One of them might hold a knife to me, but perhaps I can kick it out of his hand. My muscles are spry enough from playing softball. They can't get out of these bungee cords, but they can kick someone, pretty hard. I should save my strength for that. But how numb will my limbs be once I'm freed? I might not have enough time to let the feeling rush back to warm up. My legs don't feel as numb as my arms, though. That's where most of my strength lies anyway.

They might give me time to get ready for the so-called wedding, freshen up in the bathroom, or something. That could be my chance. Search the bathroom for something I can use as a weapon or escape through a window. Get help, and then come back for Jared.

Maybe he's already in the middle of escaping from his own restraints, soon to be breaking down that door, rescuing me. I can't see my ring with the way they tied my hands, but I can sort of feel it on my finger. Even though nearly every part of my body is numb with a dull buzzing sensation, I can still feel the ring, the metal pressing against my skin.

I glance at the red, white and blue pinwheel on the wall, and a memory from our early days flashes in the corner of my mind. It was the Fourth of July and we kissed while the fireworks went off around us—we were so into each other we didn't even notice them.

I let myself cry and breathe through the thickening snot in my nose. The taste of blood in my mouth is waning. Or I'm just getting used to it.

My tongue presses against the gag while I try to move it down. I grind my jaw up and down, rub my cheek against the mattress, and slide against the bed. It's not working. I try the other cheek; move my head around, and then something snaps in my neck like I hit a nerve the wrong way. Not so much painful but it comes with a heavy numbing sensation, and the gag feels no lower on my lips than before.

I wonder where Jared is. He could be in the next room, tied to a bed, wondering and worrying about me too. Sometimes it takes a situation like this, something life-threatening, to make you truly appreciate someone. I can't wait until we're out of this mess and back home. Snuggling underneath his down comforter, making love with nobody watching us.

Maybe Jared and I will become a famous survivor couple. They might even make a movie about us. I can't wait for the moment when we kiss while wrapped up in those thick blankets that rescue teams always have in their trunks.

I'm so dehydrated, but sucking on the rag in my mouth helps, as gross as that is. Dehydration sometimes makes me loopy. When I focus on the dress, I realize the skirt is a mismatched lacy patchwork pattern. But the unmatching parts aren't so much from a spotty dress pattern, but holes in the fabric. Moths maybe?

The wind picks up outside and hits the window, making it creak. Something taps and scratches the glass. I turn my head toward it but I can't see much. The shadow on the wall looks like a jagged tree branch.

The light in the room getting darker makes me nervous. I thought that help would've arrived by now. We've been missing for almost an entire day.

What is taking them so long?

I didn't go to work, neither did Jared—shouldn't people be looking for us? My manager should have called my emergency contact when I didn't answer my cell phone. I'm pretty sure my emergency contact is Courteney but if not her then my parents, which is just as good to get the ball rolling. I'm sure Jared's parents will be worried about him too. The whole firm will wonder where he is. Unless he told them about his plans to pop the question, and they assume he took the day off work to celebrate. But doesn't he have some big meeting with Abigail's father to relinquish their business dealings or something? They'll be looking for him, I'm sure.

Maybe it takes a bit of time to get the cops moving. They're probably already out looking, and just haven't gotten this far in their search yet. Our phones weren't getting signals up here, so maybe they won't be able to trace us. I'm not sure how that works anyway, if they have to call the phone to put a trace on it or something. Maybe they can use the "Find my iPhone" thing?

What if Jared is still unconscious, and that's why he hasn't escaped and gotten to me yet? That does worry me, that he may be knocked out that badly. Being unconscious for this long is not good. I don't want to let the thought creeping in take over: that Herschel and Sonny have killed him.

No. He's still alive. And we're going to make it out of here.

I'm so tired from straining my muscles trying to get out of these cords. Light-headed from dehydration. I'm drifting off to sleep, but every little creak startles me awake. I'm worried about Sonny coming in, even though there isn't much I can do about it. But I'd rather be awake and alert if he does show up.

Why the hell did Jared have to take me all the way out here? There were so many instances in my control where I could've avoided this. I could've canceled with him when Courteney had texted to ask me to lunch. I could've said no when Jared asked me to marry him. I could've said no years ago when he'd called to ask me out after dumping my sister.

Now I'm just beating myself up, when I should direct my anger at those two psychos for kidnapping us.

I wonder what time it is and feel the need to pee so badly

my back teeth are floating. A dull throb pulses through my bladder and I'm getting used to it, but I'll have to relieve it soon. I don't know how much longer I'll be able to hold it in before I have to let go.

My eyes drift over to the portrait of the blonde woman, and wonder if she'd ever been held captive, tied to a bed against her will.

I drift off to sleep, and then jolt awake. It's getting harder and harder to keep myself awake and alert. There's only so much I can do to stop myself from sleeping. It's not like I can fix a pot of coffee or do jumping jacks to get my blood pumping.

Footsteps outside the room. Loud creaks of floorboards, and then the footsteps stop at the door.

It creaks open, and Sonny is standing in the doorway. His shadow makes him appear larger than he is. His eyes are wide and bright, and they travel up and down my body.

He takes a step in and stands at the foot of the bed with his hands behind his back. He doesn't move. He just stares at me.

It's almost creepier than him actually doing something.

After a while, he pulls his hands from behind his back. He's holding a stalk of celery. He giggles and waves it back and forth like a pendulum. Even though it's only one stalk, the entire room fills up with the odor of celery. It wafts into the air like it's coming out of an aerosol can.

He moves the stalk between a hole he made with his thumb and forefinger. He blows a kiss at me. I scream, but no sound comes out. I writhe around in the cords but it's completely futile. I can't tear them. There's nowhere I can run to. The only thing I can do is pray for a miracle.

Sonny leaps across the room and lands on the bed, squishing me. He fondles my breasts through my blouse and unbuttons my pants. The pressure of him on top of me releases my bladder. I pee all over Sonny as he pulls down my pants, my last leg of defense and defiance against him. I squirm and struggle in the cords, but there's nothing I can do to stop him. So I piss all over his hand that's trying to jam the celery stalk into me, but he doesn't seem to care as he laughs, and a hazy gray fog fills the room.

I wake up sucking in air through my nose.

Sonny isn't on top of me.

He's not even in the room.

The door is closed, and it's not as dark in here as it was earlier. It was just a dream, and hopefully not a premonition one. My pants are still on, though they're wet around my thighs. I take a deep breath and smell urine. At least I don't have to go to the bathroom anymore. I made the bed my bathroom. I'm not sure what's worse, the smell of urine or celery. The two mixed together is one of the worst odors I've ever experienced.

Renewed urgency to get the hell off this bed rushes over me and I jerk upward stretching my arms. It's quiet in the house. If everyone's asleep, maybe they won't hear the bed scrape against the floor.

The bed bounces up and scrapes against the floor. It sounds even louder than it did before, amplified by the silence of nighttime.

I don't hear any footsteps approaching the room.

I do it again, with a bigger jump. The bed moves, but the cords don't feel like they've loosened at all.

Distant creaks outside the room. Sounds like someone walking upstairs. I stop moving as the floorboards creak closer to the room.

The footsteps stop outside the door. The doorknob turns, making a soft squeak. I hold my breath as the door nudges forward. A beam of light from the dimness of the hallway inches into the room. A whiff of celery enters along with it.

Creaks in the floorboards, and then a soft grunt and the footsteps move away from the door.

Did he forget something? Or change his mind? I'm sure he'll be back, whichever one it was, since the door is still open a few inches. I take some quick breaths through my nose and smell wet dog.

FOURTEEN

THE HOUND RUNS into the room panting and sniffing and circling the bed. He licks my hand. Maybe I can get the dog to chew through these cords!

I edge my hand closer to him, but all he does is lick it. Then he runs around the bed and jumps up on it. His nails scratch me. His nose is in my crotch. Guess it was the scent of urine that attracted him.

Soon the dog loses interest in my pee-soaked pants and starts to lick my face. He licks the rag wrapped around my mouth, his big eyes widening.

Yes, that's it. Come on dog, just tug it down a bit.

He gnaws at the rag. His teeth scrape my cheek. He can bite me all he wants, just chew through these restraints and set me free!

Creaks from the hallway. Someone whistles and footsteps pound the floorboards outside the room. A large shape appears in the doorway.

The hound whimpers and jumps off the bed and runs out through the door. A meaty hand reaches in and grabs the doorknob. The door slams shut.

"Sonny-boy!" Herschel bellows from the other side of the door. "Get that damn dog outta here and tie him up by the fence outside!"

Muffled whimpers from the dog. A couple more doors slam, and then it's quiet. Nothing but the creaks of the house settling, while the wind outside whips through the walls making the tree limbs sway in a shadow dance around the room.

If I can get out of these restraints and go through the window, I'll have to leave without searching for Jared. I can always go find help and come back for him. But what if they kill him during that time?

What if they've killed him already? I can't let myself think like this.

The room lightens little by little as the sun rises. Will this be the day they untie me, or will they continue to starve me? They'll have to give me water at some point if they plan on keeping me alive.

I wish they'd hurry up and get this "wedding" over with. What are they waiting for anyway, the caterers? RSVPs for a head count?

I stare at the portrait of the blonde woman in the dress, wondering if it's the same woman from the photos in the kitchen. The dear departed wife. I wonder if she was just as crazy as those two, or if she'd been drugged like me. Maybe they kidnapped her too. Maybe she woke up tied to a bed, and pregnant with Sonny.

I shudder in the restraints. I need to get out of here. *We* need to get out of here.

Footsteps climb the stairs and approach the room. There's that awful pig-donkey guffaw that comes out of Sonny. Sounds like he's right outside the door.

I kick my feet in the cords as well as I can. My mind is sending signals to my feet to run, but I can't. All I can do is lie here, just like a nightmare. Fully conscious sleep paralysis.

The door opens. Sonny takes a step into the room. The dog trots in behind him, and breezes by his knees.

"I told you to keep that dog outta there!" Herschel shouts from somewhere close by.

Sonny comes over and grabs the hound by the scruff of his neck. The dog whimpers, and his back claws scrape against the floor as his master drags him out. The door is still open, and I can see the hallway. It's just as dingy as the rest of this place.

Sonny comes back after a few minutes. He stands in the doorway making kissing noises at me. Smacks his lips and then blows a wet raspberry my way. I turn away and shut my eyes. I open them back up when the floorboard next to me creaks. Sonny is standing just a few feet away from me.

He leans forward and rests his hands on the side of the bed, and it sags. His chin is right over my arm, and a long piece of drool hangs down from his mouth, much like his dog. He guffaws. The slab of drool shakes and breaks off and lands on my arm. He leans in closer. His upper body almost completely covers me.

That slouchy look is gone from his eyes, replaced by a dark, intense stare that bores right into me. Like he knows something I don't know, and it's not something good. At least, not for me.

I close my eyes when his foul breath reaches my nose, hoping that will somehow lessen the wretched scent. But of course, it doesn't. My mouth is gagged—I can only breathe through my nose. So I have to smell this thing leaning over me, his hand reaching up my waist.

I hold my breath to give myself a brief reprieve. Squeeze my eyes shut, as tight as I can, and try to picture myself in Paris with Jared. Pretend we're kissing by the Louvre.

When his hand grazes the bottom of my breast, I hear pounding footsteps getting louder.

My eyes snap open. Sonny is standing a few feet away from the bed again, and his dad is standing in the doorway.

"I told you to stay out, now! Not just your dog, but you too, Sonny—it's bad luck to see the bride before the wedding. Go on, now."

He gestures for him to leave. Sonny walks out with his head down, and his father smacks him when he reaches the door.

Sonny slinks into the hallway and the dog barks.

Herschel shakes his head. "Sorry he bothered you, young lady." His eyes are cold and black with creases around the edges, and heavy bags under his lower lids. I look into them, trying to find sympathy.

He takes a step into the room. "I was gonna bring you a bed pan, but I can smell that you already went in the bed!"

He looks at me with his head tilted to the side. Does he expect me to apologize?

"It's all right," he says "Ain't the first time that bed's been peed in!"

Great. I'm lying in someone else's urine as well as mine.

His eyes light up and he claps his hands together. "Almost time to get ready! You got a big day ahead of you. We'll officially be family soon, even though we sorta been family already."

He winks, then leaves and closes the door behind him. I shudder in the restraints. Maybe this is the day they're planning on marrying me to Sonny, which means they will have to untie me, to get me into that awful wedding dress.

Every second after they untie me is crucial. I have to make a run for it as soon as I'm free. I'm sure I can outrun those two—but how far will I get once I leave this house? I don't remember seeing another house around for miles when we drove here.

I wish I knew where Jared is. Maybe I should hide first, at least for a bit. Let them think I ran out of the house and once they leave to look for me outside, I'll search for Jared, a weapon of my own, and a phone to call 911.

The sound of footsteps on floorboards grows louder outside the room accompanied by maniacal giggling.

CHAPTER

FIFTEEN

THE FOOTSTEPS STOP outside the door. "Hush up!" Herschel's loud voice bellows and Sonny's giggling ceases.

The door inches open and they walk into the room, grinning. Sonny looks like he's holding in a huge bout of laughter, trying hard to keep it inside.

He is also holding a pistol.

When did they get a gun? Did they have it this whole time? If so, why haven't I seen it before now?

I look from the gun to the wedding dress. That's how they're planning to get me inside that thing. They're going to untie me, but with a gun aimed at me.

I wish they had a knife or some sort of bludgeoning device instead. A lot easier to escape something like that since they have to be close to use it. I didn't picture a gun in any scenario. I figured I would've seen it by now.

Why hadn't they used the gun to get me here in the first place? It makes no sense. Nothing about these two makes any sense!

But it's still a gateway to getting out of these restraints. They are going to untie me. I just have to be careful with my moves. I can't simply turn and run the second I'm free. I don't know if my limbs will get limber enough, quick enough —they've been restrained and horizontal for so long that they're completely numb, and it will take a little time to get feeling back into them.

"She really is a beauty, ain't she?" Herschel looks me over with the same look I saw on Sonny when they picked us up off the road.

I stare back at him and narrow my eyes. I give him the dirtiest glare I can manage with a gag in my mouth. Sonny unleashes that noise I can't stand. The gun shakes in his hand as he throws his head back, like a demented kid let loose in a candy store.

Herschel claps Sonny on the shoulder. They both stare at me like I'm some sort of prize they just won.

My eyes fill with tears, and my insides are churning chunks. I get a memory flash of Jared as he entered me, how I sucked in my breath at the intensity of it. And these two assholes watched it. The vomit starts creeping up my throat.

"We been waiting for a girl just like you," he continues, slowly approaching me. "We never see girls like you up this way, and thought we were gonna have to go huntin' for one soon. Like I did to finally get my dear departed wife."

That poor woman. He kidnapped her and threatened her to stay. My throat contracts and I can't hold it back anymore, and I heave. Throw up a bit in my mouth. It seeps into the gag and now I'm having trouble breathing.

Sonny giggles, making the gun shake. I try to scream, "No!" But nothing comes out besides muffled groans.

"I knew we had to have you. So we started following you through the forest, shaking the trees to try and scare you." He lets out a laugh and slaps his thigh. "But you kept going in the wrong direction!"

I knew whatever was stalking us in the woods hadn't

been human. These two are monsters...but if they set this up, why didn't they just use that gun when they picked us up?

And then it dawns on me as Sonny stares at me with the gun aimed at my head. They wanted to get me here without force. They couldn't risk anyone seeing us on the road, even if it was deserted. Why would they take that chance?

These two are smarter than I thought. They're crazy *and* smart. A dangerous combination. I have to stop underestimating them.

"Where's Jared?" Nothing but mumbles come out while they both laugh.

"What's that now?" Herschel cups a hand to his ear and leans closer to me. "Did you just say, 'Screw marriage'?"

He laughs and slaps his hand against his leg. Sonny joins him, keeping the gun pointed at me. What if his finger slips from the movement, and he pulls the trigger? I squirm against the restraints, trembling all over.

I inhale deeply and the trembling stops. The heat coursing through my body turns into a tingling sensation, an adrenaline rush. The anger I couldn't release because I've been bound and gagged is festering inside of me, settling into my bones.

It's replacing the fear.

I can't wait for them to untie me. All I want right now is to take that gun out of Sonny's hand and shoot both of them.

Sonny has the gun aimed at my forehead. Herschel reaches down and unties the straps on my ankles. I flex my toes and feel a rush of tingles through my feet, all the way up my shins and thighs. I keep my eyes on Sonny. He's still smiling, but no longer giggling as he stares at my legs. He has the gun still aimed at my head, just a little lower now.

"All right," Herschel says as he straightens up. "I'm gonna undo the other straps. Now you been real good 'bout not kickin' me when I untied your legs, so let's keep up the good faith while I untie the rest, got it?"

It's not like I can kick him with a gun pointed at me. I can't figure these two out. They're smart enough to hatch this plan to abduct me, but they seem to have trouble with common sense.

I keep my eyes on Sonny and the gun while his father reaches down and unties my wrists and hands from the excruciating straps. Hot pins and needles travel up and down my limbs and fingers as the senses come back. I tug my arms down to my sides and wiggle my fingers to speed up the process. It's almost making the rest of my body numb all over again, but then the feeling comes back, little by little, while I flex and relax.

"You been tied up awhile, so take your time gettin' up," Herschel says.

I bend my arms at the elbows, and when I reach up to remove the gag Sonny takes a step closer. He points the gun at my face while his father wags his finger at me.

"Now now, not yet," he says. "No talking 'til you're given permission. That's a rule you're gonna have to get used to in this house, missy. Good farm wives know their places, got that?"

I'm not going to give him the satisfaction of nodding. I pull myself into a sitting position while staring at the gun. Sonny lowers it a bit more, though I can't tell if he's doing this on purpose. I move my legs over the side of the bed and rest my bare feet on the floor. It's sticky. Of course it's sticky.

As soon as I put weight on my legs to stand, the room spins and I fall back on the bed. Herschel takes a step forward and holds out his hands. I ignore him and try to stand on my own again. I'm shaky, but solid. More pins and needles careen up and down my legs once I'm on my feet.

I feel a little woozy so I grab the bedside table to steady

myself and sit back down on the bed. My head is buzzing. I take a few deep breaths through my nose, trying as hard as hell to control my gag reflex, and stand up again. This time I'm steadier on my feet.

I stand with my hand inches from the gag and glare at them. Sonny hasn't lowered the gun. I glance at my left hand and the ring isn't there.

How could it not be there? I felt it. The whole time I was tied up I felt the ring on my finger, the hard metal against my skin. Did it fall off when I stretched? I would've heard it hit the floor. It must not have been there on my finger this whole time. But how could I have still felt it there? Was I imagining it?

Sonny takes a step closer, the gun steady. His smile drops and his eyes darken. I drop my hands to my sides, away from the gag. Until that gun is aimed away from a vital organ, I have to wait until I'm permitted to do anything.

Herschel nods. "Good. Now undress and put on the wedding gown."

I shake my head.

He slams a hand down on the bedside table and moves his face close to mine. "C'mon now! We ain't gonna let you get dressed alone so you can try to escape, think we're stupid or something?"

I want to nod at that, but I continue shaking my head. I cross my arms over my chest and glare at them. Are they planning to keep a gun aimed at me for the entire marriage?

I look at Sonny. He smacks his lips and drops the gun a couple of inches. It's not aimed at my head anymore, but at my neck which is just as deadly. He jumps in place while giggling, causing the floor to shake.

"Pipe down, son. You'll have plenty of time for hanky-panky later. We have to do this proper—it's a family tradition. Now keep still and keep that gun pointed at her!"

Sonny raises the gun a bit higher, but not by much. Herschel takes the wedding dress off the hook and holds it out toward me. I shake my head and stay in my spot. He takes a step closer. I back up, and stumble, but don't fall.

"Put it on!"

He shakes the dress, as if that's somehow making it more attractive. It looks even more disgusting up close. The lace is so yellowed it looks like nicotine stains. Parts of the dress are torn and there are brown stains on the bodice. I hope it's dried chocolate, and not dried blood.

Herschel takes another step toward me. He's almost on top of me at this point. He smells awful, like celery, sweat, and dirt. A diluted version of his son's body odor.

"If you don't put it on," he says, his voice taking on a low sinister tone, "I'll have to put it on for you."

He grabs my blouse and tugs at it. Sonny claps his free hand against his knee. I bat his father's hand away and take the dress.

I check the gun's new position, now aimed at my chest. Sonny is getting tired. Maybe all I have to do is stall. I inch toward the foot of the bed to face the scratched mirror on the wall, next to the bronzed baby shoes. The door is just a few feet away, and they left it open.

Sonny is on my right with the gun pointed at me. Now it's aimed at my stomach. Still not a good spot but getting lower. I take a step closer to the door and keep my eyes on the gun. It moves with me.

"Don't even think about runnin' off missy. We'll find you out there, easy, just like I always did every time my dear departed wife tried to run away."

Herschel stares at me and raises his fist. I stop, take off my blouse and toss it on the bed. Thankfully I'm wearing a camisole over my bra.

The gun is aimed a few inches lower. I thought seeing my

camisole would've caused Sonny to drop it completely, but it looks like I'll have to put on that disgusting wedding dress.

The dress is unbuttoned in back, and a musty scent with an underlying whiff of celery wafts into my nose. I step into the skirt and pull up the bodice, put my arms into the sleeves and wince. The inside smells and feels about as good as it looks. I keep my pee-stained pants on beneath the skirt of the dress. The sleeves are so long that I have to push them up my forearms, and the hem of the dress drags several inches on the floor. I clutch the skirt, ready to hike it up and run from this room.

Herschel comes up behind me and I try to step away, but he pulls me back and reaches out to button up the back. When he's done he takes a few steps back, whistles and claps.

"Ain't she a beauty?"

Sonny claps along with his dad, while still holding the gun, staring at me in the wedding dress. He slaps his free hand against his wrist. I really hope the safety is on.

Then he stops clapping, letting his arms hang at his sides. He's still holding the gun but it's not aimed at me anymore, just toward the floor. It also looks like he loosened his grip on it.

It takes a split second for me to realize this is my chance.

I leap toward the door and bump into the stand holding the bronzed baby shoes. They hit the floor with a loud clunk, making Sonny drop the gun.

Herschel lunges at me from across the room, but I'm already out the door. I yank up the skirt of the wedding dress as I run.

I'm in a dark hallway. I go left, hoping it's the right way. I hear Herschel scream that Sonny is an idiot and then there are heavy footsteps behind me. I pump my legs to move faster and tear the gag from my mouth as I escape.

SIXTEEN

THE HALLWAY IS SO dark I can barely see a foot in front of me—I don't notice the staircase until I almost fall down it. I stumble halfway down the stairs, then get my balance and run down the rest.

Heavy footsteps still sound behind me, getting louder. I want to get out of this hell house as soon as possible, but I can't leave Jared here—I have to find him.

There's a door on my left. I turn the knob and it creaks open to a dark room. I slip inside and close the door just as they bound around the corner. They run past the room and I hold my breath. The footsteps fade as I exhale, glancing around the room.

A chandelier flickers dim light every few seconds. Patches of torn wallpaper reveal stained walls. A couple of flies are buzzing about the room. There's a plate of half-eaten chicken in the middle of the long, lopsided table with a book wedged under a leg. I'm in the dining room.

I feel along the wall and find a door, open it, and go inside. A strong whiff of celery hits my nose. I take a piece of the wedding dress to cough into it, and my hand slips into a pocket. Inside the pocket is a book of matches. Maybe she was a smoker—guess I would be too if I had those two to deal with. I want to light a match to give myself some light, but then worry the smell of sulfur will lead them right to my hiding place.

A dim light shines beneath a door on the opposite side of the closet. As my eyes adjust, the light reveals rows of canned goods, dried goods, a bag of potatoes on the floor, and stalks of celery bound with twine. It's not a closet, but a pantry.

My first thought is to look for something to drink. Only there isn't anything to drink, just food from what I can make out. There are some canned peaches, and I think about just drinking the peach juice. Better than nothing until I can get to one of the faucets in the kitchen or bathroom.

I crouch down to see further, my knees creaking. Tucked underneath the bottom shelf is a dusty blue cardboard box with the *Capri Sun* logo. One of those giant wholesale club packages. I rip out one of the straws and stab it into a pouch, forgetting to breathe while sucking up the entire thing in seconds. Between the fluids and vitamin C getting into my system, I feel energized. And somewhat comforted, at least for a second. I open the box and stuff as many juice pouches as I can fit into the pockets of the dress, which aren't very large.

There's a cabinet built into the wall at the back of the pantry. On a closer look, it's a dumbwaiter, big enough to fit a small adult like me. I'm not crazy about the thought of getting inside that thing, but it can work like an elevator and get me through the house unseen to look for Jared. As long as it isn't too noisy.

I take a step closer and my foot lands on something that crackles like a bag of potato chips.

Foot shadows appear in the light underneath the door. Muffled voices come from the other side as the knob turns. I climb inside the dumbwaiter and tuck myself into a ball. The door opens and I hold my breath.

"What're you doin' in there, boy?" Herschel's voice creeps into the pantry. "Forget about gettin' a snack! Let's get in the truck and look for her. C'mon, now!"

The door slams shut and the porch creaks as they pound down the steps. The grating motor of the truck revs, and tires squeal as they drive away from the farm.

I move to climb out from the dumbwaiter and something pulls me back. The dress is caught. I pull and tug at the skirt, trying to just tear it. My hands slip and I slap myself on the forehead as I snap backward. A few seconds later, I'm moving upward.

"Shit!" I try to jump out, but it's already moving and making a loud whining noise. At least I didn't try to do this while Herschel and Sonny were still here. Where is this thing taking me?

It's so dark in here. This is so much worse than being locked inside the closet when I was a teenager. I thought *that* felt like a coffin. That closet was nothing compared to this, and it's moving to boot, at a slow pace, making the whole experience even scarier.

My pulse gallops inside my wrists and I'm breathing in too quickly, beginning to hyperventilate. I feel along the walls searching for a button, but I just find slats of wood. The suspense driven by the slow movement is agonizing. I have no idea if this thing will hold my weight or crash down and kill me. I tuck myself into a tighter ball and close my eyes while I wait for it to stop, gasping and sobbing, on the brink of passing out.

After a few minutes, the dumbwaiter stops moving.

I catch my breath and open my eyes.

This looks like an attic, with an angled ceiling and rows of dusty boxes and crates. I climb out with a sneeze and move past the boxes. Most are unmarked, but a couple of them have writing on them. One has "Toyz" scrawled in marker and another, "Pichers". The box of "pichers" is open, and on top is a large collage frame with dozens of pictures of Sonny's mother, and in several of them, she is holding a plush Tweety Bird with a big grin on her face.

Creaks come from the other side of the attic. I turn toward the noise, but don't see anything. I hold my breath—it's quiet. But when I turn back around, more creaks. I whip my head around—nothing there. Worrying that it might be Jared, bound and struggling, I rush over.

Nothing but cardboard boxes covered in dust. A couple of old shovels and a broken sled. Some cracked plastic crates. Maybe it was just the house settling. I don't know what could be up here, anyway. The dog couldn't be here, I'd not only hear him but smell him. Unless someone else is here, like another kidnapped victim? A crazy old grandfather?

I don't want to go back down in the dumbwaiter but can't find any doors. I scan the floor for a hatch, seeing none. Just boxes and crates filled with clothes and knickknacks.

The closest thing I find for a weapon is a broken tennis racket, why they would have this I have no idea, but it's too bulky for me to wield. Either of them could get it out of my hands in seconds before I could do any real damage with it. But I take it anyway. It's better than nothing.

I finally find what must be the hatch that leads out of the attic, and it's blocked with a large box. I shove my shoulder against it and push. It doesn't move. I take a deep breath and try again. This time, the box barely budges, and I get a splinter in my foot.

I have no other choice but to climb back inside that tiny coffin to get out of here.

Next to the dumbwaiter is a button. Holding my breath and bringing the tennis racket with me, I climb inside, push the button, and lean back. It inches downward in what feels like a half-hour trip. At one point it pauses and my heart pounds. I shut my eyes and begin to take in short breaths again. Just when I'm certain this is where I'll die, it restarts its descent down to the pantry. My heart resumes a somewhat normal pace.

I climb out of the dumbwaiter feeling shaky. Regaining my stance, I step back through the door and into the kitchen. It's the one room in the house that should have a phone, but there isn't one.

Knives. That's something they'll have in the kitchen. I pull out drawer after drawer until I find the silverware. A medium-sized butcher knife is tucked away in a tray. Small enough for me to wield, but still big enough to do some damage.

I should get outside and find help. But how close will help be? This house is the only one around for miles. I don't know how much time I have before they give up looking for me out there and come back. They probably won't search for long. As soon as they don't see me within a certain radius, they'll know I didn't escape, that I'm hiding back here somewhere. It's not like I'd have much cover out there, anyway. I'd be a running target with my bobbing blonde head.

I make my way through the lower level, checking every room for Jared. Besides the dining room and bathroom, there's a den with a television set, an older model with a big back that juts out. A mudroom with some jackets on a coat rack, and not much else. In the living room, the floral print couch and loveseat are swaddled in dust-covered plastic.

On the wall above the loveseat, there's a wooden wall clock that looks a bit familiar. I take a step closer.

Painted along the bottom edge of the wooden clock is a row of shamrocks. The same way my father paints them, the same billowed shape, flattened edges.

I take a step back, nearly knocking into the television set. My blood runs cold. What the hell is going on here? Why do they have one of my father's shamrock clocks?

I suppose they could've bought one randomly from his online shop. But still, that's one hell of a coincidence. It's not like he advertises. The people who typically buy his clocks are neighbors, relatives, and coworkers.

People he already knows.

The suspicion enters my psyche so suddenly that it festers like it belongs there. As if it's a truth I've known all along and just couldn't admit it.

It's possible this was a random kidnapping of two people, just to abduct a woman for nefarious reasons. I have no idea if they've made any ransom demands, but it's doubtful.

But this could also have a backer, someone behind it all who hired them to do it.

Someone who wanted Jared out of my life, and to pay him back for what he did to Courteney. That's...that's so diabolical. But then again, so is locking your teenage daughter inside of a closet for two days for ridiculous reasons.

Did my parents set this whole thing up? Did they hire these two men to do it?

Oh my god. That explains why they haven't done anything to me yet. That's why there is this pretense of marrying me to Sonny and doing a proper wedding, all the stalling and waiting for it. No way would two kidnappers have *not* raped me or molested me by now. They were told to just tie me up and leave me alone while they killed Jared.

He must already be dead.

SEVENTEEN

MY THROAT CLOSES in a knot and the tears stream down my cheeks. I can't stop them. The realization sinks in, reality hitting me so fiercely I can't see straight. I back up to the closest wall and slide down until my backside slumps to the floor.

My heart finds its way to my throttled throat full of knots and I can't escape this feeling grasping my soul. Jared is dead, and my parents had something to do with it. It's careening toward me, this uncertain reality of a heinous nature that sutures itself to my very being.

As I wipe my eyes I glance up, away from the shamrock clock. This feeling begins in the pit of my stomach, like a stone just landed there and it begins to grow warmer and denser by the second.

I've known, ever since Herschel said they watched us, that this has been a total setup. They stole Jared's car. And then waited until we were wandering down the road looking for a ride. But they didn't just come up with this plan all on their own. They didn't just see us out in the woods and pick me as their prey.

I stand up, my legs shaky. I don't want to give up hope on Jared yet—there are still some rooms I've yet to check. Even if what I find is his dead body, at least I'll know for sure what happened to him.

I open a door to the right of the kitchen, finding a staircase down to the cellar. Even up here, it smells wet and dirty with a pungent, rotten meat odor. It's so awful I have to breathe through my mouth and hold my breath to keep myself from throwing up all the juice I'd just chugged.

I flick the light switch on the wall but nothing happens. I leave the door open and walk down the stairs. The sunlight streaming in from the kitchen gives very little light in the basement, but it's better than nothing. I focus on what's in front of me, then I remember the matchbook inside the pocket of the dress. I take it out and light a match. At the foot of the stairs is a giant heap of potatoes, with a dusty-looking blonde wig on top.

Another scarecrow? Whatever it is, the putrid stench makes me gag. And flies are buzzing around it.

As I get closer, I have to pinch my nose. But when I lean forward and my eyes adjust to the darkness, I see that it's not a giant bag of potatoes with a wig on top.

It's not a scarecrow. It's a woman, dressed in a burlap potato sack.

And she's quite dead.

I blow out the match when the flame reaches my fingertips and hold my nose to block out the smell. I swat at the flies buzzing by my head with the knife in my other hand. I can still see her shape in the dim light from the kitchen. I back away. My heart is going a mile a minute and I forget to breathe for a few seconds.

I've only seen a dead body once before, at my uncle Marty's wake. It rattled me, to see a body without life. There is something so unnerving and surreal about it. I've had a difficult time going to wakes and funerals since. It's hard enough looking at an embalmed body in a coffin. It's even harder to witness a rotting corpse like this.

Her skin looks like a rotted crayon color. Flapped open in some corners around her mouth and elbows, with sores all over her arms and legs.

Was this the mother, who used to be the owner of this wedding dress? She looks like she might be the same woman from the photos in the kitchen, but it's hard to tell with how decomposed she is.

As my heartbeat settles along with my breathing, I take a deep breath and the scent of rot hits me even with my nose pinched and makes me cough. That's what the smell has been all this time, what I first thought was the dinner they were going to serve us. I can't hold it back any longer. I lean over and throw up on the floor.

I use the tears streaming down my cheeks to wipe the bile from my lips. I need to give up on finding Jared, get out of here and go find help.

Pulling myself up, I grip the knife in my hand. It feels good to run my finger along the blunt part of the blade. The side that can't cut me. It's like walking along the edge of somewhere without a safety net blocking the danger below.

The best thing I have on my side is the element of surprise. I don't think those two expected me to fight back, but now they'll be on their game. Maybe I can hide somewhere and jump out at them, or something to that effect. Especially since I have to be close enough to use the knife. I wish I had that gun Sonny had been holding.

As soon as I walk back into the kitchen there's that wet dog scent. And it's the hound himself, eating potatoes from a torn open bag on the floor. He turns toward me but doesn't bark. He goes back to eating potatoes after giving me a sniff.

I'm back where I was before, in a kitchen with no phone.

While I'm debating searching for a phone in other rooms over searching for a bicycle in the barn, there's the sound of tires crunching on gravel.

I waited too long.

At first I'm pissed I didn't leave before they got back, but the potential opportunity of taking the truck is now my best option. Hide, wait until they go upstairs, then make a run for that truck.

There's a broom closet next to the fridge. I go inside and close the door, clutching the butcher knife. I step on something sharp and plastic and cover my mouth to diminish the gasp. Most of the stuff inside, brooms and mops and rags, are covered in as much dust as the rest of this place. I have to hold in a sneeze.

The door to the kitchen opens and someone walks in. I don't know which one it is, but it smells like Sonny. He shuffles around opening cabinets and drawers, looking for something.

Creaks of footsteps come closer to the broom closet. The dog whimpers, and the footsteps fade. I have to hold back a cough. When I take my next breath, it's harder to suppress. I hold my breath for a few seconds. I let my eyes water with a tickle in my throat.

The dog barks, and then trots out of the kitchen. I wipe my eyes and release a shaky breath with a cough on the outskirts, but I'm able to hold most of it in.

The kitchen door creaks open, and someone walks in. The dog comes back into the room, panting and whimpering.

"Hush now!" Herschel says.

The dog quiets down, and Herschel shuffles around the kitchen mumbling to himself. He walks by the broom closet with the dog trotting close behind him.

I hold my breath for as long as I can. A cough is coming. My eyes water and I cover my mouth with my palm. The porch door opens and closes as the cough comes out. I just hope the creaking door drowns out the sound.

The dog is still in the kitchen, panting and sniffing. Only a dog would still be hungry after eating a bunch of potatoes. But at least it's just the dog.

I should make a run for the truck—I hope they left the keys inside. They might, especially on a farm, because who is gonna steal it? Besides the escaping kidnapped victim.

If I can get to the truck I'll drive around until I find the nearest police station. Then I'll bring them back here to arrest these two hillbilly assholes. At least, that's the plan, before the hound comes closer to the broom closet. He sniffs a couple of times. Is he sniffing me out? The floor creaks with footsteps a few feet away. Did one of them come back into the kitchen? Why didn't I hear the door open?

The dog makes a weird noise. Like a cross between a howl and a yawn. I hold my breath and tighten my grip on the knife.

He trots away, his unclipped nails clicking against the floor. It's quiet in the kitchen. I can't hold my breath any longer and let it out with a soft cough.

The door to the broom closet bursts open. Herschel is standing before me. We stare at each other with our mouths open. He doesn't have a gun or any other weapon.

It happens before I can stop it.

My arm shoots out with the butcher knife.

It goes into his torso.

He falls to his knees.

Blood spurts from his mouth.

The knife is still inside of him.

And he's still staring at me.

EIGHTEEN

My arm draws back and hangs at my side.

What just happened?

I didn't give much thought to what I was doing. My arm got a mind of its own and took over while the rest of me stayed frozen. It felt like someone else did that, took control of my body when I couldn't.

I take gulps of air into my lungs and my eyes water. I can't seem to steady my breathing. It feels like the wind has been knocked out of me. Vomit creeps up the back of my throat and it contracts, and I breathe through my nose that's filling up with snot. But the smell in here isn't helping keep the vomit down. I hold my breath, letting the freeze overtake me, my heart in that strange state of pounding without oxygen for a moment.

A wet sigh escapes me and I feel spittle dribbling down my chin, that overwhelming feeling of helplessness of the human body functioning beyond control. Much like my arm did when it reached out just now and stabbed Herschel, who is still staring at me on the floor as I step out of the broom closet with my back against the wall.

His bloodshot eyes are open wide and his bottom lip is moving up and down. His hand flails out at the knife inside him, but he doesn't touch it. Blood oozes from his wound. His arm falls to the floor.

Is he dead? I think it takes a long time to die from a stab wound to the stomach, but there is so much blood pouring out of him. It makes a dark splotch in his coveralls, and seeps into the rest of his clothes, spreading in a little pool around him. The room begins to waver as I stare at the blood, so I look away and continue backing toward the door.

Blood clings to the wedding dress that's dragging on the floor. It seeps into the fabric and spreads like a fractal as I creep by, keeping my eyes on him.

The door to the porch is right in front of me—I lurch forward and leave, not looking back. The hound is lying there by the crooked swing. He gets up and barks, and I leap over him, running down the steps and nearly tripping on the dress.

The dog rushes up behind me and bites the hem. He growls and tugs me backward until I turn and kick him in the face. A little whimper and then he retreats toward the house.

A grating scream comes from the kitchen. Sonny must've found his father. I make a run for the truck, past the celery scarecrow on the fence, not even looking close enough to see how rotted it is by now. Not even thinking about how much that celery scarecrow seems like me: tied to a fence, held captive, and deteriorating. No, not at all like me.

I'm getting the fuck out of here.

When I get to the pickup truck, I yank the door open and climb inside. No keys in the ignition. Flip the sun visor down, check under the seat, and the glovebox—no keys.

I slap the steering wheel. "Dammit!"

A loud bark and the screen door opens—Sonny is standing there holding a shotgun. I slouch down in the truck. As soon as he turns and walks down the other side of the porch, I bolt out of the truck, the door hanging open behind me, not looking back.

But a few yards away, I take a look back, and then trip and fall onto the grass. The overgrowth of the unkempt lawn cushions my fall. I get up and stumble again. Finally get my balance and bearings, bunch up the skirt in my hands, and take off.

My foot lands on a sharp rock, and it tears a gash in my heel. My legs don't stop moving, and a searing pain shoots up my calf when my bleeding foot lands on a patch of gravelly dirt. But I don't let it slow me down.

When I allow myself to turn around and check, I don't see Sonny anywhere. But he must have seen me running away. If he was hired by someone to kidnap me, but not kill me, he might just let me go. Or have some scout taking tabs of my whereabouts, reporting back to him. Maybe Sonny's stupidity and clumsiness are just an act. Or maybe he's about to get in the truck and chase me down.

There has to be a road leading to the highway, or at least a house with a phone so I can call the police. I see no other houses, just more trees. The closest place might be miles away. I grit my teeth and run into the forest so he at least can't follow me in the truck.

The sun is so high it must be near noon. For a fleeting moment the thought of the last time I realized it was noon, was the day when Jared and I were driving up to this godforsaken place. It feels like forever ago. I swallow a lump in my throat and pick up my pace. I focus on my feet, one step at a time, and the trees in front of me, one branch at a time.

Each step brings a searing pain to my gashed foot. I swallow the pain down along with the lump in my throat. Sometimes there's a clearing, but a small one, and more trees that all look the same. I keep running, my eyes open for signs of life somewhere.

The forest doesn't scare me anymore. The rustling tree branches and bird caws fall into a backbeat behind me and are nowhere near enough to harm me. I'm moving too fast this time.

My nails scrape the lace of the wedding dress as I pull up the skirt and pump my legs as I run. I focus only on getting past the trees in my path, with no sense of direction. I don't care where I'm going as long as it's away from here.

Branches scratch the sleeves and tear the dress, and twigs and rocks jab my bare feet but it doesn't slow me down. I'm used to the pain by now. The forest thickens and dims the sunlight. A growl comes from somewhere distant. I'm short of breath, but I keep running for what feels like hours.

Soon the sunlight brightens and the forest opens to a brief clearing, and the edge of a cliff looms up—I skid into the ground like I'm stealing bases in softball and slide on my hip. A big rock saves me from going over the edge.

I pull myself down to my knees and peek over the edge. The waves crash against jagged rocks, and the cliff's edge curves inward to a clearing lined with trees.

No one could survive that jump. Least of all me. And what if I hit that clearing instead? I'll be lying there with broken bones and gangrene before anyone finds me.

My throat closes in a knot. Tears fall onto the stained wedding dress, refreshing the dried blood. My stomach churns and I hold back the bile creeping up my throat. Take some deep breaths, close my eyes, and feel the sun on my face.

When I said yes to Jared, despite my misgivings, I'd never imagined something like this would happen. The ring isn't on my finger anymore, but it feels like it is.

Twigs snap behind me. Did he follow me out here? I whip my head around—nothing there. I turn back toward the cliff as a seagull glides down to the water. Right before it reaches the surface, the bird pumps its wings and flies back up in a glorious arc.

I stand up at the edge of the cliff, my legs shaking. The water looks so inviting, as if I can just dive right in, maybe do a cannonball, with no repercussion. Pretend I'm diving off the raft at the pond—no big deal, just a quick dip and then I'll head home. To that final resting place.

I'm waiting for my life to flash before my eyes, but nothing is happening besides the sounds of waves and nature around me. Maybe remembering that base I stole at last week's softball game when I slid into the ground is all I got.

A twig snaps, more loudly than the last one. He must be getting closer. I move along the edge of the cliff with my eyes on my feet. The waves crash against the jagged rocks that I'll probably land on if I go over.

I don't know if that's better or worse than facing what's behind me.

It's sort of appealing, the thought of throwing myself over the cliff. Take that bungee jump, only without the cords. I'll probably pass out before I hit anything anyway. That's what I've heard happens, at least.

Somewhere along the way I lost my fear. Maybe it was getting lost in the woods, or fighting back and escaping the farmhouse, likely a combination of it all—but I don't feel afraid anymore. It's something different. Something darker. I feel almost as numb as I was in the restraints.

I envision myself falling over, hoping it's true that people pass out before hitting the water. I'm inching toward the edge—a couple of pebbles tumble down the side. My feet are taking over like my arm had when I stabbed Herschel.

I hear a rustling behind me. I creep away from the edge of the cliff and crouch behind a bush. The rustling gets louder.

I hold my breath and keep my eyes open.

What if it isn't Sonny or his father? What if something

else was stalking us in the woods, along with those two? Maybe they weren't the only ones. What if multiple stalks were happening?

What made the claw mark in the tree?

A vague whiff of that animal-hide smell accompanies more rustling leaves. I hold my breath and peek over the bush.

A small bear trundles out from between the trees. I let out the air in my lungs, hoping the bear will just pass me by. The bear takes a few steps near the bush I'm behind. A black nose peeks through the leaves and sniffs. Its inhale is like a vacuum, and I can almost feel my scent drifting away from me and into its nose. My lungs feel like they're about to burst and my eyes water.

A bird caws nearby. The bear's nose goes up in the air and backs out of the bush. I let out a lungful of air and cough. I glance around the bush and watch the bear trundle back into the forest.

Was it that bear rustling the leaves and snapping twigs behind me all along? I haven't heard the hound barking. Maybe Sonny gave up chasing me.

But I still don't know where to go from here. I don't want to jump off the cliff. But I don't want to go back the way I came. I don't even know how to get out of here. I escaped the hell house only to get lost in the woods again.

I'm just so tired. It feels like my body is shutting down on me. I yawn and want something soft for my head to rest on. Everything around me is getting hazy. I shake my head and blink, but the haziness doesn't dissipate. I place my chin on my knees, just for a second. In the next, I topple over to the ground.

CHAPTER

NINETEEN

WHEN I WAKE UP, the light in the sky is a bit darker. I'm still wearing the bloodied wedding dress and my head is pounding. I peel myself off the ground and turn away from the cliff.

Hunger claws its way through my stomach. I want a burger. A greasy fast-food cheeseburger, something I haven't let myself have in a while. And I want to sleep, for a long time, on a big bed with the freedom to move my arms and legs around as much as I need to.

I reach behind to undo the buttons of the dress, but I can't reach them. Instead, I pull my arms through the sleeves and then yank the dress off over my head. I toss it on a bush, bloodstains and all, and go back into the woods wearing nothing but my camisole and pee-stained pants.

There has to be somewhere, someplace nearby that will save me. I'm near the ocean, why aren't there rows of cottages and summer homes with leftover vacationers hanging about? It's late September and technically off-season, but there are always people around somewhere after Labor Day, locals and kids and retirees.

A flash of movement through some trees out of the

corner of my eye makes me turn left—and I swear I just saw red taillights. There must be a road over there.

With renewed strength in my legs, I run through the trees, not even noticing when twigs scratch my arms.

The spot through the trees where I'd seen the headlights is too dark now. I think I'm focusing on the right spot, but I'm sure I'll see the lights of another car as soon as one goes by. I just need to surge forward, straight ahead, and don't let myself stop.

Finally I find the road ahead, but no one is driving down it, and I lose hope that anyone will for a while. Maybe those taillights were just a mirage.

When I took off the wedding dress, it didn't quite marinate in me that I might need it later. I'm already shivering, wishing I'd held onto that wretched thing for warmth.

With my arms wrapped around my waist, I keep moving down the road. After a while, I see a car heading my way, a hatchback. I lean out into the road, waving my arms, when someone calls my name.

"Elizabeth! Elizabeth Martel!" The voice is familiar. It sounds like a man's voice.

I turn around to see a car several meters down the road, parked along the right shoulder, with the backseat doors ajar.

"Elizabeth Martel!" a different voice shouts—this one isn't familiar.

"Liz!" The familiar voice again.

Wait—is that Jared?

I try to say "I'm right here" but my mouth won't work. My throat contracts and I heave. There is no saliva in my mouth right now. Nothing I can do to make it, either. I can't swallow. I can't even seem to speak.

"Elizabeth!"

"Liz Martel!" A new voice. Sounds like a woman.

"Elizabeth! Liz!"

Blurred spots come into focus on the faint figures ahead of me, yards away from the car with the open doors. There's a group of people, about four of them, and one is a tall, lanky man with a confident stride.

It's Jared.

"Jared!" I try to scream, but my throat is still too dry. I jump up and wave my arms so he'll hopefully see movement and come my way.

"Liz! Oh my God, I've found her!"

Jared runs toward me, and the closer he gets the more detail I can see in his face. But there's no chiseled chin, or tousled brown hair. The face looks a bit like his, and the tall frame is the same, but he has a pointed chin and close-cropped, military-style cut hair.

It's not Jared. It's his brother Preston.

"Liz! Thank God!"

Preston reaches me and scoops me into his arms, the same way Jared used to. I haven't felt this safe and comforted in a while.

"She's here! I've found her!"

I look up to see who Preston is talking to, spotting Bradley, along with another man and a woman. The man looks like a paramedic, and the woman is dressed in a police uniform.

"How did you find me?" My tongue is heavy and my mouth is so dry I can't even hear myself. My words sound like mumbles, like I still have the gag in my mouth. I'm not sure he can even understand me.

"She needs some water!" Preston says.

Someone hands him a thermos. Preston brings it to my lips, and I sip the water, holding in the desire to rip the container from his hand and gulp the whole thing. I'm cognizant enough to realize I'd probably throw up again if I did that.

Everything feels so surreal, more so than the rest of this ordeal. It feels like this isn't happening to me, but a character in a movie that I can't turn off and walk away from, because I'm starring in it.

Someone puts a thick blanket around my shoulders, and it's warming me so wonderfully. I tug it around me closer, letting it soothe the shivering that's been enveloping me.

As soon as I can talk, I tell them everything, starting with the proposal on the picnic, and then how Jared's car was stolen. The pickup truck with the two men who offered their landline to call for help, and then took us to their celery farm not far from the picnic spot. The police officer radios this in, saying there are potential suspects at large.

"We knew where Jared was taking you for the picnic," Bradley says, his forehead creasing. "Same spot we had that big Galbraith family reunion years ago."

Preston nods. He rubs my shoulder, but the blanket around me is so thick I can barely feel him. The paramedic leads me to a gurney and helps me climb into it.

"We got worried when Jared didn't return our messages. We all knew he was proposing and Mother was dying to know Liz's answer. But when no response from him came the next day, and he didn't show up at the office—"

"And you weren't answering your phone either, Liz," Bradley says. "At first, I thought you'd lost your phones or ran out of gas or something like that. We started a search party and have been looking through these woods—I can't believe this is what happened." He gestures to me as if *I'm* what happened, though I know he doesn't mean it like that.

"Have you found Jared yet?"

Preston shakes his head, resting his hand on the side of the gurney. "No. Still no sign of him yet."

"I searched through the house as best I could before I had to run." I sniffle and look down. "But I couldn't find Jared."

The officer's radio crackles, and she turns away as she speaks into it. Are they going to blame me for leaving Jared behind to save myself? I certainly am.

"Liz, you should've run the second you had the chance," Preston says. "I can't believe you tried searching for him. You've got guts."

"Looks like they found the house you described," the police officer says as she turns back to us. "It's the only celery farm in this vicinity."

I nod. "Did they find Jared?"

"They found an injured man inside, he's being taken to the hospital. Happen to know anything about that?"

Guess I didn't kill him after all. "That was me. I stabbed him when he came at me."

The cop shares a glance with Bradley. "We'll be questioning him along with the other man on the premises."

"Sonny," I say. "That's his name. The other man, the one I stabbed, is his father Herschel."

She nods. "We'll continue searching the surrounding areas for Mr. Galbraith."

Preston gets into the ambulance with me to go to the hospital. The paramedic starts putting an IV in my arm, and I look away. Never been a fan of needles.

A blanket of exhaustion covers me as I lay back on the gurney. The paramedic straps a seatbelt around the bed, and one around my waist. They feel like restraints.

I ask him what's in the IV, and he tells me it's just fluids to keep me hydrated. But why do I feel like I'm about to pass out? And why is everything looking so blurred, out of focus?

I look over at Preston, and his face is blurry too. I can't seem to keep my eyes open. My lids are so heavy. Someone shuts the door to the ambulance. It makes me nervous. It feels too familiar, being in this small, enclosed space, strapped to a bed, feeling groggy.

"Will she be okay?" I hear Preston ask. He sounds so concerned. He's thinking of me as a sister already.

"She's probably in shock," the gruff voice of the paramedic says. "Dehydrated too. She's lost some blood, but we gave her some fluids and they'll run tests at the hospital."

"Don't worry, Liz." Preston's voice is muddled, like he's speaking through a mouthful of food. "You're going to be just fine."

It's the last thing I hear before everything goes black.

I'M LYING in an unfamiliar bed. I can't sit up, can't seem to move. Something's stuck to my arm. And something is inside of my nose.

Am I back in the hell house, tied to the bed?

Was that rescue just a dream?

My heart pounds. I open my eyes wide and see a white blur. I look for the pinwheel. It's not on the wall. No flypaper in the corner. These walls are too clean. And it doesn't smell dank in this room. It smells like ammonia.

It's so cold in here. I bring my arms up to hug my chest, and the thing stuck on my arm tugs and pinches me.

"Liz, are you awake?"

The voice sounds familiar. It's not Jared, it's not even a man's voice—it sounds like Courteney. I turn toward it, and there's a blonde, pink blur moving in front of me.

"Wait, I'll come back with a nurse."

With what? It sounded like she said a nurse.

I blink and see a TV mounted on the wall, in the corner. The bedside table has a remote control, and another control pad with a bunch of buttons on it.

There is an empty chair facing me. Resting on the chair is a phone with a rose gold case. It looks like Courteney's phone.

The door opens and in walks my sister followed by a plump woman in blue scrubs.

"Hey there," the nurse says. "How are you feeling?"

"I'm so happy she's awake!" Courteney clasps her hands.

I stare at them both. I can't tell if they're real or not. I sort of want to pinch one of them to find out.

"Mind if I just check a few things?" The nurse looks at Courteney, who nods. The nurse turns and looks at me with a smile. I'm still not sure if she's real. She takes a step closer, and then she walks over to a machine next to my bed. I'm half-expecting her to morph into Sonny any second.

"Okay if I change this?" She points at my arm.

I look to where she's pointing and notice the tube coming out of me. It startles me. I yank my arm closer to my face.

"That's okay," she says. "We don't have to do that just now." She smiles at me. She has a calming presence. I'm starting to believe she's real, and not Sonny in disguise.

"Liz," Courteney says with a frown. "Are you okay?"

The nurse turns toward Courteney. "She's had quite a shock. Her vitals are good, and she hasn't suffered any serious injuries."

Courteney nods.

"She's dehydrated, though, and we want to make sure she's got plenty of fluids."

"I'm going to bring her back to my place as soon as you say it's okay for her to leave," Courteney says. "She can stay with me."

There's a knock at the door. Courteney turns and opens it. A man wearing a crumpled gray suit walks in. He's almost as tall as Jared.

"Where is Jared?" I ask.

Courteney looks at me with a slight shake of her head, and then she starts crying.

"What's wrong?"

"Liz," Courteney says through sniffles. "I'm so sorry."

"Ms. Martel," Gray Suit says as he takes a step forward. "My name is Ed Rawlings, I'm a detective with the Boston Police. I'm very sorry to be the one to tell you, but Mr. Galbraith was found deceased."

The sound that comes out of me is like a giant puff of air trying to escape my insides, but I don't hear it because my ears are ringing.

"What?" My eyes sting with tears and my throat tightens and I can't breathe. I pound the bed and I hear myself scream his name. But it doesn't sound like it's coming out of me, it sounds like I'm hearing it from somewhere far away.

The nurse rushes over and holds me down. The tears pouring out of my eyes are hot, and I taste their salt when they reach my lips.

"Just sit back," the nurse says. Her eyes are big and brown, and kind. "We don't want you to strain yourself."

I look over at Courteney. Still crying, she pours a cup of water from the pitcher on the table and brings it to me. My hands are shaking and she helps me bring the cup to my lips. The water coats my tongue and throat, and makes the room look less foggy.

"Where was he?" I wipe my eyes and stare at the detective.

"He was found about fifteen miles east of Interstate 95, not far from where you'd reported his car had been stolen."

"How...how did he die?"

"Looks like he suffered a bad fall. There's a rocky clearing around a hundred feet above where he was found. I'm sorry, Ms. Martel."

I crumple the empty paper cup in my hand and throw it

onto the floor. "They pushed him, I know they did! Or they killed him and threw him into that clearing!"

"Who did?"

"Herschel and Sonny! The same men who kidnapped me!"

"Ms. Martel, I know that you gave a statement to the local police and they questioned Herschel and Sonny Johnson. They are denying picking up a young couple with a stolen car and bringing them to their house to use the phone."

I stare up at the detective. What did he just say?

"Are you...are you being serious? They abducted me and my boyfriend! They kept us captive and tied up and...and... almost raped me!"

"They say they were at a community pot-luck dinner that night. The local sheriff, Charlie Colts, was there with them the whole time. He confirmed this to me."

An alibi? "This is insane! The sheriff is lying for them, they must be friends or something! Don't you see it's a coverup!"

He's shaking his head. The tears coming down my cheeks are fiery and sting when they reach my chin.

"They can't get away with this!" I pound my fists into the bed. "What... what about...."

"I'm sorry, Ms. Martel. They have an alibi, and we found no evidence of what you're saying occurred. Is it possible that you witnessed your fiancé fall to his death, while you were out searching for the car?"

I'm shaking my head. My memories are fuzzy when I try to trace back every detail of what happened. The time we were lost in the woods is one big blur. I just remember the basics: going on the picnic, the giant basket, the proposal, the ring, getting lost, the car gone. And then the pickup truck.

"Look," the detective says. "You have been through hell, anyone can see that. Something terrible happened to you.

Maybe it wasn't the Johnsons, maybe it's someone else and it's a case of mistaken identity, it happens."

I want to scream. As if the hell I'd just gone through wasn't bad enough, now everyone thinks I'm crazy and delusional. Part of me is wishing I'd walked over the edge of that cliff.

My mind is reeling and I can't help but let the thought creep in that maybe he's right, and I imagined it after passing out from dehydration or something. Maybe I am losing my mind. It certainly feels that way.

But no. I *know* what happened. I know it wasn't all in my head. It can't be. My head shakes from left to right, trying to release the doubt coming in before it settles.

"But...I stabbed him!" I stare at the detective. "Herschel, in the *gut*! When I was escaping! The cop who found me in the woods with the search party said they found an injured man in the farmhouse."

"According to his statement, it was self-inflicted. He was so distraught over his wife's death, that he decided to take his own life. But his son found him and brought him to the hospital."

"What? That's ridiculous! And you believe that he attempted suicide by stabbing himself in the stomach? Who does that?"

"Liz," Courteney says, patting my arm. "Please calm down. You've been through a lot and I don't want to see you pass out again."

My eyes light up. "The wedding dress. The one they dressed me in, that would have Herschel's blood on it."

Detective Rawlings looks at me with his head tilted.

"That would be evidence! The wedding dress, I tore it off after I ran from the house...I think I left it in the bushes near where they found me."

"I remember seeing that in your statement. We did search

that whole area and found nothing. No dress, no other pieces of clothing."

"Sonny must have found it first and gotten rid of it! Don't you see they're just covering their tracks?"

I also forgot to tell him about hiding in the dumbwaiter. Maybe a piece of lace from the dress is still there from when it had torn? But is that evidence enough? Am I looking even more crazy to the detective right now?

The detective cocks an eyebrow. "To be frank, Ms. Martel, it's suspicious. That he just happened to have stabbed himself with a knife at the same time you've accused him of kidnapping. This is why I am still investigating this case."

I breathe out through my nose while Courteney leans down and squeezes my hands. This is a nightmare. If Herschel and Sonny get away with this, I don't know what I'll do.

"There was a dead body in the basement! A woman!" I blurt out.

He takes out a small notepad from his pocket and flips it open. "A dead body? That wasn't in your original statement."

"I was a little out of it."

The detective flips through the notepad and nods. "However, the sheriff states they searched their home—and found no evidence of what you say happened. No mention of a body either."

"I'm quite sure it wasn't a thorough search. Don't you have a forensics team that can find something, like a fiber from mine or Jared's clothes, a piece of my hair? Or our cell phones?" I look around the hospital room as if searching for a lost thought, and nothing comes. I glance down at my hands. "The engagement ring."

Courteney stares at me, her eyes wide. "Engagement ring?"

"He asked me to marry him right before they abducted

us," I say to her, before turning toward the detective. "They must have my ring. It's a princess-cut diamond with an inscription. J + E in block letters."

He scribbles in his little notepad. "That's helpful. I'll get a new search warrant based on your statements regarding the body you found. Where did you say it was again?"

"The basement."

"Thank you. I'll be in touch if I find anything."

"Thanks, Detective." I nod, trying to keep myself from screaming.

"But we don't have enough to hold them right now. The Johnsons have an alibi, so my hands are tied until I can find more evidence of your claims."

I start shaking. "They did this to me. They killed Jared. They need to be in jail! And they're not the only ones!"

I glance over at Courteney, to see her reaction. Her head is tilted down and she's wiping her eyes. But just because she was scorned by Jared, that doesn't mean she would want him dead. Courteney may have been a tattletale kid, always taking our parents' side, but that doesn't mean she was in on this. I don't believe she'd planned this with my parents.

Where are they, by the way? Wouldn't you think they'd come visit me in the hospital? It makes me even more suspicious. Especially knowing that Jared is dead.

"We're going to get to the bottom of this," the detective says. "So if you remember anything else, please just call me."

The clock with the painted shamrocks flashes in my mind. But I keep quiet about that. especially with Courteney here. I take the card he hands me, thinking I'll get in touch after I'm out of the hospital.

Detective Rawlings mentions the district attorney being friends with Jared's family, and my heart starts pounding. I can't face his parents. Not yet. No matter what they say, no matter how they act, I know they will partly blame me, the middle-class girl Jared was slumming around with, who ended up getting him killed when he asked her to marry him on a picnic in the back-woods of Maine. It sounds like a bad made-for-TV movie.

When the door closes behind the detective, Courteney pulls me into a hug. The silence is filled with our muffled sobs as we shake into one another's embrace. She pulls away and grabs a box of tissues from the bedside table. She blows her nose and hands me the tissues, also insisting that I drink more water.

"Court, I didn't imagine this." My eyes widen as I look at her, taking deep breaths. "It happened."

"I believe you, Liz, I do. But...think about the possibility that it was just a horrible, extremely vivid dream that happened after you witnessed Jared's death. It happens to people all the time."

I shake my head, unblinking. "But I have no memory of seeing Jared die. How can that be?"

"The human mind is a very powerful thing. It blocks out horrible things, and makes you believe in false realities. Some people live inside entire worlds they create inside of their minds, outside of the real world. It's a common effect of post-traumatic shock."

I can't let myself believe that whole ordeal was nothing but a dream.

Courteney offers to get me some takeout so I don't have to eat the crappy hospital food. My mouth waters. The thought of eating a big cheeseburger with fries and a milk-shake is making me just a little bit happy.

And then I feel guilty, for feeling even just the tiniest bit happy, because Jared won't be there to share any of it with me. He won't ever be there to share anything with me. We'll never try out new foods together again, or sleep in a bed together again. Even the last time we made love is now tainted with the knowledge that those two perverts watched us.

I'm starving and ask Courteney to bring me a burger and fries. She throws in an apple pie which I find when I open the bag, grinning at her.

With every bite, I feel a little bit better. Enough to get my heartbeat down to a normal level. The world in front of me loses the filmy haze and returns to a normal clarity. I no longer feel like I'm in a surreal movie, but I still feel a hollowness that the food doesn't fill. Reality sinks in faster than I can process it.

Jared is dead. I'll never see him again. And there are so many things I could've done differently to prevent that.

Courteney's voice pulls me away from my thoughts. "They said you can be discharged tomorrow."

I can't even manage a fake smile at the news. How am I supposed to sleep at night knowing the Johnsons are out there and free to come after me? How can I do anything knowing Jared is dead? Get up and go to work, make breakfast, do the dishes? None of it seems possible. That sinking feeling is overwhelming me. I just want to drown inside of it for a while, and maybe let myself die a little bit, a piece of me going into the void where Jared is now.

"Mom and Dad wanted to take you back home, but I insisted you stay with me for a while."

"Thanks, Court. I appreciate that."

But it's only for a while. I'm going to have to go back to my apartment alone eventually. Whenever I shut my eyes, I see Sonny's face. His slouchy eyes. That laugh.

He's going to come after me, I just know it. Regardless of who paid him, whoever set this up, he's going to come after me. I can just tell by the way he was looking at me—this is different for him. It's not about money or revenge or anything. He thinks he has the right, because he was supposed to have me on his wedding night.

I can already see the sleepless nights ahead of me. Checking every door and window seventeen times before going to bed. Tossing and turning despite the tranquilizers the doctor will hopefully prescribe.

I wish it had been Sonny who'd opened the door to the broom closet. I wish I'd stabbed him through the throat and watched him die. I want him to lose his chance at life, just like Jared did.

A dark part of me wants to see him suffer even worse than that. I want him to be afraid, tied down and helpless, unable to move, with no food or water for days.

After I stabbed his father, I should have grabbed another knife and hid in the closet again. Waited until he came into the kitchen and surprised him in the same way. I could've said that was self-defense. I could've killed them both, and no one would question my story.

No one would be coming after me.

TWENTY-ONE

AFTER THEY RELEASE me at the hospital, Courteney takes me to her place. I haven't been to Courteney and Chet's townhouse in a while, and they've spruced the place up—plush carpet in the living room, ceramic tile in the bathroom, and the fireplace with a stone mantel.

Chet hugs me. "How you holding up?" he says as we break the embrace, a worried frown on his face and brow.

I shrug. "Okay, I guess. Thanks for letting me crash here. I can't face my place just yet."

"Anytime, you know that." He winks at me and squeezes my shoulder. Courteney hugs me, and they lead me to the guest room. It has no windows, one of those small rooms in an apartment meant for an office or a den, but the bed looks cozy with fluffy pillows and one of Courteney's crocheted quilts.

"Let us know if you need anything," Courteney says. "There are fresh towels in the bathroom."

"And feel free to help yourself to anything in the kitchen too," Chet says.

"Thanks, guys. I really appreciate it."

I hug them both, and they leave, closing the door behind them.

Panic settles into my chest and stomach, similar to when the ambulance doors were slammed shut—the feeling that I'm being closed in, cut off, trapped.

I open the door, just a few inches. I can see bits of light streaming in, from the streetlamps through the windows outside the room, and it puts my mind at ease. I sink into the bed, a million times more comfortable than the last one I was in. I fall asleep the second my head hits the pillow. But that doesn't stop me from seeing Jared's face as I drift off, and it doesn't stop me from dreaming about him.

My dreams turn into something else. Memories of being tied up and unable to move, no way to escape. I wake up covered in sweat.

I get out of bed and tiptoe into the kitchen. After checking a few cabinets, I find what I'm looking for above the sink. I grab the bottle of Hennessy and pour a dram. Usually I just sip it, but this time I tilt my head back and down half of it. The warmth trails from my throat to my stomach. After a shaky breath, I finish it.

It feels nice. Brings that tingling warmness to me quicker than wine does. But I don't know if a dram will be enough tonight, so I take the bottle with me into the living room and curl up on the couch with a blanket.

I snap on the television and turn to The Weather Channel. Something about that station soothes me. It's nice to have a live person talking on the TV that's not depressing news, and it's not a talk show, but someone chatting about the most common small-talk topic in the world: the weather. It just makes me feel grounded to have this station on in the background. I don't have to pay attention to it, but it's there, and I can focus on the screen when my thoughts swarm at me too much.

According to the wall clock shaped like a star, I got a full hour of sleep. I guess that'll have to do for tonight, because there is no way I'm going back in the enclosed room right now. It felt like I was back in the hell house all over again. I pour another dram and focus on the tornado warning in Kansas. I tuck the quilt around me and drift off just before dawn.

It feels like only minutes have passed when the garbage truck outside wakes me. For a moment, while I'm first waking up and stepping out of the dream world and into reality, I forget that Jared is dead. I forget everything the last few days have brought to my life.

When reality sinks in, I start to cry. I have a feeling this will happen every time I wake up, for a long time.

I'm drawn into the kitchen by the delicious scent of brewing coffee. Chet greets me with a smile, and I try to hide the bottle of Hennessy behind my back but I'm pretty sure he can see it.

"Good morning," I say. "That coffee smells incredible."

"French press!"

I sneak a shot of the Hennessy into my mug when Chet opens the fridge and leans down looking for something. Just a little bit, to get me by. It helps take the edge off.

Courteney comes in and tells me that Jared's mother called a couple of times. The thought of facing her right now makes me shudder. More so than usual.

Courteney frowns. "She sounds worried about you."

She hands me a couple of aspirins. I take the pills with some water, though the thought of having a little more Hennessy in my coffee sounds so much better than aspirin.

"I'm not trying to push you," Courteney says. "But I think you should go see them. It will be good for you. For all of you. You sort of need each other right now."

I shake my head. "Do you think that they think I had

anything to do with this? That, like, I killed him and made up the story about being kidnapped?"

Courteney tilts her head. "I don't think you killed him, Liz. I think he had a freak accident. And it's possible that you're suffering from post-traumatic memory loss and your mind made you believe you were kidnapped. It happens to people, Liz."

"I didn't imagine what happened, Courteney!"

She nods and looks away from me. I can tell she doesn't believe me. Why doesn't anyone believe me?

Courteney puts an arm around me and squeezes my shoulder. "At least consider talking to them."

I should face them at some point, but that isn't happening anytime soon. I also know I have to go back to my apartment eventually, but that isn't happening anytime soon, either. I can't look at the pictures, the memories, the reminders of Jared.

I might just have to move, because every inch of my apartment will remind me of him. The kitchen table he helped me pick out. The sofa we used to cuddle on. The corner in the hallway where he pressed me up against the wall and kissed me. The photo of us on a harbor cruise is on the end table in the front hall, and it'll be the first thing I see when I walk inside.

Maybe Courteney can go over there for me. Either store the photos away or throw them out. Or we could give them to his parents. Though I'm not sure what it matters anyway. I don't have any pictures of Jared at my sister's place and still can't get him out of my mind.

I will wait until the funeral to face his family. It will be easier to avoid them in a big crowd, with my sister at my side. We can put in an appearance, and then I can come back here and hide underneath a blanket with a cup of something yummy, and spiked.

TWENTY-TWO

T HE NIGHT BEFORE THE FUNERAL, I go to bed with a full stomach and a few sips of warm milk to wash down an antihistamine to help me sleep. But it doesn't stop the dreams.

I'm tied to the bed and Sonny and his father are fondling me. Jared walks in, and then Herschel shoots him. Sonny climbs on top of me while his father takes the gun and holds it to my head. Suddenly Sonny has a knife in one hand, stalks of celery in another, and I'm free from the restraints. I grab the knife from him and stab his father. Jared walks in again, only he looks like a giant scarecrow made of celery, and his watch is wrapped around his stalk wrist. He takes the knife out of Herschel and places it in my hand. He tells me to use it on myself, so that we can be together again.

I wake up hyperventilating. I'm tangled up in the sheets and have a minor panic attack trying to escape them, believing I'm tied to the bed, back in the farmhouse. It takes a few minutes for my heart to settle down. I get up, take a shower, and pour a double shot of cognac. I down the whole thing.

My hands shake when I try applying some waterproof

mascara, and wind up with black specks around my eyes. I don't even care. Courteney loans me a basic black dress and stuffs some travel-size tissues into my purse for me. I squeeze her hand.

"Thank you. Thank you for everything, Court."

"Of course. I'm always here for you."

I sit in the backseat of Chet's car and fall in and out of napping while we sit in traffic on the way to the funeral. Courteney makes small talk along the way, while I stare absentmindedly through the window. Nearly every street we pass reminds me of Jared. We spent a lot of time walking through the streets of Boston together, hand in hand.

When we reach the church, a really nice place in the Back Bay, I can't get over the flowers, the people, the limousines— it's like something you'd see when a celebrity dies. The Galbraiths have over five hundred guests. I didn't realize Jared had such a huge family. And apparently, many fans of the supermodel Elizabeth Martel thought it was *her* boyfriend who died, because they're standing near the church trying to snap photos of me. I hear one fan say, "She's so much shorter than I thought!" Another says, "She looks awful!" when I walk inside. I'm quite sure I do. I keep my head down, ignoring everything around me besides the ground in front of me until I step inside, Chet holding the door open.

It's hard to step into this crowd, this room full of people who knew Jared for so much longer than I did. Nearly everyone has a story about him they want to share with me, which I don't want to hear, like the time he fell off a horse and broke his femur. It didn't even scare him away from riding once it healed. He literally got right back up on that horse.

An uncle of his tells me how Jared came in second place in a dance-off in middle school. Jared and I danced at events, but we never danced like that, and apparently, he used to love learning all the new dance moves. I would've loved to see that side of him.

It's difficult meeting and hugging all his family members and friends within a short period, and introducing them to Courteney and Chet who stay by my side. I've met some of them before, but only about five to ten percent of the people here. Maybe Jared planned on introducing me to the rest of his relatives after we got married. I feel hollow inside at the thought. These are the same people who would've been at our wedding ceremony, and I'm meeting them for the first time at Jared's funeral, wearing a black dress instead of a white one.

Jared's brother Preston and his wife Lacey both hug me for what feels like an eternity. Preston's eyes are bloodshot, his skin pale. I can't help but think about what Jared had told me, how they had an arranged marriage. It just doesn't seem like it. They look like the perfect couple. But maybe that's the point. Their families had thought the same thing.

They chat with my sister and Chet, and I turn around to see Bradley, who gives me a tight-lipped smile and a small nod. I'm not sure what to make of it, but then again, how else do you greet someone at a funeral?

"I...I'm...so sorry."

What else can I say at a time like this? How many sorrows can you convey with a moment, a look, a gesture, and words? How can you make anyone who's lost a child feel any amount of better, ever? I wonder if that grief ever goes away. I'm sure it dulls over time as you go through each day, but it's an underlying thing that simmers just beneath the surface, waiting for a memory to bring a moment to the forefront of your mind and you can think of nothing else.

I turn around to see Katharine. She looks like a different person. Older, jaded, and junked out like a beat-up car, only wearing a tasteful Louis Vuitton dress.

I've always been intimidated by her, with her austere

regality, her old-world money mentality. And now, she just looks *done*. She appears a couple inches shorter, too. But there's something else. A walled barrier, an iron curtain. I look into her eyes and swear there's a flash, like violent lightning striking through a dark night.

"Katharine," I say with my hands splayed. "I'm so sorry."

"I'm sorry too." Her voice, through those three small words, grates into me like nails on a chalkboard. This woman hates me. She blames me. I shift my feet a couple times and wring my hands. I glance at Bradley, who seems like the more stable one.

"We all are." Bradley glances away from us, either staring at the entrance or lost in a trance.

Katharine looks at me with her ice-blue eyes. I take a step backward, and my breath catches in my throat. "I-I'm just so, so sorry, for everything."

"I know it's not your fault, Liz." Katharine takes a deep breath. "And I hope you don't *blame* yourself for it." The emphasis she places on the word "blame" sends a chill down my back. Her voice hardened on that word, as if it were something vile and unspeakable she hated to utter.

"No," Bradley says, with a sigh. "You really shouldn't blame yourself." He looks at the floor and presses his fist to his mouth, as if he's holding back tears. I shake my head and shrug. I don't know what to say except that I'm sorry over and over, repeating it like a chant, until I have to press my lips together so tightly my grinding teeth gash my inner cheeks.

Katharine blinks, and her eyes are glossed over and filling with tears. She brushes her finger underneath her eyelids, and the smallest sniffle escapes her. Her face is creased with wrinkles, and her icicle eyes turn to stone.

I might be misconstruing her reactions toward me. She's probably holding back tears in that stone-faced manner women grow to learn when we're in public settings. Perhaps she does blame me for her son's death, but she's also a mother who's just lost her son, and I was—maybe in her mind—with him when it happened. I should probably be more sympathetic toward her.

Bradley wanders off to greet someone who just arrived. I wish he were still here. The way Katharine is looking at me and teetering on the edge of collapsing in front of me, I don't feel comfortable being alone with her.

"I just wish..." She shakes her head and steels her shoulders. Part of me wants to tell her to just let it all out, cry as much as she likes—this is her youngest son's funeral after all, but she doesn't want to do that here. She'll wait until she's safe at home, in her private bathroom, maybe in the shower, before she'll let the tears truly fall.

"I know," I say with a sigh. "You keep thinking about what could've been done differently, and he'd still be here. I know that feeling all too well."

Katharine stares at me. And then I see that the edges of the daggers in her eyes are glimmering with tears. I can't tell how this woman feels about me. She either hates the sight of me or sees me as a way to relive the last moments with her son. She might equally want to see me all the time and never see me again. Duality becomes a lifestyle when someone you love dies suddenly.

I could chalk up her behavior to the shock of grief. After all, who am I to judge how someone handles grief? I'm not stepping foot inside of my apartment until every photo of Jared is gone, and the furniture moved around. I haven't gotten around to asking Courteney and Chet to move the furniture as well as the photos, but I'm sure they will. They've been letting me do pretty much anything I want in their house, including sleeping anywhere I like, and single-handedly cleaning out their liquor supply.

Katharine clears her throat and leans closer to me.

"We're going to find out who did this to Jared, mark my words," Katherine hisses. "We've hired a private detective to investigate what happened."

My eyes light up. "You believe me about the kidnapping? The police were trying to make me think I imagined it or something."

Katharine nods. "Of course we do, Liz. I know in my heart that there is something fishy going on here, some sort of local law coverup."

I feel so relieved. If this rich, powerful family has hired private detectives the truth is going to come out.

Then Katharine gives me a brief, but extremely tight hug. My ribs feel like they're going to fracture under her tight squeeze. When she lets me go, the air rushes in and out of my lungs rapidly. She gives me another tight-lipped smile and a clipped farewell before moving off to the other side of the room.

As I step into the vestibule for a break from the crowd, a familiar face enters the church—my old roommate, Andi Kearns. She sees me and tilts her head with a slight shake, her dreadlocks swaying slightly.

She comes over and hugs me. As I sniff back the snot from my nostrils, it's obvious that she hasn't quit smoking. It's one of the reasons I moved out. Even though she smoked outside, the smell was somehow still in the apartment, all the time, in her clothes and purses and things. Even the paper grocery bags smelled like cigarettes. It's a strange sensation, feeling comforted by a scent that used to bother me.

Andi steps back, looking at me. "How are you doing?"

"Hanging in there." I shrug and wrap my arms around myself. "Feels like I haven't seen you in a dog's year."

Andi chuckles. "I was seeing this guy I met on a dating app. We took a lot of trips to Vegas. I'm broke now."

The first smile in a while creases my face. I've missed her, smoke stench or not. I remember going out for Thai food on Friday nights and getting drunk while watching chick flicks. How we used to find a small "Charlie Brown" tree to decorate for Christmas. Sometimes, I really miss those days.

Andi holds my hand and we move toward the main chapel, joining Courteney and Chet. The four of us walk up the aisle to our pew. I keep my eyes on the floor, letting Andi guide me until we reach the altar. After I greet his family I turn, and the casket is in front of me.

Thank god it's a closed casket. But that doesn't keep my stomach from tightening in a knot, with noises in my gut. Painful noises like butterflies made of iron, scraping the lining of my stomach with their wings, threatening to tear through my insides.

Jared is inside there, and he's dead.

TWENTY-THREE

AFTER THE SERVICE, the Galbraiths invite everyone to the reception at their grand home in Brookline. The last time I'd been there was the day Jared and I stopped by to pick up things for our picnic, and I know that I'll have a hard time going there. I invite Andi to join us since my sister and Chet have to get back to work. I really need her there. I'm not a part of the Galbraith family, and no one from my family will be there.

Andi stays by my side the whole time. I have a bit too much to drink, and I can't seem to eat anything even though the buffet looks delicious.

"I'm so sorry," I say for the hundredth time to another Galbraith and finish off my drink in a swig.

"Want a refill? I'm taking you home, so feel free to get hammered," Andi says as she takes the empty cup from my hand and moves to the bar to grab me a refill.

I smile at her as the soothing warmth of alcohol runs through my blood, making everything a little better. Numbing me so I don't have to feel anything for a while.

One of Jared's older relatives comes by and kisses my

cheek, telling me how lovely a Galbraith I would've made. I thank them and say, "I'm sorry" for the hundred and first time.

"I'm sure you are, Elizabeth," a steely voice comes from behind me.

The voice unnerves me. I turn around, biting my lip.

It's the gorgeous, statuesque Abigail Adams.

"Pardon?"

"I'm sure you're sorry, just like we all are," Abigail says as she takes a step closer to me, looking down at me with her heels giving her even more inches over me.

What a weird thing to say, almost accusatory. Does she think I killed Jared? For what, his money? Wouldn't it have made more sense for me to do that *after* we were married?

"Yes, we all are." I wrap myself in a hug. "We will all miss him."

"Some more than others, of course. I know you two were serious, but he had roots with the rest of us. Our families go back a long way."

I nod. "So I was told. Listen, Abigail, I-I'm sorry things didn't work out the way you had planned."

Her eyes narrow and darken. "Maybe if you hadn't gotten in the way, he'd still be alive."

I can only manage a blink. "What?"

"You don't fit in with this family."

Abigail turns and walks away from me. I turn and stare after her as Andi leaves the bar holding two fresh glasses of white wine.

"You won't believe what just happened."

I grab a glass from Andi's hand and pull her aside, telling her everything.

"Wow," Andi says, once I've finished. She takes a large swig of her wine. "That's...insane."

As I speak, a horrifying thought starts forming in my

mind. Something unthinkable. Something unreal, but potentially possible.

Did Abigail hire Herschel and Sonny to kidnap me?

No, that's crazy. Why would she have Jared killed, not me? Unless it was payback for turning her down? Or they killed the wrong person?

Andi shakes her head. "And I thought your family was nuts."

I chuckle. "They're a bit toxic too." It's on the tip of my tongue to mention the shamrock clock I saw in the farmhouse, but I decide it better to keep to myself.

"I never thought either of your parents were playing with a full deck, not since we were in college. Remember that time they decided to just 'pop in', without calling you ahead of time?"

I completely forgot about that or blocked it out since it'd been so mortifying. I picked a college far away to keep them from just popping in, but they went and did it anyway.

The night before, I'd spent the night at my boyfriend's dorm, like we always did on Saturday nights. And the next morning, I got a text from Andi saying that my parents were there. She was just as mortified since she had a boy in her room.

"And remember how your dad flipped out when he found out you were with your boyfriend for the night? It was creepy."

"He flipped out a lot." I swirl around the wine in my glass. "I guess I was just used to it."

"The way they treat their own daughters is appalling to me, always has been. Courteney just lets them control her."

I hate to admit it, but she's got a point.

"I mean, where are your parents anyway? Why aren't they here supporting you?"

I glance around, not sure why I'm expecting either of my parents to suddenly show up.

"At least Courteney was here. She just had to leave early."

"I'd still be more suspicious of them being behind this, or maybe even Courteney or all three working together, than this Abigail woman."

"I don't know. Maybe."

"Look Liz, more likely than not, those kidnappers were just some crazy randos who decided to do this. Some guys are nuts like that. All the true crime podcasts out there is the proof."

"Maybe." She's probably right. I take another sip of wine, savoring the wonderful numbness it brings me.

"It sucks that it seems like they're getting away with it, too. Why does that happen so much when a woman is assaulted? People never question someone when they've been mugged or had a home invasion, when they could just as well be lying about it so the insurance company gets them a nicer TV or something. But when a woman is assaulted, people are always suspicious that she's lying. It doesn't make any sense."

Maybe I've just had too much to drink and I'm connecting dots where there aren't any. Because she's right, it's more likely the Johnsons just targeted us out in the woods. It's not like I was thinking or seeing very clearly after being held captive and dehydrated for nearly twenty-four hours. It's too crazy of a coincidence, anyway. The thought of anyone setting this up is diabolical.

And I can't help but think that maybe it *didn't* happen.

Was it just some horrid, vivid, inexplicable nightmare?

I suppose I could've been unconscious, from...something. Exposure? Hitting my head on something? And dreamed I was tied up and put into a wedding dress. It does sound like something out of a crazy dream.

I shake my head at the thought. I can't accept that. I

know what happened to me. I couldn't have envisioned that. Or even enhanced it in any way.

"Listen," Andi says, as people are beginning to clear out of the dining room. "I want you to know that you can stay with me for a while, if you like. You're always welcome."

"Thanks. I appreciate that. I'm staying with Courteney for now, trying to muster up the courage to go back to my place."

"Hey, why don't I do some redecorating for you? Make it look new, so it doesn't have as many memories."

Damn. She always reads my mind.

"That's amazing, Andi. I...I don't know what to say."

"Say nothing. Give me the keys and consider it done."

I smile. I really have missed her.

CHAPTER
TWENTY-FOUR

ON MY LAST night at Courteney's, we play board games, order takeout and get tipsy. It feels really good to do something like that, a stay-at-home fun night with people I love, who care about me. A down-homey vibe that I haven't had with Courteney in a really long time. If there's one good thing coming out of this, it's that Courteney and I are getting close again. But that's the thing about sisters. We never really lost that closeness, it was just laying dormant. I'm sure if Jared and I wound up married, we would've found a way back to this closeness, at some point.

Andi calls me once she rearranges my place and offers to go home with me.

"I can't thank you enough, Andi, you're a doll. But I need to do this alone the first time. I can't explain it."

"I get it. Just let me know if you change your mind."

I thank her again and after we hang up, I reconsider. Maybe I should have some moral support upon my first entry into the place that will hold the most memories of Jared.

But in the end, I decide to go back home alone to face it.

When I open the door, a memory of the first time Jared

walked into my apartment comes at me full force. It was after our second date, and he admired the antique end table I kept by the door for mail and keys. I shake off the memory, swallow the choking sob in my throat, and step inside.

Andi replaced the end table with an orange triangle wedge and mounted a shelf for my keys and mail. I'm not sure what she did with the antique table, but I hope she kept it for herself.

As I walk into my tiny living room, I notice the television hanging on the wall instead of standing on the wooden chest, which is now adorned with framed photos of me and Courteney when we were kids. She covered the sofa with a faux fur blanket and two oversized fluffy pillows. I also have new beige curtains. Not my color, but at least they're different.

In the kitchen, she moved the cups and dishes to different spots. Why would she do something like that? I'll have to get used to it, but I can always move them back if it gets too annoying when I'm looking for a glass.

I close my eyes and visualize having just woken up, wandering into the kitchen. I open my eyes and instinctively go to the cabinet right above the coffee machine. Inside that cabinet are wine glasses, not mugs—I find those in the cabinet above the stove, so I switch them back. It'll make my mornings easier.

Last is my bedroom, the room that will hold the most memories of Jared. Including the first time we made love. I take a deep breath, slowing my trek down the hallway and forcing myself to look inside the already-open door.

Andi did a nice job here. I have new bedding with cream-colored sheets and a comforter with roses in different shades of pink and red. The tops of my two dressers have doilies on them. The curtains in here are lace, and she hung pictures of Southwestern landscapes over the bed. It reminds me of a classy hotel room. Nondescript, yet cozy and comforting.

But it's not working like I hoped it would. When I look at the new bedding, all I can picture is me and Jared together on the plush comforter, making love and holding each other. The image is so vivid, but then it becomes blurry from the tears forming in my eyes.

With my arms crossed over my stomach, I rush out of the bedroom. In the living room, my mind pulls away the faux fur blanket on the couch, and there Jared is on the bare white sofa holding a coaster under his drink, criticizing the curtains with a grin.

And I forgot about the Clark Gable DVDs and other random things Jared left here, like the umbrella by the front door. I pick up his umbrella with the wooden U-shaped handle. My fingers trace the grooves in the wood, tiny nicks that Jared's hands had caressed while waiting for a train or taxicab. I sniff the folds of the fabric and somehow smell him inside the umbrella, a subtle hint of that mix between soap and pine needles that was distinctly Jared. My throat tightens.

My eyelids press against each other, but I hold back the tears. Maybe I'm getting better at that. Practice makes perfect. I take the umbrella and the DVDs to my bedroom closet, and shove through my clothes until I find a spot in the back.

There's a pink shoebox wedged into the corner. My face gets warm—I know what's in there. I shouldn't open it.

I pull off the lid.

Pictures of Jared and me from our early days, the ones that had been stored away and replaced with the more recent ones on display on end tables and walls. The first picture on top is the two of us dressed in red carpet garb for a Hollywood-style party. We look so young in that photo, even though it was only taken a couple of years ago. I trace his chin with my finger and a tear falls and lands on the picture.

This photo catapults me back to when we were falling in love, and he was up on that pedestal. Things were so wonderful then. I throw a blanket on top of the shoebox and run into the bathroom with more tears streaming down my face. I wash down a Benadryl with two shots of vodka and eat a microwave pizza. Sometimes food helps, especially junk food, so I've gained some weight. But that concerns me about as much as the amount of alcohol I've been drinking, which has probably aided in the weight gain. But I don't care. I'll do whatever it takes to get the type of slumber where I can stay asleep, even when the nightmares come.

I pack up the box of photos, DVDs, and things that belonged to Jared and take them down to my storage locker. That way, I'm not throwing it all away, but it's out of my apartment and out of my sight. I tuck the box far in the back of my locker and place the skis I never use in front of it.

I take the stairs back up to my apartment, and as soon as I walk out of the stairwell and into the hall, I see my door is open. I know I didn't leave it open. I remember balancing the box on my hip to close it. And I can hear the television coming from the living room. I know it wasn't on when I left the apartment. I haven't even turned it on tonight.

I don't want to go inside, but my phone is on the coffee table and I definitely want that. I should just leave the building and run to the nearest police station. I still want my phone, though.

I tiptoe inside, my eyes darting left and right. I pick up my phone from the coffee table, grab the remote, and turn off the TV. The sound of rain pelting against the windows gets louder. I catch something shiny out of the corner of my eye. Something tiny is glinting on the end table. I take a step closer. It looks like my engagement ring. Where the hell did that come from?

The air smells faintly of celery. A hand clamps over my mouth. Foul breath in my ear. And then that awful guffaw that is unmistakably Sonny. I scream, but no sound comes out. He licks my earlobe and tightens his grip around me.

CHAPTER

TWENTY-FIVE

I JOLT UP IN BED, panting like a dog.

Sonny isn't grabbing me from behind. No one is here. I'm alone in bed, and I start to steady my breathing. I've been getting better at that. But these nightmares aren't getting any better. They're getting worse. So vivid I'm having trouble getting back to a state of reality when I wake up.

The clock says I've been asleep for only three hours. The sheets are so damp with sweat, that I either have to change them—which I don't feel like doing—or lay down on the sofa. I take a pillow from the other side of the bed and plod off to the living room. The floor creaks and I sidestep the dip in the kitchen floor, which I have to cross to get to the living room.

The creaks in the floor, even though they're coming from my own feet, still send shivers down my spine. My mind can't seem to fully come out from the dream. It all felt so real, Sonny and a celery smell inside my apartment.

I throw my pillow on the sofa and double-check the deadbolt on my door. I check my closets and every dark corner, turning on lights, with Jared's umbrella in my hand for a weapon if needed.

I pace back and forth from the living room to the kitchen, double- and triple-checking every corner, feeling like I'm going in circles.

I head to the bottle of vodka waiting for me. I put one in the freezer last night, to keep the liquid ice cold. I like the way it slices down my throat.

Leaning back in the living room, I take a sip from my tumbler. A couple of gulps and my insides are buzzing. That first burst of booze hitting me does that. Especially on an empty stomach after waking up in the middle of the night.

I'm not sure when I started drinking straight vodka, but somewhere along the way, screwdrivers and Irish coffee stopped doing it for me. I like the lightness of vodka. It's a nice, clean path to the joyful numbness that I need. Getting drunk every night seems no more remarkable than getting to the gym on the weekends or going to work in the morning. Both of which drinking really aids in doing.

I feel cold all over and hug myself. I take a sip and enjoy the buzzing sensation it brings to my lips. But it's brief, and I need another sip when I slip back into the dark hollow minutes later.

Sometimes I get so angry with Jared. For driving us to the middle of nowhere to propose, just to be different. He could've proposed anywhere. A restaurant, ball game, one of the many beaches in New England, but no. He had to drive us straight into the lair of those two.

He was just trying to be romantic, it's not his fault this happened. But it's easier to be angry with him. He should've known not to surprise me with a proposal. We never even talked about marriage. We never made jokes about growing old together, never spoke about having kids, none of that. Don't couples usually talk about marriage first, before proposing? I thought they did. But maybe some guys catch us by surprise on purpose to see what our initial reaction is, to see how we truly feel.

I sort of always knew I was going to be an old maid, that minimalizing moniker given to women who choose their own lives instead of becoming wives. Marriage always terrified me, not just from seeing my parents' marriage, but other stories I've heard over the years. How someone you love can turn into someone you hate so easily. Maybe that's what happens when you spend nearly every waking hour with the same person for decades. And the way people complain about their spouses makes me wonder if some people don't show their true colors until they're married. Or they hold their significant other to an ideal, put them on a pedestal, and once the real world of everyday life settles in, that pedestal topples and they're left with a regular old human being, who has hopes and fears and makes mistakes that are simply unforgivable to the person who'd had you up on a pedestal.

I take a sip and look at the clock. It's four in the morning. I'm almost through another night, and another bottle. Sometimes it's better to stay up and wait until morning instead of falling asleep, because it's just too damn hard when I wake up. Reality creeps in during that in-between state of sleep and waking, and clobbers me all over again when I remember that Jared's gone. Waking up is one of the things I hate most about going to sleep.

I tip my glass to my lips but it's empty, so I pour more. The numbness it brings helps me so much. And I don't care that it does. If chocolate cake helped, I'd eat it all the time. Whatever gets me through each day, each night, every hour, every minute.

I wonder if this is what other people do when they lose someone. Because the days go by, nothing we can do about it. We can stay in bed and mourn for weeks, but that doesn't change life from continuing around us. We still have to eat, go to work, do laundry, pay bills, and go to the doctor—it never stops. We find our own ways of dealing with the trauma that makes the carousel stop when we lose the person we were riding the carousel with. We get off the ride while we mourn for them, but the carousel never stops. That's why it's so hard to jump back on it after it feels like your whole world has stopped.

Rain patters against the windows. Headlight beams from passing cars illuminate and sparkle against the glass. It's been raining a lot this fall. We're probably going to have a wet Christmas this year, as the forecasters are saying. I remember last year it didn't snow on Christmas but a few days after, just before New Year's. We had a snowball fight in the Common that only lasted a few minutes. It was such a carefree moment, and I start to sob but re-steady myself to keep the tears back.

The fingers of my right hand reach over, expecting the ring to be there on my left to twist around and play with—but the ring still isn't there. It's odd to get that phantom ring feeling when I only wore it for a few hours. It's as if the ring had soldered itself onto my finger and made its home there. And then, when it was removed, my finger went into a strange kind of numbness where I couldn't feel my hand, but I could feel the ring, the entire time I was strapped to the bed—and it'd never even been on my finger.

I have to deal with the Monday morning sales meeting tomorrow, and I'm not looking forward to it. Part of me wants to call out sick, but by now I'm completely out of sick time, not to mention vacation time.

I curl up on the sofa, and a chill comes over me. It feels like a cold hand is touching my cheek, then my forehead. I get these surprise chills, when there is no explanation for one coming through, no open window or door, no draft whatso-ever. I wonder if it's Jared trying to hold me. I wonder if his ghost will always be stalking me, hovering over me for the rest of my life.

Sometimes I get wisps of that feeling while I'm in bed, just before falling asleep. I can almost feel him lying beside me. Telling me we should be together. Whispering to me to join him.

Maybe I should.

I don't believe that stuff about going to hell if you commit suicide, because sometimes it's a noble act, like the monks self-immolating in protest. Or the Native American women who took their own lives to save themselves from Columbus and his men.

I could drive up to the Zakim Bridge. Run right to the edge and jump. Or I could get a gun. I've heard a gun to the head, through the mouth, is a surefire way to do it. Get my license to carry, go through the classes and background checks, for the sole purpose of using it on myself. Seems like a lot of work, but probably worth it for the foolproof method of doing it.

But sometimes, when I think about getting a gun, my thoughts shift from using it on myself to using it on someone else. Usually after having one of these nightmares about Sonny coming after me. He's someone I'd like to point a gun at, more so than myself. Is that any healthier, though? Killing him instead of myself, I'll probably end up in hell after all. But I'm already in my own personal hell anyway, so what does it matter?

Everyone gets their own personal hell. It's all for you, a personal set of problems made just for you and only you. Only you have to deal with them, nobody else. You're alone from day one, your birthday, and you're alone on your death day too. You can talk to people, friends, relatives, shrinks, it doesn't matter—you're always in this alone. Nobody is there with you inside of your mind. Nobody else is there to fight the demons in your dreams. So it's better to toughen yourself up, right? Better to be strong alone since no one is really there, anyway. People will always leave without warning.

A stronger chill passes through me. I sit up, my breathing shaky and my heart pounding. I'm shivering so badly I throw a blanket around my shoulders. It must be nearing dawn. I look for my phone to check the time and can't find it.

My laptop is on the coffee table. I open it, and a picture of a sandy beach fills the screen behind the time showing half past three A.M.

I click the "Don't like what you see?" prompt in the corner, and the picture changes to Big Ben in London. I find myself smiling. London has been on my bucket list for years. I've been to Paris, but not London, with its double-decker buses, Buckingham Palace and of course, the chimes of Big Ben.

I open up the web browser and my first instinct is to check the travel websites for deals, but instead, I search for job postings. Specifically, the ones that require travel.

My page results are pretty good. I find listings for sales, recruiting, and property management positions with some travel required. I'm so sick of my job. I'm sure eventually I'll get sick of whatever my new job might be, but it'll at least be a change. If I'm traveling for work, I'll probably just see the inside of hotels and conference rooms for business trips, but maybe on my own dime, I could do an extended stay over a weekend, and get in some sightseeing and exploring, wherever I go.

I'm starting to get that warm feeling in my gut, but it wanes as quickly as it shows up. Part of me feels so guilty whenever something makes me happy. Why do I have the right to feel happy when Jared is dead? Nothing feels right about it. The brief few seconds when I forget about it all make me feel so guilty for not letting it constantly stay in the forefront of my mind.

The open browser page on my laptop refreshes, and a new job listing appears at the top, for a "Business Travel Sales Manager" and my stomach does a little flip. I skim the job description and it sounds perfect for me. It's for a big hotel chain, requiring travel to different hotel locations to coordinate events for business conferences, train and oversee the staff, stuff like that.

Before I lose the nerve, I hit the "Apply" button and fill out the forms. Upload my resume. I cough when I hold my breath for too long, and then take in some air.

Something about this feels right. I'm getting a similar feeling I had standing on the cliff watching the waves crash against the rocks, the feeling like I was about to take a plunge —only this one is much better.

CHAPTER

TWENTY-SIX

When I wake up in the morning, the first thing that pops into my mind is the new job I applied for last night. Not Jared. This new job possibility is giving me a light at the end of the dark tunnel I've been traveling through since I woke up in the hospital bed.

While waiting for my coffee to brew, I sift through my wallet, checking to see how much cash I have left after my last visit to the liquor store. I find the card the detective gave me, Ed Rawlings. I wonder why he didn't put his full name on his business card. It just says "Ed Rawlings." Makes me think about putting "Liz Martel" on my stuff. Why bother putting your full name if you don't go by it?

Scribbled on the back is his cell number. After a few sips of coffee, I decide to give him a call to check in on the case. I'm about to hang up after several rings when he picks up.

"Rawlings here."

"Hello, Detective Rawlings? This is Liz Martel. We met—"

"Yes, Liz, of course. How are you doing?"

"Okay, hanging in there. I was wondering if you'd made any headway in your investigation of the Johnsons?"

He sighs. "Not much, unfortunately. I'm sorry. I wish I had more news for you."

I nod, even though he can't see me through the voice call. "I think I have some more information that might be helpful. Things have been coming back to me, like remembering a dream."

"Really?" I hear him shuffling papers. "What is it?"

My family history is something that needs to be discussed in person, but I don't want to go to a police station.

"I don't know if this is something we're allowed to do, but is there any way we can meet in person? To talk about it over coffee?"

He chuckles. "Of course we're allowed to meet—you're a key witness in an investigation I'm conducting. Do you have a place in mind?"

"There's a café on Newbury Street called Trident."

"The book café? I know the place. They have some great food."

"Are you free at all today?"

"Sure, I can move some things around and meet you in about an hour. How's that?"

"Perfect."

"See you then, Liz. And the coffee is on me."

I haven't been to Trident in a while but have always loved the place. They have a diner and bookshop on the main floor, and an entertainment area on the second level for events. I've been to some poetry readings and a Roaring 20s party with Jared. But most of my memories there occurred before I met him, so it's not a special place for us.

Yet the second I walk in, the memory of Jared and me dressed up like Jay Gatsby and Daisy Buchanan on New Year's Eve hits me fiercely. That was such a fun night.

I rush to the bathroom in the back and open the door before even knocking. Luckily no one was in here anyway. I lock it behind me and lean against the wall as I fall into sobs. Memories hit me harder than I'd anticipated. After a few moments, I lever myself upright and splash some water on my face. The paper towel I use to dry with is too thin, so I grab another. Then I inspect my face in the mirror—eyes still puffy and nose red. Whatever. I have a feeling the detective won't care if I'm a basket case, anyway. I'm sure he's used to that in his line of work.

When I walk out of the bathroom and into the café, and see people strewn about the shop ranging in age from college kids to elderly retirees, I'm reminded of how much I love this place. It brings people together. Between the timeless comfort of having coffee while sitting at a countertop, to the décor of being surrounded by books reminiscent of a library, this spot has been a place I've gone to whenever things are bad, like they are right now.

I see Detective Rawlings standing at the diner counter scanning the menu.

"Detect—Mr. Rawlings." I catch myself before saying, detective. I don't know if people will care there's a police detective here, but probably best to keep that to myself.

"Liz." He turns to me and extends a hand for me to shake. "Please call me Ed."

"Okay. Ed. Thanks for meeting me."

Ed gestures for me to sit at the counter. He asks for a regular coffee and the Mega Benedict, and I get a cappuccino. My appetite is non-existent still.

"I love the food here," he says and sits down on the stool next to mine. "Glad you mentioned it. I don't get to come here as often as I'd like."

"Your job must keep you pretty busy."

"Pretty busy is an understatement." He snorts and shakes

his head. "But that's because I like to give my cases one-hundred-and-ten percent of my attention."

I smile. "That's good to hear."

Our coffees arrive and I sip mine gingerly being mindful of the foam on top. I dab my upper lip with a napkin just to make sure there's nothing there.

"I was happy you called," he says. "I've wanted to make sure you were getting on okay. But I didn't want to disturb you, since I don't have any new information for you. Not yet, at least."

"I understand." I smile at him. There is something about him that makes me feel at ease. He reminds me a bit of my Uncle Jack. "So you are still investigating the Johnson family, even though they have an alibi?"

Ed looks me in the eye and leans in closer.

"Liz, between you and me, that sheriff up in Maine is covering for them. I don't know why, I don't know their history, but I don't buy that alibi. Just like I don't buy that Herschel Johnson stabbed himself in the stomach in a suicide attempt."

My heart pounds and for the first time in a while, it's in a good way.

"Really?"

He nods. "I've been suspicious of it all along. But my hands are tied—if a sheriff gives a statement that he was with them, during the time you state you were held captive, I have to accept it as their alibi, which clears them."

I'm shaking my head in disbelief even though I believe what he's saying. I'm sure this stuff happens all the time.

"However, the investigation is still ongoing—the Galbraiths also hired private investigators to find out what happened to their son. I get the feeling they don't think I'll do as good of a job, but a PI will only botch up my investigation, so I asked them to hold off until I've researched all the leads. Until we find out exactly what happened to your boyfriend, this case isn't closed."

"I still don't know myself. One minute he was sitting next to me in the Johnsons' house, the next he was gone and they were restraining me. I never saw him again."

I wipe a tear away. Ed clears his throat and sips his coffee.

"So, you said you've been remembering things that might be helpful?"

I nod. "I remember seeing something at the farmhouse when I was searching for Jared."

"Hold on a sec." He sets his mug down with a clatter and takes his phone out of his pocket, pausing with his finger hovered over the screen.

"Do you mind if I record this? I don't want to miss anything."

"No, not at all."

"Thanks." He unlocks his phone and places it on the counter between us, then hits the record button. He turns in his seat to face me. "So, what do you remember?"

I take a deep breath and tell him about the clock with the shamrocks along the edge, the same type of wooden clock my father makes and sells.

"It's entirely possible that the Johnsons simply bought one of your father's clocks at his online shop. I mean, anyone can find something from anywhere with the internet."

"I know, and I agree, but it's a strange coincidence. And with the history with my sister and Jared—"

"Wait, what history is this? Your sister had a relationship with Jared?"

"Yes, before I met him." I glance at the phone and tell him how Jared and I met, the tension that's been in my family ever since he dumped Courteney and asked me out.

He lets out a low whistle as the food arrives. He digs into his meal and devours it. I concentrate on my cappuccino, impressed by the man's ferocious appetite. It's been so hard to eat these days. But the coffee is warming me nicely.

"Sorry," Ed says in between bites. "I'm famished. But I find it very interesting that there's a history of animosity between your family and your boyfriend. That's very interesting indeed."

He turns back to his food and finishes it in a few more bites. I wonder if all detectives eat this quickly. Maybe they have to since they have so much work to do and little time to eat.

"So." Ed pushes his empty plate aside and takes a sip of his coffee to wash it all down. "Tell me—has your sister, or anyone else in your family, said or done anything recently that would lead you to believe they still carry any animosity towards Jared?"

I glance to the side. Since I hadn't spent that much time with my parents or Courteney since dating Jared, it's hard to give him a direct answer. All I can think of are the snide remarks she and my mother made at the Christmas party last year, but that was quite a while ago. And it's not like they're locking me inside of closets anymore. Just because they're capable of doing things like that doesn't mean they would still do it to their adult daughter who no longer lives under their roof.

Maybe I'm reaching here with this theory.

"Not recently, but—" I sigh as I look into Ed's eyes. He has deep brown eyes, a bit droopy and weary, but kind. "There was a tense scene when I brought him to my parents' place for Christmas last year. Courteney was there, and my mother made it clear she didn't think much of Jared, even when he dated my sister. I have to admit, though, that I'm not very close with my family. They're very controlling. I couldn't wait to get out of there when I got out of school."

"What about your sister? How's your relationship with her?"

"We're two years apart, and growing up, it was always more competitive than friendly. She was the beloved angel, and I was the troublemaker. But we enjoyed a bit of closeness after we both moved out—we used to take Sunday brunches and shopping trips back when we were both single, living in the city."

The memory makes me chuckle. I do miss those days of our early twenties, going on bad dates and talking about it over mimosas. Sometimes Andi would join us.

He takes a sip of his coffee and asks, "How about now?"

"It's been strained since I started dating Jared. She seemed fine about it at first, but after I became more serious with Jared, she and I stopped the Sunday brunch-and-shopping thing."

"That's not surprising."

"And I got a few late-night drunken phone calls from her telling me I betrayed her, and that Jared was the one who got away. I stole him from her, blah blah blah."

Ed winces. "Damn. That's rough."

"That's why I thought it was odd that she texted me out of the blue the morning we drove up to Maine for the picnic."

His face lights up. "What did she say in the text?"

"She asked if I was free that day to go out to lunch with her, something we haven't done in a long time. And every time I think back to that moment it kills me, that if I'd just made that simple choice of bailing on my date with him to go out to lunch with her. None of this would've happened."

Ed cocks an eyebrow and swigs the rest of his coffee. He motions to the server behind the counter to refill his mug.

"Tell me about your parents and upbringing. You mentioned that they were very controlling, which can be toxic, but there's a difference between toxic and overbearing. Were they helicopter parents, or something worse?"

I let out a sigh as my memory reel flashes nearly every moment of my childhood when my father flipped out and yelled, my mother trying to placate him only to have his ire redirected to her. I wonder how many times he laid his violent hands on her. The night I heard her scream about him choking her was the only one I witnessed, but I'm certain there were other instances.

"When I was fifteen, they locked me inside of a closet for dating an older boy from another school."

Ed's eyes widen as he turns toward me. "For how long?"

"Two days."

"Jesus! Did they at least feed you?"

"Yeah, my dad had built a little slot into the door, like a doggie door, that they put food and water and milk through."

"He built a slot into the door? For Chrissake. How many times did they lock you in there over the years?"

"Not many, and not for very long. It was like the last straw punishment. The worse the crime was, the more inclined they were to put me or Courteney into the closet. But with her, I only remember it happening once or twice when we were really small. Don't even recall what she did, but she wasn't in there for long. The one I remember the most was the time I was fifteen, probably because I was so much older and in there for two whole days."

Ed shakes his head and sips his coffee. He gets a little crinkle in between his eyes that reminds me a bit of Jared, only his face is wrinkled, older. He has a bit of a receding hairline that gets accentuated when he raises his eyebrows, which probably happens a lot in his line of work.

"Were they physically abusive?"

"Not outside of spanking us when we were younger. They preferred isolation forms of punishment, like grounding us by removing things from our bedrooms. Books and laptops. If we had to do schoolwork, we'd have supervised computer time. Or they would isolate us by making us feel like we weren't being a 'team player' in the family. I remember Courteney ganging up on me with them a lot growing up, telling me I was shaming the family by doing something like wearing red lipstick at school or skipping class."

"I'm hoping your family didn't do this to you and Jared, but this might hold a little water. I'm going to investigate this further. Can you tell me the name of your father's shop? I'll see if I can get a court order to see their orders over the last few months."

I nod, thanking him. And for the first time in a while, it feels like I've got someone on my side. Ed Rawlings believes me, and he is going to get to the bottom of this.

"There's something else too," I say, "another suspicion I have." He nods for me to go on. "I mean, it's entirely possible that the Johnsons randomly picked me and Jared out in the woods to terrorize us, like crazy men sometimes do, but I just have this feeling that they weren't the masterminds. My own family is one theory, that I really hope isn't true, but I do have another. Another 'enemy' so to speak."

"Who?"

I tell him about Jared's arranged marriage, and Abigail Adams. How snippy and short she's been with me in our two interactions, and what Jared had said about her family's special bodyguard operation.

"Jared did say it was just a rumor, but you never know. These bluebloods have more money than God and I wouldn't put it past them to do something like this. Especially since he seemed to scorn the entire clan by not marrying Abigail."

Ed chuckles. "I know what you mean. They don't make movies like *Taken* and *Hostel* for no reason. The ultra-rich can do pretty much anything they want, to anyone they want."

"I've seen *Taken*, the one with Liam Neeson? I didn't see the other one."

He snorts and shakes his head. "Don't. It's not for the faint-hearted. But I wouldn't be surprised to learn that those torture places exist for whoever has the money to do it."

I shudder, imagining what that movie must be about. Ed asks for the check and waves away my offer to pay.

"You just had a coffee. This one is on me. Next time we'll go somewhere fancy and then you can pay."

I stare at him, and then he grins, and I laugh. "So there will be a next time?"

"This is an ongoing investigation until we nail the bad guys. Until then, I'll keep you posted." He gets up from his chair and smiles down at me. "It's nice to talk face-to-face, so I'd be happy to meet for another bite when I have news for you. And please, if you think of anything else that may be helpful, call me any time."

"Thank you, Ed, I will. It was nice to talk to you about this."

"Like I said, I don't know why that sheriff is covering for them. It's part of the investigation. But I'm glad you gave me something else to go on, because every little piece of the puzzle will help me solve it."

With that, he winks at me, and it makes me smile.

CHAPTER
TWENTY-SEVEN

I FINALLY BREAK down and agree to see the Galbraiths. It takes two vodka sodas that morning to summon the courage to visit their huge house in Brookline. I don't want to drive, so I take the train.

When I get there, I ring the gate. Seconds later it buzzes open and I walk under the trellis. The cobblestone path that leads through the manicured lawn doesn't fill me with a sense of reminiscence like I thought it would. Jared and I didn't spend that much time at his parents' house, but we did come here on the last day we were together. I expect a rush of emotion to rise up and consume me. But it doesn't.

Yet regret still pools in my stomach, since I'd give anything to go back to that morning and leave him standing here on the walkway holding the giant picnic basket, so none of this would've happened.

With a sigh, I knock on the front door and wait. When no one answers, I turn the knob and it opens to an empty foyer. I step inside.

Where is everyone? Usually the second I walk into this

house, a butler or the housekeeper opens the door and offers to take my bag and jacket. I shift from one foot to the other, taking a moment to look around the foyer. The first thing I notice—the first thing anyone would notice upon looking around the foyer—is the shrine to Jared.

A long mahogany table covered with photos of him from infancy through adulthood. A school photo from every year, wearing the same bright smile and a pastel polo shirt. Flanking the table are tiered shelves housing items from his childhood: fencing trophies, plaques from academic decathlons, and a pair of bronzed baby shoes.

I notice there are no pictures of me and Jared together. I take a deep breath, and sweat begins to line my underarms and my chest constricts. I pull on the neckline of my shirt and clear my throat. Still, no one comes to greet me. Should I leave, or just walk around this gigantic house calling out "Hello?"

I take a step into the closest room, the library, and the housekeeper comes out from the kitchen.

"I'm so sorry!" she says while wiping her hands on her apron. "The oven was overcooking the roast."

"It's okay!" I reply. I never know how to act around people in situations such as these. Should I act sympathetic, because she has a tough job? Or should I act annoyed because she wasn't there to greet me? Both of these things fall under her job description, and as someone who's had jobs requiring me to wear many hats, I decide to feel sympathy.

She takes me to the drawing room where Katharine is sitting on a divan. She looks stylish as ever in a classic Chanel suit, but she also looks like she's aged several years, even since I saw her at the funeral.

"I'm so sorry I haven't been by to see you sooner. It's just been...rough."

Katharine grazes a finger underneath her lower lid. She keeps her eyes downcast for a moment before lifting them to make contact with mine. "I lost my son. You lost the man you loved. I think we're close in our levels of grief."

I sit down on the edge of the divan, trying to take up as little space as possible. "I think you're right."

"We were the two women who loved him the most. The women *he* loved the most." She pours tea into two tiny cups on a side table, and hands one to me. I take a burning sip, and my tongue threatens to blister right there. I place the cup on the saucer and my hands shake so badly the China clinks. I set it back down on the table.

"Jared asked for my help picking out your ring. He was so excited, and nervous about it."

Now it's my turn to brush a tear away. "He certainly did take me by surprise."

"Do you still have the ring?"

I shake my head. "I don't know what happened to it. I asked the police to keep a lookout, but they haven't found it yet."

She picks up her cup of tea and gestures for me to do the same, ignoring the fact that I'd set it down in the first place.

"We have hired private investigators to find out exactly what happened to you both. I don't believe my son was just found dead in the woods—someone killed him, and whoever is responsible for this will be brought to justice."

I take a deep breath. "The thing I want to say, most of all...is how sorry I am. I'm sorry for everything. I'm so sorry for being the reason Jared was even in that situation."

"Elizabeth, please stop blaming yourself. If there's one thing I cannot stand, it's a self-blaming victim. I see this all the time in the women's shelter...they blame themselves for what their attackers did to them."

I forgot she volunteered at shelters. I wonder if I would've done something like that as Jared's wife, as a Galbraith. If you don't have to work, it seems like a good way to spend your days. Certainly more meaningful than shopping and visiting spas.

"This one woman I met at the shelter, she said it was her fault for paying more attention to the children and not spending enough time tending to her husband, and that's why he hit her. Can you imagine that?"

Actually, I can. It sounds like something my mother would say. Hearing that sort of stuff over the years is one of the things that always soured me on the idea of marriage.

"You and Jared would've had a wonderful marriage. And you would've had beautiful children. It's such a shame."

I don't have the heart to tell her I never wanted children, or that I'd been considering calling off the engagement. When is the polite time to leave? In five minutes?

"We would love to have you over for Christmas," she says. "Are you sure you can't come? We have plenty of room, and always too much food."

"That would be lovely ...but I think we have family from out of town coming up this year, my Aunt Rose and Uncle Jack from Texas. My mom has some big thing planned."

"Well, if you have a chance to drop by, please do so."

When I look into her eyes, the icicles melt with fresh tears. It hits me hard just how much this death has affected her. I thought I had a lot of memories of Jared, but she has half a lifetime's worth.

"I want to show you something." She stands up and gestures for me to follow her, taking my hand. We go upstairs to Jared's room. Her hand is just as cold as I would expect.

Chills travel through my whole body. This is giving me the sad sense of reminiscence I've been expecting. I recall the first time Jared showed me his bedroom, and we fooled around while his parents were downstairs, just like a couple of high school kids. The memory doesn't make me feel sad, but wistful. Like the taste of a lollipop on your tongue, or the whiff of cotton candy in your nose, something that brings you back to a time long ago when things were simpler, happier. Something you wish you could live inside of forever.

Katharine opens the door to Jared's room. I'm overwhelmed by how cold it is in here. It's like a drafty cabin in the woods during a blizzard and reminds me of the feeling I sometimes get at night of an icy hand caressing me. I shiver and wrap my arms around my chest, then notice Katharine hugging herself too.

When I was downstairs looking at the shrine of Jared in the foyer, I was surprised there weren't any pictures of me with him. I thought it was because his family blamed me for what happened to him, but I'd been wrong. Jared's bedroom is filled with photos of the two of us. Every trip we'd taken, every holiday we'd spent together, and several of just me. Some of the pictures are poster-size, framed and hanging on the walls.

"I can't believe you did this."

"Elizabeth," she says. Her soft gaze reaches my own and she puts a hand on my shoulder. "Jared did this. *He* had all these photos of the two of you."

"He did?"

There are pictures here I didn't even know existed and have no idea why he never told me about them. Some I recognize, like the one of us holding hands walking through the Common. We looked so good in that picture, Jared with his blazer and cashmere scarf, and me in the red trench coat he loved. I remember when he asked another couple to take our picture under the trees, and we reciprocated by taking their photo for them. That was a great day. One of those moments kept in a time capsule buried in the corners of my memory, available to dust off and open at any time. It's the same as it's always been, sitting there waiting to be remembered, enjoyed and brought back to life again. Because it's always been real. It's always been there.

My breath catches in my throat, and I choke back a sob. I don't want to be in this room anymore, though I don't want to be rude.

"That one." Katharine points toward the wall to our right. "He always said was his favorite."

It's a picture I remember, the two of us on his friend's boat on the Charles River, one of the photos he'd blown up to poster size.

It was the Fourth of July, and the fireworks blasted behind us. His friend got a candid shot of the two of us on the deck. Jared and I were looking at each other. Our eyes were shining, and we shared that secretive smile that couples tend to have. The smile that said we were connected and living in a different world from everyone else around us.

That picture had been one of my favorites, too. We were so into each other, we didn't even notice the fireworks going off around us—we were making fireworks of our own.

I glance down and notice a hardcover book lying on the floor and a piece of paper jutting out from underneath. I can see "UPTIAL AGREEMENT" on the page. Is that a prenuptial agreement? I glance toward Katharine as she takes my hand and leads me out of the room. She closes the door.

Jared never mentioned a prenup, but he probably wouldn't have during the picnic. He'd wait to ask me to sign a prenup later on, probably while we were planning the wedding. Maybe I can sneak back to his room later to peek at it. I'm curious what the conditions would've been.

It is noticeably warmer in the hall and my lungs loosen.

Katharine asks me to stay for dinner. Preston and Lacey are coming over with the kids, and she says they'd love to see me.

And then Bradley comes home and greets me with a hug as soon as he walks through the door. It is nice to be with them. I don't know why I've been avoiding it.

"I would've liked being a part of this family," I say.

"Liz," Katharine says, calling me Liz for a change, which fills me with warmth. "You *are* a part of this family. You've been an honorary Galbraith all this time."

I'll never tell his family I was considering ending the engagement. Just like Jared never found out either. I'm glad he died thinking I was going to marry him. I probably would have, eventually. I did love him. Even with that temper of his, that was just a part of him. What made him so special, was the guy who got a giant picnic basket and swept me off my feet with a diamond ring, that's who Jared was. That's the person I loved.

I walk over to the Jared shrine in the foyer and pick up a picture of him at a dance when he was a teenager. Looks like a fall formal from the colors and setting in the background, leaves and trees, with earthy tones.

At the other end of the table, there are a couple photos of an older blonde woman. She looks vaguely familiar. There is one picture where she's wearing a bright yellow dress; the color is so vivid it almost looks neon.

There is also a plush Tweety Bird resting in her lap.

My heart begins to race and I try not to drop the photo. She looks like the woman in the portrait at the farmhouse, that I spent so much time staring at when I was tied to the bed. The blonde hair, the large build, curved chin—it's uncanny.

It's not just a similarity, it's the same woman.

I'm trying hard to keep the expression on my face neutral, but I can feel my eyes widening by the second. My hands are shaking as I put the photo back on the table, and almost knock over another one in the process.

In that photo, she's with a very young Jared holding a birthday cake. Written on the cake is:

Happy Birthday Aunt Jolene.

TWENTY-EIGHT

MY HEART FEELS like it falls to my feet and there's nothing but an empty lump in my chest. My spine ripples, and then the ripples reach the back of my neck and creep up to my face in a tingling sensation. The floor almost feels like it's moving.

There's something so strange about this. It's *too* coincidental. It feels like another piece to a puzzle I don't have an image for to help me complete it. I look around for Katharine as Preston and Lacey arrive with their toddlers.

"Liz!" Lacey says and hugs me. "It's good to see you. You look great."

"Thanks." She's just being nice. I have such dark circles under my eyes the cover-up wouldn't even mask them.

"How've you been?" Preston asks.

"Okay, I guess. You?"

He shrugs and gives a sad smile. He looks so much like Jared. "One day at a time, right?"

Lacey smiles and greets Katharine with a hug, then excuses herself. She walks over to her children climbing all over Bradley and tells them to leave their grandfather alone, but he protests that he loves it.

"Katharine," I say. "I was just admiring the photos of young Jared with his Aunt Jolene. How long has it been since she went missing?"

"Over twenty years. We searched for her for a long time. Police, private detectives, we tried everything. But when someone doesn't want to be found, you will never find them."

"You think she ran away?"

"It's possible."

"What makes you think she ran away and that she wasn't...taken?" I can hear the tremble in my voice.

"She'd made a huge withdrawal in the joint account Bradley's father set up for her, and some of her clothes were missing. I suspect she planned to take off in a show of defiance."

"Defiance?"

"From what Bradley told me, she'd had a big fight with their father. He wanted her to marry someone he'd picked out. That's fairly common in this family, you know."

Katharine looks me in the eye. Is she wondering if Jared told me about Abigail? I'm not sure, but the narrowing of her eyes as they scrutinize mine tells me she's trying to find out how much I know about something.

I turn away from Katharine's gaze. "I'm guessing she didn't want to marry the guy."

"One thing I remember about Jolene." She picks up a photo of her. "Was her laugh. It was such a unique sound, like nothing I'd ever heard before."

A wave of that maniacal laughter appears in my head, the cross between a pig oinking and a donkey braying.

Did Aunt Jolene laugh like that? I certainly can't picture it. She looked too nice to have such a horrific laugh. Ran away from home to avoid an arranged marriage only to wind up kidnapped. Maybe she traveled up to the same spot of the family reunion picnic, just to get away for a while, and encountered Herschel out hunting in the woods. She must have woken up tied to a bed just like I was. I can only assume Sonny was the result of rape.

My lips move up and down, but no words come out. I'm literally speechless. I don't know what to say to her. These poor people are grieving enough. Do I really need to add to it by telling them the man who'd kidnapped and murdered their youngest son also kidnapped and possibly murdered the aunt who's been missing for years? Herschel had said Jolene had passed away, which could mean anything. She could've had cancer or killed herself. Or *he* killed her.

I remember the dead woman in the basement. Is it possible that was her? The body was so decomposed it was hard to tell, especially in the dim light in the basement.

I try to hold back the shudder escaping through my shoulders, but it slips out anyway. Hopefully Katharine will think I'm just shaking over memories of Jared. I cover it up by making myself cry. That's not too difficult these days. And then Katharine is crying too.

All I want to do is grab a bottle of vodka from the nearest liquor store, keep it inside the paper bag while I take swigs from it on the subway, and then finish it off when I get home, hiding safely underneath my covers, where all that can hurt me are nightmares.

Bradley comes over with glasses of wine and hands one to me. He looks like he's holding back tears as he gazes down at the floor, his eyes glassy, his fist pressed against his lips. I want to tell him about Aunt Jolene, but he seems like he doesn't need another heavy blow right now. I feel so bad for these two. I take a deep breath and sip my wine.

Katharine puts her arm around me, and Bradley smiles. I can't help but feel warm all over. Maybe it's the wine, but I like to think it's something else. A sense of comfort from being among those in pain. They're hurting just as much as I am, trying to take each day at a time. Finding their own ways of dealing with the grief. I think my sister was right, we kind of need each other right now.

They bring me to the dining room and seat me across from Preston and Lacey. I notice an empty chair with food on the plate. I wonder who else is joining us.

The housekeeper walks in holding something and carries it over to the vacant chair. She turns and puts it next to the place setting. It's a framed photo of Jared.

Preston glances my way with a frown as Katharine gets up and walks over to the photograph. She places a napkin at the base of the frame, making a little bib.

"Now, now, Jared darling, we don't want you to get stains on anything."

And then she actually starts spooning peas onto the photograph. They drip down the frame and onto the napkin.

"Mom," Preston says, with a tremor in his voice. "Do you have to do that now?"

"He can't miss any meals, now, can he?" Katharine snaps at him.

Preston's face is in his hands and his shoulders are shaking, silently crying. Trying to hide his face from the world. Poor guy lost his brother, and now his mother is doing *this*. How does he get through it?

His wife doesn't seem to be any help. Lacey is busy feeding the kids, keeping her back turned, and her voice overly cheerful. That must drive Preston even crazier.

I glance over at Bradley, who picks up the table wine and fills his glass to the brim. Maybe it's just the hollowed-out grief Katharine is dealing with. I know that feeling well. Everyone has their own way of dealing with grief. Some people drown their sorrows in alcohol, some build shrines of their lost loved ones and feed photographs of them.

It's hard to watch Jared's mother spoon-feed a framed picture of him while everyone else is eating, though. Part of me wants to stand up and offer to help so she can sit down and enjoy a hot meal, but I don't want to feed a photograph. Just the thought of doing that brings me to a level in my psyche I simply don't want to visit. I'll just sit there, nibble at the food on my plate, and count the minutes until I can leave.

Stifling silence surrounds the dinner table. It's so quiet all I can hear is the sound of chewing. One of the toddlers belches, and the sound seems to bounce off the walls. The clinks of silverware sound louder than they should, as if we're in an echo chamber.

Finally, Katharine stops feeding the photograph with the napkin draped around the bottom covered in food. A collective intake of relieved breath surrounds the table, and the noises of eating and drinking are no longer magnified. We can pretend we're a normal family enjoying a normal dinner, and not a group of people trying to deal with grief over losing someone we all loved.

After dinner, while they're busy playing with the toddlers, I tiptoe upstairs to Jared's room. A draft whispers by my ankles at the bottom step, as if the ghost of a cat slipped by my feet. It gives me a start. I take a deep breath and continue forward.

The stairs seem to get lighter as I walk. I don't think about it much as I move upward until I reach the landing, keeping my eye on the bottom level in case anyone comes by.

I reach Jared's room and open the door. Cold air rushes around me and hovers over me. Slipping into the scenery of our relationship, spread out over the walls, is astounding in the silence it brings. There's not a sound inside of this room, no hum of life at all. Yet life surrounds me along the walls.

Our happiest moments, our beautiful bliss. Every special memory we shared, captured in time, in print, and papered onto the walls like proof of existence.

I see the corner of the page I'd glanced at earlier, underneath the thick hardcover book. "UPTIAL AGREEMENT" peers out at me. I crouch down and pull the paper out, holding just the barest tip of the book, to make it look as if nothing has been disturbed in here, not even a line of dust.

The words "PRENUPTIAL AGREEMENT" are printed on top of the page with a logo for an attorney's office, in huge font. Jared's name is listed below, but the name next to his isn't mine.

It's Abigail Adams.

I turn the page to check out the rest of the document and find another document paper-clipped to it. I remove the clip and look at the other set of pages—it has the same attorney's office on the letterhead, and this one says "FINANCIAL AGREEMENT". I skim through the top page, my mind barely processing the date on the top, a week before the date on the Prenuptial Agreement.

I, Jared Julius Galbraith, being of sound mind and body, do hereby relinquish all financial holdings of my inheritance to Bradley Kirk Galbraith

"Elizabeth?"

Katharine's voice comes from behind me. My heart stops beating for a second. I clutch the pages and turn around to stare at her standing in the doorway, looking like an apparition with her skin paler than ever.

"I'm sorry. I was just...coming in to look at the pictures..."

Katharine's lips are pressed together tightly, and she takes a step into the room. She reaches toward the documents I'm holding.

"These pages...fell to the floor. And I was just picking them up." I'm amazed at how well I'm able to bullshit on the spot.

She takes the legal documents from my hands. I'm feeling so weak all over that I just give in and let her have them even though I really want to read what they said.

Katharine sighs. "I didn't want you to know about this... and I don't want you to take it the wrong way." She folds the documents and tucks them under her arm. "There was someone else Jared was supposed to marry."

I tilt my head and wait for her to continue.

"You see, Liz...we wanted him to marry the Adams girl, but he said he was in love with you. You were the woman he wanted to marry."

"But why was he relinquishing his inheritance to Bradley?"

She sighs and looks down. "When we told him we'd cut him off if he married you instead, he called our bluff—said he'd give up his inheritance to be with you. He drew up these financial agreement papers relinquishing his money to Bradley."

My mouth drops open, and my bottom lip trembles. Tears brim beneath my eyelids. "I—I can't believe this," I manage to stammer out. He was going to give up all that money, just to be with me, and I'd been questioning whether I wanted to marry him. I feel like throwing up. It's such a sickening shock I feel as if I'll simply faint on the carpet in this cold room.

"He said money didn't matter as long as you had each other. Jared planned to live off the money he'd make from his law practice, like a commoner!" She scoffs and clucks her tongue.

I stare at Katharine, and take a deep breath. "Jared told me about Abigail Adams."

Katharine's eyebrows shoot upward. "He did?"

"He said the woman he was supposed to marry was a distant cousin, from your side of the family. He seemed a bit...repulsed over the thought of marrying someone he was related to."

"In our family, we traditionally marry people within our circle. And sometimes, that circle can include a distant relative."

I raise my eyebrows at her, my lips pursing.

"There is nothing wrong with that," she says. "People all over the world marry cousins and distant relatives!"

I shake my head, letting out a little laugh. "Incest is best, right?"

Katharine presses her lips together so tightly they disappear. If she'd been wearing pearls, I'm sure she'd be clutching them right now.

"I can't believe he was going to give up his inheritance," I say. "I don't know why he never told me about that."

"Perhaps he thought you would've turned him down if you knew he wasn't going to inherit the Galbraith fortune."

My eyes narrow as I stare at her—I feel the top of my nose crinkle. Did she just accuse me of being some kind of gold digger? Rage simmers beneath my skin. My face is getting warm, and I'm sure my eyes are blazing. Katharine's hands are splayed, and her bottom lip trembles. She looks at me, and I see fear in her ice-blue eyes.

Is she afraid of me?

"I was never with Jared for his money. I never thought we were going to be anything more than a long-term fling, and meanwhile, he was planning his life with me. He was going to give up everything for me."

"Liz," Katharine says. "Jared called our bluff. He had those papers drawn up when we showed him the prenuptial agreement we'd prepared. As soon as he handed us the financial agreement, we gave in, and gave him our blessing to marry the woman he loved."

"And I didn't even want to marry him."

"What?" Katharine's mouth drops open.

"I enjoyed his company, I cared for him, loved him, even, but I didn't see myself marrying him. Or anyone, for that matter."

"So you were stringing him along after all? Getting his hopes up!"

She looks like she's going to vomit. The bile coating her throat reminding her that Jared chose me over her. Not every girlfriend is in direct competition with her boyfriend's mother, but it's an age-old Freudian thing that never really goes away. You replace the woman in your man's life, and that woman is his mother.

"It wasn't like that at all. He was my boyfriend." My voice falters and I shake my head. "But I didn't deserve him. None of us did."

I take one last look around the room, at the photos of me and Jared, and walk downstairs, ignoring Katharine's calls behind me.

On my way out, I glance at the photos of Jared in the foyer. Bradley walks by as I'm heading to the front door.

"Liz, are you leaving? Would you like a ride home?"

I stare at him. The man who was cutting off his son because Jared wanted to marry me. I shake my head and narrow my eyes. Katharine will fill him in soon enough.

I slam the front door behind me as best as I can since it's quite heavy. I march down the stone path and pass beneath the trellis, a wave of cold air enveloping me. I stop and look back at the house, the last time I hope I'll see it, and let myself think of Jared. How wonderful he was. How he didn't want to follow in his family's footsteps, and how much he must have loved me. When I feel tears brimming I blink them back, turn around, and leave.

On my walk to the train, surrounded by college-age kids concerned with nothing but their classes, my phone rings. I don't recognize the number, but the mood I'm in makes me answer it right away.

"Hello?"

"Hello, may I speak with Elizabeth Martel?" a smooth, professional voice comes through.

"This is she."

"Elizabeth, hello. My name is Amy Stuart—I'm the recruiter for Accord Hotels. We received your application for the Business Travel Manager position. Do you have a few minutes to talk?"

My heart races. I should've let it go to voicemail, then I could've called her back when I was at home, and off the busy streets of Boston. I start to panic, and it hits me—I don't have to do this right now.

I take a big, deep, confident breath. "Hi Amy, thanks for the call. I'm actually about to get on the train. Mind if I call you back?"

I'm surprised and impressed with this newfound attitude. Instead of freaking out over how I'm going to get through this call, I'm choosing to end it and pick a better time for me to talk. Amy Stuart doesn't mind at all and gives me her direct dial line.

I have a feeling I'm going to get this job. And I can't wait.

CHAPTER

TWENTY-NINE

THIS ENCOMPASSING FEELING of power came over me at the Galbraith house when I faced Katharine. It almost makes me feel taller, my limbs a bit stronger, able to take on anything. It gives me even more courage to face my parents.

Not sure what I might encounter when I get there, or what I'm even looking for since I'm sure there's no journal titled "How I did it" with a full confession. I just feel this urge to go over to my childhood home, maybe even walk into the closet they'd locked me in and face it for the final time.

No matter what, I'm never coming back to this place again. If this job falls through, my plan B is to take off for parts unknown soon. I just have a few things to take care of first.

The Lyft driver pulls up to the curb, a block away from my parents' place. I step out, seeking no solace from my surroundings, but a sense of estranged comfort washes over me as I turn toward the house that holds the remnants of my childhood.

It's a special, sacred place, the home in which you were raised. It can be a house, an apartment, an alleyway, a foster home, or another temporary dwelling that is never forgotten. It's a fondness that emanates from the soul, this longing for childhood, going back to those carefree days when summers actually meant something.

Walking closer to the high, primly trimmed hedges that make up the fence full of thorns reminds me of when I was a teenager trotting and skipping home from school right at the beginning of a vacation week or summer break.

The closer I get to the front door, though, the wonderful memories of summer breaks and fun-in-the-sun feelings dissipate. I take a deep breath and stop in my tracks.

The front door is as austere as I remember, with its chunky nicked wood and three tiny diamond-shaped windows cut in a diagonal pattern at the top of the door.

The scent of oregano hits my nose as soon as I step onto the front porch. The windows are open, letting in the warm fall breeze. Memories of sitting on the sofa, listening to music, and ignoring my homework as I daydreamed about what I was going to do that summer vacation or what boy I would flirt with at school hit me full force, and I almost can't walk for a second.

Just as I reach the front door, it swings open, and there my father stands. He looks older than the last time I saw him. He has a crew cut, as always, but it's faded and graying on top. Soon he won't have much hair left to cut. It breaks my heart for a moment, until I envision his hands around my mother's throat.

"Elizabeth! Thought I saw you walking up."

"Hi, Dad." I wave, hoping I look casual as hell, even though both of us know me showing up here on a random Tuesday evening is, well, weird. Especially since I hadn't called ahead.

"Sorry we couldn't make it to the funeral. Come on in, your mother's making spaghetti with meatballs."

The sound of that makes my stomach rumble. Mom's spaghetti with meatballs was a comfort food I was never able to emulate in my cooking. My spaghetti is always too rubbery, and I can't seem to make a decent meatball to save my life.

"Thanks," I croak out, my throat closing into a knot I wasn't expecting to appear. It's just...he looks so old, and frail. He's still tall and intimidating, but not like he was when I was younger. Has he aged this much since I saw him last? Or am I just seeing the effects of age in him for the first time?

Teetering on my spot, I steady myself and walk into the house. Dad closes the door behind me and all the warmth that had consumed me moments ago vanishes. I shudder as a draft of air hits me from the open windows. I'd forgotten how much colder it always was inside of this house, even on sunny days. I sometimes would bring my homework and listen to music on my iPod on the porch, the warm sun hitting my face.

"Your mother's in the kitchen," Dad says, his voice gruff as he gestures for me to follow him. As if I don't remember the way to the kitchen in the house I grew up in. Typical of him. But I follow anyway, since I'm not here to argue about that. I'm here for closure, and to hopefully get some answers. If they are behind all of this, I've got my phone in my pocket recording everything they say.

"Judy, honey? Liz is here," Dad says. He clears his throat, coughing into his fist. Maybe he went back to smoking a pipe.

"Liz?" My mother's voice floats in from the kitchen. Soon she enters the room, wiping her hands on her apron. Just like when I was a kid. The childhood memories hit me with a force that nearly staggers me. My mother, now so much older, with gray hair and wrinkles, her hands gnarled and veiny.

"H-hi, Mom!" I try to say cheerily, even though the eeriness of it all is trying to encompass me like a blanket.

I'm here to try to prove that my parents had something to

do with my kidnapping, but standing in my childhood home, with comforting smells wafting out of the kitchen, my mother with gray hair wearing an apron and my father looking older by the second standing nearby, is absolutely killing me.

How could they have done this? It makes no sense. They were harsh on me when they were raising me—by being controlling and overbearing, telling me what to do, and who to spend my time with—only because they thought it was best for me. Very much like how Jared's parents thought arranging his marriage with Abigail was best.

And I know in my heart that they couldn't have possibly had anything to do with Herschel and Sonny Johnson abducting me and Jared.

"Liz, how are you doing?" My mother asks as she leads me into the kitchen and sits me down in a chair. They've gotten new seat cushions. Makes sense. It's been almost eight years since I've lived here.

"I'm...doing okay, considering." I ease into the chair, making myself feel at home. It's hard not to, with the décor in this kitchen. Warm wooden cabinets with soft mauve oven mitts hanging from the handles. And there's an underlying scent of cinnamon that's always been in the kitchen, ever since I was a girl. I used to wonder if my mother would boil cinnamon the way people did on real estate shows to make houses feel warm and inviting, or if there was some cinnamon-scented plug-in hidden somewhere. I've searched but never found a source. Maybe some spilled cinnamon behind a cabinet that was never cleaned up?

"You know, this apron belonged to your grandmother," she says, fingering the green vines stitched along the hem.

"Really?" Even though she's told me this about a dozen times, I still pretend it's news to me. "Amazing how it's stayed intact all these years."

"I take good care of it. Handwash it, line-dry, low-temperature iron. But it's true, they just don't make things the way they used to. Clothing falls apart so much more easily these days."

"Very true."

"I don't know if I've ever told you this, but your grandmother wasn't exactly the nicest person around. Though I don't want to speak ill of the dead."

My father stomps into the kitchen, and my knee-jerk reaction is to cower, but I stay in my seat, gripping the edges with my fingernails digging into the wood.

What's got him in such a bad mood now?

"Damn wood saw is too dull. I gotta go to the hardware store."

"Can't you go tomorrow? Your daughter is here visiting. I thought we could all have dinner together."

"I'll be back before you know it—the store's not far. I'll be in and out and when I come back we'll have a nice dinner. Is Courteney coming, too?"

I shake my head. "No, Dad, I just popped in for a visit. I wasn't planning on staying long, but the food does smell good."

"Well, maybe we can do a Sunday brunch, and I'll invite your sister and Chet over. How does that sound?"

"Great."

He turns and leaves, his hand in the air in a backhanded wave.

Mom turns back to the stove. "Maybe you'll meet someone new soon."

"It's a bit too soon right now, Mom."

She shakes her head and clucks her tongue. "I just knew that Jared was trouble from the start! The way he drove a wedge between you and your sister...no man should come between two sisters."

She does have a point, I suppose. But it's not like Jared cheated on Court with me. He did officially break up with her before asking me out.

"Maybe now you and Courteney can start getting closer again."

"We are. But you have to understand, Mom—it's just not the same now as when we were fresh out of college. She's married now. We're not two single gals living a Boston version of 'Sex and the City' only without the sex."

I chuckle, looking for a tongue-in-cheek reaction from her, but she's still staring at me in a very similar way that Katharine did.

"I don't want you and your sister to be single forever, Liz. I'm happy that she has Chet now and is settling down. I want the same thing for you, but I can't say I'm disappointed that it won't be with that awful, two-timing Jared!"

I startle at the statement—so much for not speaking ill of the dead.

"If nothing else, we can see the silver lining to come out of this whole ordeal, and that's that Jared is gone for good."

That's a horrible thing to say, even for her. I glance over at the closet, the one I'd been locked in. It was designed to be a utility closet. The door is closed, and the slot Dad built into the door to pass food through is now boarded up—but it still scares me to stare at it.

A chill washes through my body and my earlier suspicions are starting to creep back in—they hired the Johnsons to kill Jared. I need to get out of this house as quickly as possible.

Pulling out my phone so it's in my hand, ready to call for help, I see it's still on video recording everything. I stand up from the chair, staring at my mother.

"Mom," I say, and take a big breath. "I need to ask you something. It's important, and I want you to tell me the truth."

"What is it, Liz?" She turns from the stove, wiping her hands on the apron.

"Did you and Dad have something to do with my kidnapping, and Jared's death?"

She lets go of the hem and the apron falls to her thighs like a curtain. I look into her eyes. They're so dark and narrow, it makes my blood run cold and I take a step back. The back of my knees hit the seat of the chair, but I remain standing.

"You think that your father and I had something to do with Jared's death? Are you serious?"

"I'm sorry, but you're talking about how much you hated Jared and that you're *glad* he's dead. I'm just trying to figure it all out, why this happened."

"Why this happened? Are you still under the delusion that you were kidnapped by those men who have an alibi? The sheriff vouched for them, Elizabeth. I think you need psychiatric help if you're still suffering from this delusion that you were kidnapped, and not somehow responsible for Jared's accidental death in the forest."

My mouth drops open. "What did you say?"

"You certainly do have a wild imagination, Liz. You imagined that your father locked you inside of a closet when you misbehaved as a child, but that never happened."

I involuntarily back up and fall into the seat. My back is to the wall, and my mother is between me and the door.

How in the hell did I let myself get trapped inside this house again?

"That did happen, Mom. I was fifteen and you both locked me in there for two days!"

My mother chuckles, shaking her head. "You're still trying to claim that, are you? Well, it's your word against ours. Courteney's too. Because I know for a fact that she doesn't recall any of that happening, either. Only you do, Liz. Just like you're the only one who remembers being kidnapped by those poor, innocent men."

I'm shaking my head, my hands clenching into fists, and then unclenching, my palms sweaty as my nails dig into them.

"Nobody believes you, Elizabeth." She takes a step closer to me. I scrape back in the chair, my phone still in my hand, recording everything.

"Somebody does. The Boston Police Department does, and we're going to find evidence to put those men in jail for life."

"Keep telling yourself that. The more you repeat it, the truer it is, right?"

I rise from the chair and stare at her, my mother who isn't much taller than me, but still somehow holds an amount of power over me that makes my knees shake.

"You and Dad locked me in that closet." My voice shakes along with the finger I point at the door. "The slot he built into it, that you pushed food through, is still there in the door! It's just boarded up."

She rolls her eyes. "You were always so dramatic, making up these tall tales. This is an old house with all sorts of nooks and crannies. Your father didn't put that slot into the closet door, it was already there."

"Now who's making up stories? I didn't imagine Dad choking you that night when I was seventeen, either."

Her eyes flash for a second, and then she smirks. "I do hope you get the help you need, Elizabeth. I can recommend a therapist for you."

I push past her and leave the house, thanking the heavens that my father isn't around. He's a lot harder to stand up to than her. Even though I don't have to put up with them or their gaslighting anymore, it still affects me. It still hurts me.

I walk a few blocks to call a Lyft, my hands shaking as I tap the screen.

CHAPTER

THIRTY

I CALLED Ed on my way home but he was in the middle of something and said he would call me back. I'm feeling a bit better once I'm home and have some vodka in my system, but I can't seem to stop my hands from shaking even with the heat on high and wrapping myself up in blankets. I stare at the street below as the sun goes down and the streetlights come on, wishing for the hundredth time that I could see the stars from my window.

My phone dings with a reminder: my job interview for the Business Travel Manager position is at nine o'clock in the morning. I'm so shaken up and nervous, I'm going to have trouble falling asleep. My instinct is to pour another drink, but I don't want to be hungover tomorrow.

I order some takeout but can't seem to eat more than a few forkfuls of rice before my stomach winds itself into knots. After pacing up and down my place for a couple hours, I go for a walk around my neighborhood. It's starting to get chilly at night, so I bring a jacket and my earbuds and listen to music as I walk.

There aren't as many people out and about as there would've been a couple of months ago. I like walking the streets when they're nearly empty like this. You can only find that in the middle of the night, or very early in the morning. Or during a blizzard, but no one wants to be outside then.

The streets are dark in that mysterious way city streets appear, with streetlamps showing the path but much is shrouded and unclear. You can see a few feet in front of you, and the vaguest glimpses of silhouettes in windows and corners, but everything else is a mystery. Lonely late-night wanderers, people with pets to walk, nighttime joggers, and insomniacs roaming, but everyone is a mystery. Anyone is a potential threat or victim, if the thieving and nefarious minds hiding in the shadows make themselves known. Even though they are not always there, the threat is. The worry is always there when you walk the city streets alone.

On the next block, as I cross the street, I get the sensation that someone is behind me, like a late-night jogger about to come down my path. I turn around—no one is there.

I turn forward and continue walking, quickening my pace. The next block has a 24-hour convenience store that seems deserted. I glance inside but no one is behind the counter. Maybe they're on a bathroom break. I don't know how someone could stand working the overnight shift at any job. How would you meet people, keep up relationships? It would be tough, that's for sure. You'd probably have to hang out with other overnight shift workers. Maybe there's a dating app for that.

As I pass the convenience store, I get the feeling that someone is coming up behind me again. I turn, but the street is empty.

I take out my earbuds and listen. I can hear footsteps behind me. I turn around. No one is there, and the footstep sounds are gone.

Just my imagination? I move forward but keep my earbuds in my pocket. My soft-footed steps from my sneakers make for a quiet walk, especially now that I've stopped listening to music. Sirens rise and fall in the distance. Horns honk at one another. But it's so quiet where I am. Even in the cool fall weather, there are usually at least a few college students running amok. But no one is out here tonight. The streets are too deserted, too silent. An eerie feeling begins to course through my veins.

The footsteps are behind me again. I don't hesitate and break into a sprint.

I don't care if it's just in my head. I don't care if I'm running from nothing. I'm not taking chances anymore. No more hesitation. No more indecision. My choice is to survive.

My sneakers hit the pavement nice and easy like running shoes should, and I quicken my pace. Much better than running barefoot through a forest. I try to keep my energy up as my breath shortens. My heart is pounding too quickly.

If I turn the corner at the next block, I'll loop back to my apartment. I reach into my pocket for my keys and grip them between my fingers for a makeshift claw weapon. I don't look behind, but I can still hear the other footsteps pounding against the pavement.

I'm running out of breath. I'm only a couple blocks away from my building and that helps me pick up the pace. The footsteps are getting louder, closer. I don't look back.

When I see the stairs to my building I almost cry out in relief. My downstairs neighbor Lenny is sitting on the top step smoking a cigarette.

"Hey Liz, where's the fire?" he asks.

I'm so out of breath I can't speak. I reach the bottom of the stairs and look back. I see no one there, but there's a slight shift, a shadow down the alley I just passed. I double over, catching my breath.

Was someone following me? There *were* footsteps behind me. But whether they were real or not, it's hard to say these days. It could've just been my imagination, thinking someone was following me. Taunting me. Trying to drive me crazy.

"I think...that someone...was following me," I say to Lenny between gulps of air.

His eyes widen. "Damn, you okay?"

"I think so." I walk up the stairs and sit next to him. His grayish skin, wrinkled from so many years of smoking, illuminates as he takes a drag.

"Probably shouldn't be out walking this late at night."

"I just had to get some air."

"I hear that. Although when I say I want some air, what I really want is one of these." He holds up the smoldering cigarette in his hand.

"I'm glad you were here."

Lenny smiles and offers me a drag from his cigarette. I thank him and decline with a little laugh. I tried a cigarette once in college. It made me throw up.

I stay with him until he finishes his cigarette, and he walks me up to my apartment. I thank him, and once I'm safe inside, the walls start crumbling down on me.

Everything makes me jump. The shadows on the walls when a car passes by. The sound of the elevator doors opening and people walking by my front door. Worst of all the creaks from the floor above me, since that apartment is supposed to be empty.

This is such an old building. A brownstone built just after WWII. Bound to have lots of creaks from the building settling. There's the dip in the kitchen that I've gotten used to. I automatically sidestep it when I go by.

I'm too jumpy, too wired. Going for a walk was a bad idea. My insides are pulsating as the adrenaline rushes through.

And the need for a drink outweighs the need to look fresh for my interview tomorrow. I'm not going to look good with zero sleep tonight, and some vodka will at least help me get a little rest. Find a couple pockets of shut-eye that'll see me through the day, or the morning at least, until I fall back into a world where I can just relax.

In the kitchen, I take the bottle out of the freezer and a glass out of the cabinet, but then I pause. The glass hypnotizes me with its clearness, it's cleanliness. It's blank slate of nothingness...a clear glass, a see-through portal. Vodka, too, the clear liquid you can see straight through, to the other side, another world, another realm that this clear substance can lead you to.

I stare at the bottle. It's mesmerizing me, taunting me, tempting me to fall into its blank well. I tell myself to stay strong, tell myself it's not worth it. My hand stays clutched to the bottle as I stare at it longingly inside the freezer, the tiny Jack Frosts crusting on its bottom. I let go and close the freezer, then place the glass back in the cabinet.

I plod to the living room and turn on the TV. Hoping the mellow mind fuck of television will help me fall into a numbing bliss, similar to the one I'd find at the bottom of a bottle.

But of course, an old black-and-white movie is playing, just in time to remind me of Jared. We used to love watching these old movies together. It looks like *It Happened One Night*, one of our favorites. I don't have the TV on long enough to find out for sure. When I throw the remote control to the carpet, the back snaps open and the batteries fall out.

Every time I think about Jared it comes with a new pang, knowing he was going to give up all that money and stature just to be with me. Millions of dollars, a Brahmin family post, all so he could marry me. It's such a sick joke.

The tears come before the choked-up feeling in my throat shows up. I've been crying so much that I've realized the tears have different categories. The tears when a memory gets me so choked up the tears spill over my attempt to keep them in. The tears when a private, shared moment we had comes rushing in after an association out of my control, like a movie or commercial on TV. The other day I turned on the TV and the first thing that came on was an ad for JARED, the jewelry store. A shining engagement ring took up the entire screen and sent me straight to the vodka.

Just like now.

I pour some into a tumbler, a small amount that I kick back in one sip. It's not numbing me as quickly as it used to. I need more.

When the glass is empty, I pour more. And more. I bring the bottle with me to the sofa and watch the rain while I sip. It hits the window and the city lights sparkle in a blur. An ambulance passes by, reminding me that someone out there is having a tougher time than I am. It makes me feel slightly better.

The next morning, I'm standing before the revolving doors that will lead me inside the building, where on the seventh floor there is a woman named Amy Stuart waiting to interview me.

And I'm not only terrified. I'm hungover and sick to my stomach.

I've taken antacids and I'm drinking seltzer, no vodka even though it would probably help the hangover. But I'm still nauseous and nervous, and the minutes are ticking by.

Do I go upstairs and attempt a new fate? Or do I simply go back to my current job, and count the minutes until the weekends for the rest of my life? I'm sure this job will come with its own amount of drudgery, but at least with this one, I'll get to experience life in different states from time to time.

Or do I just pack a bag, close my eyes and pick out a spot on a map, and take off somewhere to start a new life?

With a deep breath and a tingle in my gut, I move through the revolving doors and take the stairs to the seventh floor.

CHAPTER

THIRTY-ONE

THE SEVENTH FLOOR of the building opens into a modern foyer with gray slate counters, slanted windows, and plush V-shaped chairs in maroon, cream, and navy. There's a misty scent of water lilies in the air, and I wonder if there's a plug-in somewhere.

I don't see a reception desk and take a few steps into the area to look around. There aren't any magazines displayed on the coffee table in front of the multi-colored chairs, and the windows are frosted over. Out of the corner of my eye, I see a tall, sleek woman with dark brown skin and a fuchsia suit breeze by, and I move to call out to her to see if she knows where I should go, but she's already gone.

With a sigh, I take a step closer to the frosted glass windows. The streets of Boston are blurry, but I catch glimpses of headlights as cars and taxis move through the haze.

"Elizabeth Martel?" A silky voice says from behind me.

I whip around, wincing at a tiny crick in my neck, and see none other than Abigail Adams standing before me.

"Uh, h-hello. I'm here for an interview."

"Really?" Abigail says. She takes a step closer to me. This time, I don't back up. "With which division?"

"Elizabeth?" A much nicer voice comes in from behind Abigail, who turns around and there's a woman about the same height as me, only a few years older.

"Yes," I say, my eyes going from her to Abigail.

"I'm Amy Stuart." Amy moves closer to me, holding out her hand with a smile. "Thanks for coming in!"

I return the smile and keep my eyes averted from Abigail —who I sense is giving us side-eye—and shake Amy's hand. "No problem at all. I'm happy to learn more about the position."

"Great! Come right this way."

She gestures for me to follow her, and I trail behind, feeling Abigail's eyes burning into my back.

Once we're safely inside the conference room with soft mesh-back chairs, a Keurig, and a purified water cooler, I look Amy in the eyes and ask who the woman in the lobby is.

"That's Miss Adams. Her father is on the board of directors here."

"Ah," I say. Great. There go my chances of ever getting this job.

She pulls out a chair at the head of the table and I pull out the one beside her. She places a notepad and pen on the table and leans forward, smiling politely. "So, tell me what brings you here. What interested you about this position?"

"I've been at my current company for several years and I love the people I work with, but feel it's time to branch out and do something a little different."

Over the next twenty minutes, we discuss my current role, the duties of the new role, and the general travel expectations which Amy says are roughly six to eight times a year.

"You'd be traveling to our different locations in Seattle,

San Diego, San Antonio, Atlanta, and Philadelphia, and of course here in Boston. Do you have family here?"

"I do, and some family in San Antonio as well."

"Oh! How lovely. Well, the time of your stays, depending on what the hotel needs, could be lengthy, so it's nice to know you have family in two of our locations."

I smile and nod. I'm practically frothing at the mouth over this job, where I could spend time in cool cities for weeks or even months at a time by the sounds of it. Live a nomadic life and get paid well for it, which sounds pretty great to me right about now. I'm hoping Abigail has no say whatsoever in who gets hired at this company, but with the way my luck has been going, I doubt that.

Amy has me wait there to meet their Human Resources Director to go over benefits and all that jazz, and I get up to make myself a coffee.

The door opens, and I turn around expecting to see Amy, but it's Abigail standing there, staring at me.

"I heard you're applying for the Business Travel Manager position." She sneers at me.

I square my shoulders and tilt my head upward, looking into her face.

"That's right. I am."

"Lots of luck, Elizabeth. Lots of luck," Abigail says with a smug, sick little smile, the kind with no joy behind it. Just a fake, plastered-on grin, her eyes crazed and tired. With that, she snickers and turns away, the door closing behind her.

CHAPTER

THIRTY-TWO

AFTER THE INTERVIEW, I buy a big bottle of cheap vodka on my way home. Abigail taunting me like that rattled me so much that I ended up blowing the rest of the interview. But she was going to stand in the way of me getting that job anyway, so I'm sure it didn't matter.

My train passes by the stop near Trident, and I pull out my phone to text Ed as I get off. He writes back immediately and says he's sorry he didn't call back last night, and he'll meet me there for a coffee in half an hour.

It's so tempting to pour some vodka into the coffee while I wait for him, but that would only work if I had a little airline bottle—this gigantic party-size bottle poking out of the paper bag would be a little too obvious.

When Ed finally arrives, he looks haggard but happy to see me. He sits and orders a coffee, and then I tell him about what happened at my parents' place and the things my mother said.

"I have a recording of it too."

"Well"—He winces and sips his coffee—"that's illegal, so I'll just pretend I didn't hear that."

"Oh. Sorry. I just thought it was a good idea. But I don't get it—don't people get put away when there is video evidence of a crime being committed? How is that not illegal to record?"

"Recording an incident in public is different than secretly recording a private conversation without the other party's knowledge. In fact, if you see a crime being committed, it's your duty to try to help or document it as a witness if it doesn't put you in danger."

"That makes sense. I didn't witness a crime, but I suspect one with them."

"I can't listen to the recording. I'm still pretending you didn't tell me that it happened." His eyes shift around the room and he takes another sip of coffee before looking at me again. "But tell me how your mother was acting."

"She seemed almost pleased that Jared was dead, which was creepy in itself. Said that I was better off without him after what he'd done to my sister and pitted us against each other. Which he didn't do. Not really."

"And you say you and your sister were closer, before him?"

I shake my head. "No, not really—I mean, we spent more time together when we were in our early twenties. But she always went from relationship to relationship and gave all her free time to whatever guy she was seeing."

"A little boy-crazy, eh?"

"Boy crazy? That sounds a little, 'old school' shall we say?" I wink at him, and he grins and finishes his coffee.

He flips his wrist over, glances at his watch and pulls out his wallet.

"Sorry, I gotta run."

"Let me get this one!" I wave his wallet away. "You just got a coffee, anyway."

"All the more reason for me to pay my share." He laughs and tosses a few dollar bills on the table.

"I'll leave that for the tip." I take out my wallet. "By the way, I wanted to mention something that might help your investigation."

"I was planning to contact you about that, Liz. I got a new warrant to search the Johnsons' farmhouse with my forensics team."

My ears perk up. "Oh yeah?"

Ed sighs. "I'm sorry to tell you this, but we found no evidence to corroborate your story. We found no dead body in the basement per your statement."

"What do you mean, no evidence? Didn't you find any, like, fibers of mine or hairs or something in the forensics search?"

"I'm sorry, Liz, but no. We found no traces of anything that matched your clothing, prints, or DNA."

"Then they must have cleaned it. Did it seem *too* clean, like covered in bleach, or something?"

"Not that I'm at liberty to tell you this, but no. It had traces of both of their fingerprints, but that's it. Nothing that matched you or your boyfrien—sorry, fiancé."

"Wait a minute, wait a minute!" I pound my fist on the counter, and the barista behind it glares at me. I lower my voice. "I peed on the bed, Ed. If there are no traces of me, then they must have gotten a brand-new mattress. Can you check on that?"

"Well...I don't know if that will change anything."

"Why can't you at least check?"

The scary thing is that my mother's voice telling me, "Nobody believes you," is grating into me. I'm starting to question my own mind. It makes me shudder and glance around the cafe, wondering if what I'm seeing before my own eyes is even real.

"Liz, calm down. I told you that I believed you, and I do. It's entirely possible the sheriff is covering for them and that he even helped them cover traces of you and Jared. But I still need more to go on to put these guys away. Please be patient. I promised I would keep you posted."

It's like I'm fifteen years old all over again and my sister and parents are ganging up on me in a lie. Something I know happened, and they're all claiming it never did.

"What was the thing you wanted to tell me?" Ed asks as he stands up from the counter.

"There was a portrait hanging in the room I was held in—Herschel's late wife wearing the same wedding dress they put me in. I think she's Jared's Aunt Jolene who went missing twenty years ago. They looked exactly alike. Herschel insinuated he had kidnapped her as well. I didn't put two and two together until I visited the Galbraiths and saw the pictures of Aunt Jolene."

"Interesting." Ed rubs his chin. "You sure it was the same woman?"

"Pretty sure. Maybe the Johnsons have some kind of vendetta against the Galbraith family?"

Ed looks off to the side and glances at his watch again. "Maybe. I do have to run. I'll keep you updated, okay?"

He pats my shoulder in what feels like a condescending manner and leaves the café. I stare after him, wondering if my theories just make me sound even crazier to him.

I *was* trapped inside that place. Just like I was locked inside of a closet when I was fifteen years old, no matter what anyone tries to make me believe.

I know the truth of what happened to me. And I need to find a way to prove it. I just need a little help from a friend to do it.

THIRTY-THREE

I CALL ANDI, who has a gun for home defense, and tell her I'm finally ready to learn how to shoot. Back when we were roommates, I had mixed feelings about keeping a gun in the apartment. It made me nervous, that it would just go off and shoot one of us, but it also made me feel safe, knowing it was there in case anyone broke in and tried to hurt us.

Turns out she has two guns now, a Beretta and a Colt Python with an ivory grip, and she offers to take me out to her friend's farm for a beginner's lesson. Thankfully it's not a celery farm, but a hay farm. I love the smell of hay.

I'm so nervous at first, just being around the guns. There's something so sinister and powerful about them, these weapons of defense and destruction, but they're also intriguing. I can see why some people are simply drawn to them, the collectors and gun enthusiasts.

"I like the one with the ivory handle," I say to Andi as she places it inside of the case. Its whitish trim matches the ivory.

Andi grins, opens the other case, and hands me the Beretta. "I like it too."

"It's heavier than I thought it would be." It feels like I'm holding a molded piece of lead.

"Hold it for a while," Andi says. "Until it feels like it belongs there."

I trace the Beretta and let my hand mold itself around it while I get used to the weight. There aren't any bullets in the chamber, and I practice pulling the trigger while aiming at the sky. The snap of the click feels sort of nice. Satisfying, in a way.

"Not sure I'm ready for you to load it yet." I take a deep breath.

It feels as if there's no going back once I fire a bullet out of this gun. Kind of like losing your virginity.

"I wasn't planning to 'til you're ready." Andi's voice is calm as ever. "Just keep practicing."

She goes over to one of the chaise lounge chairs next to the cooler she brought and pulls out a bottle of stout. She lights a cigarette, and sips and smokes while I shoot. I do a few more dry runs until I feel comfortable enough to have her load it.

Andi lines up some cans along the back fence and tells me to fire at them. I take a shot at the first can. The force of the recoil is much stronger than I expected it to be, and the sound is disorienting. I almost lose my balance when I fire, but Andi says I don't have my legs spread far enough apart. I stretch them out a bit more.

Pulling the trigger is much different once there's a bullet in the chamber. It's kind of scary. The click is heavier, more powerful. After I get my bearings, I try again. Once I'm over the first shock, it feels good to shoot. Really good. Something about that powerful click feels like putting the right piece of a heavy, steel jigsaw puzzle into place. By my seventh fire, I hit one of the cans.

There is something so soothing about holding a loaded

gun. It makes me feel powerful. In control. As if I can make anything I want to happen. It also gives me this sense that nothing bad can happen to me with the gun in my hand. Unless I want something bad to happen.

We leave the farm and head back to the city. I offer to take her out for dinner and drinks to thank her, and she wants to drop off her guns at home first. Andi still lives in the same apartment we used to share, but she doesn't have a new roommate.

"I kind of like living alone," Andi says with a smirk. "I can smoke all I want."

"I still think you should quit," I mutter, and she chuckles.

"By the way, I can go to the training class with you if you like. You'll need that certificate and three personal references when you apply for your LTC. You can use me, and probably your sister, and I have a buddy at the gun range who I could get to vouch for you."

I nod and watch her store her guns in the front closet. We walk to the Thai food place we used to order from when neither of us felt like cooking. It's one of those restaurants that looks like a dive from the outside, but the food is amazing. As soon as I walk in the delicious smells of curry and pineapple fried rice take over and comfort me.

Once we order, Andi asks me how my job is going.

I shrug. "I started looking for a new job."

"Oh yeah?"

I nod. "Had an interview the other day...but it didn't go very well."

"What happened?"

I tell her about bumping into the scary Abigail Adams in the lobby, and finding out her family is on the board of directors.

"And," I say with a sigh, "she sort of taunted me, saying 'lots of luck getting the job' in a really sarcastic way. It rattled me and made me nervous. And then I stumbled over a couple of questions after that, and when I went to shake the woman's hand at the end of the interview I slipped on the carpet and ended up accidentally touching her boob."

Andi covers her mouth, but it doesn't stop her laugh from escaping. "Sorry, Liz. I know it's not funny. But it kinda is."

I shake my head. "Maybe on a TV show that would be funny, but not when it could affect your career."

Andi nods. "You're right. I'm sorry. So what happened after that?"

"The woman, Amy Stuart, she pretended like nothing happened."

"See? There you go, you're worried about nothing."

"She's very professional." And definitely not a drunk like me.

"I bet you'll get the job. I think you're worrying too much."

"Thanks," I say. But I know I didn't get that job.

Then our drinks arrive, and our food shortly after, and we both devour it. I guess shooting cans at the farm took some energy from us both.

Andi orders a second drink, then a third with dessert, but I hold back. Better for her to get a little drunk for what I'm planning to do. When the server brings our check over, I wave away Andi's wallet when she pulls it out.

"No way, this is on me!" I hand my credit card to the server.

"Liz, you sure?"

"Of course. You did me a huge favor today. I can't thank you enough."

We leave the restaurant and I hook my arm through Andi's on the way back to our old apartment, waving at the cigarette smoke she blows through her nose.

"You sure this ain't bugging you?" Andi turns her head away on her exhale.

"Not at all. Go right ahead." Even though the smell is bothering me.

Andi stumbles as we climb up to the third floor. This building doesn't have an elevator, one of the things I always liked about it.

"How about another drink before I hit the road?"

"Sure! I got whiskey, stout, and half a bottle of wine. Help yourself. I have to pee."

Andi rushes into the bathroom. I see my chance and go into the front closet searching for the case holding the Colt Python, but I don't see it. I remember it had a whitish trim to match the ivory, but all I can see is the black case with the Beretta.

I unlock it and pull out the Beretta along with some bullets. I shove them into my purse just as I hear the toilet flush, and I rush into the kitchen. In the fridge, there's half a bottle of chardonnay, which gives me a pang thinking about Jared. I pour myself a small glass of wine and take a sip. It's pretty stale, and I purse my lips as Andi comes out of the bathroom. She goes to the fridge and pulls out a bottle of stout for herself. We clink our drinks, and she runs to the bathroom again a few minutes later. Having now broken the seal, she'll have to pee frequently the rest of the night. I pour the rest of my stale wine down the drain while she's in there.

"Thanks again, Andi," I say when she comes out of the bathroom. I've got my keys in hand, and my purse is around my shoulder. I can feel the weight of the gun.

"Are you sure you have to leave? Maybe we could have a sleepover!" She says with a laugh, her fingers twirling her dreadlocks. She looks so innocent and childlike, it makes me sad and guilty.

I shake my head. "Maybe some other time. I'll give you a call—we should have dinner again soon."

"Sure! And let me know when you want to go to the gun range for practice, once you get your LTC. You won't regret it, believe me."

A sting pricks my face. "Sure thing. Will do."

I can't believe I'm doing this. The old Liz would've never stolen her friend's property. But this is the new Liz. And I kind of like the new Liz.

When I leave Andi's place, I keep myself steady, my shoulders strong. I've got the gun tucked inside of my purse, and my will tucked inside of my soul.

THIRTY-FOUR

I'M SITTING in Chet's car with the revolver in one hand and a half-empty bottle of vodka in the other, trying to summon up liquid courage. I told him and Courteney that I just wanted to take a road trip to get out of town to clear my head, and they let me borrow the car. And now I'm here.

I don't have to do this. I can turn the key in the ignition, turn the car around, and drive home. Give Andi her gun back and maybe mention being roommates again. Our night out was sort of fun, reminded me of the carefree times when we were younger. That's what I should do. But I'm sitting here in my car fondling her gun instead. Just like I did when she first taught me how to use it. Only I'm more familiar with it now. It's like a lover I've grown to know well, all his nooks and crannies and special spots.

I remember the first time Jared and I made love. It was a bit awkward at first, as it is with most first times. Then we got the groove of one another and couldn't stop enjoying each other.

My breath catches in my throat as memory tears surface. I close my eyes and let them fall as I stare through the window. The sky is growing dark, exposing the stars. Dozens of them, so many stars and constellations visible up here, and blurred through my tears. I trace the gun in my hand. I wonder why weapons are always so phallic. Knives. Baseball bats. Guns. Probably because men invented them.

My lips are getting numb. My head feels both light and heavy. The darkness takes over and breathes into my skin, the sacred temple of my soul, and festers until it numbs me. A blackness, a blankness in my being takes over until some form of light lets itself in and I stumble into it, take the reins, and come out of the darkness, for a while at least. But that's not the case right now.

I turn the Beretta around so the barrel faces me. It looks so ominous from this angle. No wonder people freeze when they have a gun aimed at them.

I could pull the trigger and it would all be over. No more nightmares, no more looking over my shoulder, worried someone's about to grab me. It seems so simple. But instead, I turn the gun to point away from me and look back out the window.

Toward the celery farmhouse down the road.

Ed said they'd found no evidence. No fibers or traces of either me or Jared being held captive here. No proof of the kidnapping, nothing that will put the two of them behind bars.

But maybe I can find something, some piece of evidence to put these two in jail forever. Or at least take the pictures of Jolene and get them nailed for that kidnapping, if not mine.

I'm wearing a black burkini and black leather gloves, while drinking and playing with the gun. Stalling because I'm nervous. The vodka is helping me gain courage. I go back to fingering the gun.

I wonder how this will look to Sonny when I aim it at his face. Will he cower? Will it take him by surprise? Will I have the guts to shoot him? Or will he just overpower me and take the gun because he's three times my size?

He could take the gun away and then use it on me. Which means I have to shoot him as soon as I see him, without hesitating. Shoot him like a hitman would, without breaking a sweat, and walk away. Be as cool as the steel in my hand. Can I do that?

The absurdity of it all hits me, and I almost laugh—it comes out as a cough instead.

It's all just so surreal. How am I even here? Who would've thought last summer that by the fall I'd be a widowed fiancé holding a gun, dressed like a cat burglar, about to break into a house to find evidence of my own kidnapping? This messed-up reckoning brought me here. This place in eternity, the hell I escaped and keep finding my way back to.

And now I'm here. At the same house I'd been captive in, only this time I'm free. I am in charge. I will call the shots this time around. The real shots from the gun in my hand.

Anger creeps in as I picture Sonny. His fat, bulging face and slouchy eyes. Chortling out that horrific cackle of his. I take a deep breath through my nose. Exhale through my mouth.

I have to do this. I'm sick of not being able to sleep. Sick of the nightmares. Seeing Sonny's face nearly every time I shut my eyes. Hearing that grating laugh.

I take another sip. The tingling thrill running through my nerves gives me courage, along with a hint of the numbness that will envelop me later. I'm teetering close to that line. I need the right amount of alcohol to hit me at just the right time, and then I can go through with this. But if I drink too much, I'll get too drunk to do anything but pass out. It's a fine line to walk.

I want another sip but make myself cap it. Any more and I won't be able to concentrate. Sitting back, I take some deep breaths while I stare at the stars and let the blanket of confidence wash over me the way only liquor can. I start to feel invincible enough to do something so stupid I'd never even fathom it sober.

But that's what I came here to do.

A weight sits in the air as I step out of the car. It grows denser with each step I take. The bright moonlight shines down on the grass and trees in a silvery glaze. It's quiet, no crickets around anymore. It's cold out but I can't feel it. The gloves are helping and so is the vodka. And somehow the gun makes me feel warm. It's probably the adrenaline. My heart is pounding so hard it feels like my whole body is vibrating. But that could be from the vodka too.

An owl hoots. The trees around me are like an oasis with the bright moonlight behind them, illuminating the ground. Patches of fog hovering, making shawls for the tree limbs. I keep my gun aimed ahead and move closer to the farmhouse.

My feet whisper into the grass, and I keep my movements as calm and silent as I can. My eyes settle into the blunt darkness surrounding me. The surreal quality of the night envelops me, like a silver blanket flowing out from the trees. Keeping myself grounded in the reality of what is before me, I put one foot in front of the other. I wet my upper lip and keep my fingers steady near the trigger.

The pickup truck looks like it's in the same spot it was in before. The last time Jared and I held hands was in the back of that truck. He'd traced the engagement ring on my finger and it seared my mind with a sacred moment. I'm expecting a lump in my throat over that memory, but nothing comes.

I make it to the fence, and the celery scarecrow isn't there. Up ahead, dim light shines onto the porch, streaming in from the kitchen. I hold the gun at my side and keep my eyes on the porch, which is dark, but empty. I don't see the hound, but he's probably close by. I should've brought dog treats, or a steak to keep him quiet.

I reach the porch and recall these stairs are creaky. And on the first step, sure enough, it creaks. How am I going to get inside without anyone hearing me?

As if it were listening to me, the wind picks up and makes the tree limbs sway and creak. I step onto the porch amidst the creaks of the trees and duck down. Thought I saw a shadow. A gust of wind passes through and makes me shiver.

Am I really going to do this?

Taking a deep breath, I keep my finger steady near the trigger as I reach the door. It's unlocked and I step inside to the kitchen.

Flashes of Herschel lying on the floor, a puddle of blood growing bigger around him hovers over me. I close my eyes and shake the image away. Take a deep breath.

I shouldn't have kept my eyes closed for so long. I keep the gun held ready at chest level as I move out of the kitchen. Maybe the vodka was a bad idea. It's almost making these flashes harder to deal with.

Faint buzzing and voices sound from the back of the house—the electronic echoing of a television. I tiptoe closer to the TV sounds, leading me to the den. I remember seeing an old-fashioned TV set when I was searching the house for Jared, the kind with the big back that juts out.

The semi-circle of light from the screen highlights an overstuffed armchair, with no one sitting in it. The program playing is some old detective show. The room is empty and I'm getting the strangest feeling that this is some sort of trap.

I go over to the closet. Sounds of a car crash come from the TV. I yank open the door, keeping the gun steady.

Nothing but coats and sweaters hanging inside. Boxes on the floor. The floorboard creaks behind me. I turn around, but no one is there. I don't loosen my grip on the gun. I just lower it a bit. When I find myself sucking in air, I realize I've been holding my breath and remind myself to breathe.

I move down the hallway until I'm in front of the staircase. I don't want to go upstairs yet, so I keep searching the first level instead. Where did I see that first picture of Jolene on the wall, holding Tweety? I thought it was near the stairs, but I see nothing. There was definitely a portrait hanging in the room I was in, though it will be a bit bulky to carry out of there and back to the car for the evidence. I could just snap a picture of it with my phone instead.

I want to find something, anything that will prove I was here, Jared too—best thing to do is trace my steps of the rooms we were in. First place I remember being after the kitchen was the bathroom. Maybe I left my ring in there after washing my hands?

Steadying the gun in front of me, I creep toward the bathroom. The door is ajar and the light is on. I tiptoe toward it and tap the door open, the gun aimed and ready.

It's empty. Not even soap or shampoo inside. The shower curtain is still missing, and I look around the floor by the toilet and sink—nothing.

That leaves the pantry and the dining room. I brace myself, keeping the gun steady. I try to control my breathing while I get closer to the dining room. The sound of my heart pounding echoes in my eardrums.

I open the door to the dining room and several flies buzz by my head. I swat at them with the gun, pinch my nose, and peer inside. My senses feel heightened yet dulled, as I try to dim the horrid scents wafting into me from this room.

The half-eaten dinner plate that already had flies buzzing around it back when I was escaping this place, is still there. Now an entire army of bugs swarms around the rotting meat, and the stench inside the room is so overwhelming I can feel vomit creeping up my esophagus. Not nearly as bad as the stench of a corpse, but close. It makes me wonder if there is another corpse in here, and I scope out the room, but only see the chairs.

I move on to the pantry, hoping to find something like a torn piece of lace from the wedding dress in the dumbwaiter, but nothing like that is to be found.

And I'm finding it really eerie that neither Sonny nor Herschel, or even the dog, are here. I should've heard the dog by now. Or smelled him, at least. If they went somewhere why is the truck still here?

I don't want to go upstairs or down to the basement—it puts me in a vulnerable position defense-wise. Plus I'm not sure what I'd find down in the basement aside from a trap.

I aim the gun at the wall and clench my jaw while I decide where to look next. I take a deep breath and go to the stairs. The first step creaks when I put my foot down. I hesitate before hitting the next step, though at least that one doesn't creak.

But the next one does. I bite my lip and keep walking up the stairs. A loud creak comes from above. I aim the gun at the top of the stairs. No movement. But it's so dark up there, it's too hard to tell. I take another breath and trot up the rest of the stairs. I reach the top step and face a dark hallway with rows of closed doors.

When I ran away from the room, I didn't pay much attention to the other doors in the upper section of this house. I just made it to the stairs and fell down half of them.

None of this looks familiar to me. I'm not even sure which room I was in—maybe the second or third door to my right?

I keep the gun steady and blink as little as possible. There is a dim light ahead, shining under the third door on the right. I creep toward it, and as I pass the second door, I get a whiff of celery. There's a faint sound of a dog whimpering, but then it's gone, and I wonder if it's just the wind.

The closer I get toward the dim light under the door, the scent of celery comes back stronger. So strong I'm having trouble breathing through it. I have to suppress a cough.

I reach the door, turn the knob, and nudge it open. Back up and hold my breath. Go back to holding the gun with both hands and kick the door open. I keep the gun held in front so it's the first thing entering the room, and peek around the barrel.

A jar candle flickers on the bedside table. What's lying on the bed makes me blink a couple of times. I'm half-expecting it to sit up and lunge at me. But I'm pretty sure it can't move.

Dozens of stalks tied together with twine making gangly limbs and a long torso. Dressed in loafers, short pants, and a white shirt. The head is a pumpkin with triangle eyes and a nose, a mouth carved into a crooked smile. On its head is a brown hairy wig that looks like a dead animal. I don't know if this is supposed to be a giant celery scarecrow, or something else. I'm nauseous just from looking at it. I want to shoot it, but I only have six bullets.

Wrapped around a bundle of stalks is a watch. I move into the room to peer closer.

It's Jared's watch.

Is this celery man supposed to be Jared? What is this, some kind of effigy? I breathe through my mouth while I walk closer to it. The carved-out eyes follow me, watching me. There can't be a person hiding inside this thing—especially Sonny or his father, they're both too big. Still, I point the gun at it, keeping my eyes on the pumpkin head.

With my other hand, I pull out my phone and snap a couple photos of the thing wearing Jared's watch, then reach down to take it.

I tug at the watch. It won't budge. I keep checking the

pumpkin head while my hand holding the gun shakes. You'd think removing a watch from a stalk of celery would be an easy thing to do. I'll have to put down the gun and use both hands.

I place the gun on the bedside table and keep my eyes on the pumpkin head. I unstrap Jared's watch, but it still won't come off the stalks—it's tied to them with twine. I open the drawer of the bedside table, hoping for a pair of scissors, or a Swiss army knife.

The pumpkin head moves. I grab the gun and aim it at the pumpkin. Is it in the same spot it was in before? It looks like it. But I could've sworn it moved. Maybe I'm just seeing things. My mind teaming up with the vodka, playing tricks on me.

I keep the gun aimed at it as I search the drawer for something to cut the twine. I find a small pair of sewing scissors under a rag. But when I place the twine between the scissors and squeeze the handles, the dull blades slide right off. With a wince, I put the gun back down and hold the twine with my other hand. A couple more tries and I finally cut it, and free the watch. Now this thing is just a scarecrow made of vegetables. No longer an effigy of Jared. And evidence for me to take to the police.

Keeping my eyes on the scarecrow, I send the picture of the scarecrow wearing the watch to Ed, with a text that I found Jared's watch at the Johnson farmhouse. I don't know if that's enough evidence to put them in jail, but it's something. Proof that we were held captive here.

I strap the watch around my wrist, take my gun, and leave the room. I'm not sure where to look next, so I pick the next door on my left and open it the same way I did before. This room is much darker than the last. I feel around the wall and find a light switch, then snap it up. Lying on the bed is another celery-pumpkin scarecrow.

There's something almost ritualistic about this. Are they part of some cult? The scarecrow tied to the fence had yellow corn husks for hair, and I think it was supposed to be me. Like a voodoo doll or something.

I check the celery-pumpkin thing for my engagement ring, but it's not there. I open the bedside table drawer—it's empty.

I flinch when a dog starts barking. It's muffled but nearby, coming from outside. And the window is behind the thing on the bed.

There can't be a person inside the pumpkin, but this one also seems to stare at me as I walk. I move around it to get to the window, keeping the gun aimed at it, and peer out.

It's so dark outside. The dog is still barking, but I can't see it from here. Sounds like it's coming from the back of the house.

A creak sounds behind me. I turn with the gun aimed and ready. Slight shadow of movement, but nothing is there. No Sonny, and no life-sized celery scarecrows standing in the doorway.

I take one more look at the thing on the bed and leave the room. Peek into the next room, and it's the same room I was trapped in—the red, white, and blue pinwheel is still thumbtacked to the wall in the same spot. The bronzed baby shoes I knocked over are back on the shelf.

But the bed is gone. My suspicion that they got rid of the pee-stained mattress is justified. The portrait of Jolene wearing the wedding dress, the one I'd stared at when I was strapped to the bed, is also missing. There's a miscolored rectangle shape in the wall where it had hung. I snap a picture of that, at least.

The barking gets louder. As I leave the room, the smell of wet dog hair wafts into my nose, then is replaced by an all-too-familiar celery scent. I make my way down the stairs to the kitchen with my gun aimed ready, and the dog is there, wagging his tail. He trots toward me and whimpers.

How did he get into the house? I glance over to the door, and it's wide open.

The hairs on my arms stand on end.

A shiver passes through my shoulders at a scarily familiar sound. A laugh that's a cross between a pig oinking and a donkey braying.

THIRTY-FIVE

SONNY STEPS INTO THE KITCHEN, holding a gun much larger than mine. He is chortling out that horrific cackle, the only sound that ever seems to come out of him.

I aim my gun at him, glaring at his face while my knees shake. "Where's your daddy? Figured he'd show his ugly head when I got here."

He just looks at me and grins. The hound whimpers and goes over to Sonny, burrowing his nose between his shins. Sonny reaches down with one hand and pets the dog.

With his hand holding the gun, he aims it at me, laughing.

I duck, crouching behind the table. From beneath it and between two chairs, I aim for his kneecap and fire.

The laughter stops.

His heavy frame hits the floor.

Standing, I keep the gun aimed at him as I inch closer. His round face shines on the floor. His eyes are closed and his mouth is open. He's not moving. He doesn't look like he's breathing. I nudge his leg—still no movement.

Also no blood. Shouldn't there be blood forming around

his leg, pooling on the floor? It's hard to see clearly in this dim light. I move in a bit closer.

The barest shift of movement flashes. Sonny reaches out and grabs my ankle.

He pulls me down. The gun falls out of my hand and skids across the floor.

"No!"

I kick Sonny and my foot lands somewhere soft and fat. Kick again and aim lower this time. He lets out a squeal that sounds like just the pig part of his laugh.

The moonlight filtering in through the windows shines enough to show me the gun, a few feet to my right. I scrape across the floor on my elbows. The second I touch it, Sonny is on top of me, straddling my back.

The weight of him is such a dense heaviness it knocks the wind out of me. I stretch my arms as far as I can but I'm only grazing the tip of the barrel.

His hands cover my eyes. They're so big and meaty that they cover my nose, too. The tip of his pinky is on my upper lip. I open my mouth and clamp down on his finger.

The rancid taste of his flesh almost makes me let go, but I don't—I bite down harder. Until I taste blood. He squeals and shifts his weight off me enough that I can breathe better. I spit, take in a lungful of air, and stretch my arm to reach the gun.

I've got the barrel in my grip. I swing it back and the butt of the gun hits his head. Not hard enough to knock him out, but enough to make him slide off me.

My hands are steady as I turn the gun around so the grip is in my grasp.

There's a slight shuffling noise, and then it's quiet. All I can hear is the hound barking. It's like Sonny disappeared. I can't even smell him nearby.

"Show yourself or I'll shoot your dog!" My voice is getting hoarse.

I pull myself up and move forward, waiting for Sonny's meaty, bleeding paw to reach out and grab me. I listen to my own heavy breathing.

The sound of tires crunching on gravel and a flash of high-beam headlights make an arc through the room. The dog barks and trots out through the open door to the porch.

My heart pounds—someone is here. What if it's the police? Maybe Ed got my text and showed up to save me. And then my pulse races like crazy.

I creep over to the door to see who's coming up the drive-way. The black burkini helps me blend into the darkness. My eyes adjust as I peer through the slat in the door. The car pulling up the driveway is a silver Mercedes. The Mercedes stops. The person who steps out of the car is tall and lanky, like Jared. And then he turns around.

It's Bradley Galbraith.

THIRTY-SIX

MY EYES WIDEN as I stare at Jared's father. The moonlight shining behind him heightens the highlights of whitish gray in his hair. His shoulders hunch over, and he appears to walk with a slight limp. He looks even older than he did when I last saw him. A version of Jared so much older, that I barely recognize him.

"Sonny!" he shouts. "Herschel! Where are you?"

What the hell is he doing here, alone? Why isn't he here with a set of cops or lawyers or something?

And then I notice the gun in his hand. My heart stops pounding for a second and a sprout of warmth grows in my gut. A sharp intake of breath as it hits me—did he come up here to kill Sonny and Herschel for killing Jared? Did the private investigators they hired prove what they did?

"Herschel! We need to talk." He's shouting as if he's an older brother or an uncle or something—it's too familiar. Something's not right. The warm sprout in my gut expands and grows denser.

The dog trots toward him, and he shoos him away. My heart starts pounding so hard I can feel it in my throat. My head is spinning and I'm wishing I didn't drink half a bottle of vodka in the last hour. Thoughts swim in a muddy memory pool and it's taking me too long to connect them and form an answer to what the hell is going on here.

Sonny's hulking mass steps around from behind the house. How did he get outside so fast? This place must have lots of back doors.

Bradley turns toward him, pointing his gun at Sonny, who's wringing his hands. What happened to his gun?

I pull out my phone and start recording. I have a feeling it might be worth showing Ed. It's a private conversation, and I am on private property, but I'm potentially about to witness a crime. I keep my phone steady.

Bradley takes a step closer to Sonny. "That detective—Robbins is his name? Came by the house today asking me and Katharine all sorts of questions about your mother."

The portrait of Jolene in the wedding dress flashes in my mind like a strobe light. A slow, sinking realization is on the tips of tumbling over.

Bradley raises the gun and aims it higher. "You messed up, Sonny. You and your idiot father. Where is he, anyway?"

Sonny backs up, still wringing his hands. Shaking his head.

"You were supposed to kill *her*, not my son!"

CHAPTER

THIRTY-SEVEN

THE HOUND RUNS over to Sonny and howls. A chill passes through me and meets up with the blood running cold in my veins. It makes me shiver so hard my teeth nearly chatter and I clamp a hand over my mouth.

The world is shrinking as these words balloon up around me, enveloping me, making me want to float away. I feel the urge to let out a howl myself as Bradley's words echo in my ears.

You were supposed to kill her, *not my son.*

My mouth drops open. A few drops of spit fly out on my exhale. My tongue feels too thick, too heavy. The realities are not catching up to my brain. The readiness of my typical brain is just not there. But I'm sobering up quickly as my mind reels with bits of information clicking into place like a gory jigsaw puzzle, complete with monogrammed linen napkins and an old wedding dress covered in blood.

My heart falls to my stomach. All the anger I felt toward Herschel and Sonny Johnson becomes magnified, turning into the shape of a cone, the point aimed at Bradley Galbraith.

Slowly, my breathing catches up and my stomach flips.

Those iron butterflies are back and chipping away at my insides with their heavy wings.

"Well, well, well," Herschel's voice says from nearby. "Look who's here to visit us, Sonny-boy! It's your Uncle Bradley."

Herschel steps out from behind a tree. He sticks out his belly Teddy Roosevelt-style, his hands clasped behind his back as he walks. It looks like he's holding something behind him. Something long.

"Why did you have to kill my son? Why? Was it payback? Revenge or something?"

"I told you before, it was an accident! We was gonna return him to you just a little bruised and beat up. But he tried to escape! He attacked Sonny here. We had no choice."

"Then why didn't you call me? Why involve that damn sheriff?"

"For starters, I don't trust you. Why didn't you tell your own son that we were hired by you? Why didn't you let him in on it?"

"You think he would have gone along with kidnapping his girlfriend? He would've left me and the family for good if he knew what we did."

And that's exactly what Jared should have done. Taken as much money as he could, packed a bag and left that crazy family forever.

I'm compelled to stumble backward but fight to keep the camera steady. Bradley set this all up—from the beginning. For all I know Katharine was in on it too. Possibly even the Adams family since they wanted Abigail to marry Jared. These blueblood families are certifiably insane.

"We did what we thought was best, Brad," Herschel says. "Because as I said, I don't trust you. I knew you wouldn't come through with your end of the bargain. Just like last time."

"Listen, Herschel," Bradley says. I notice that he doesn't lower his gun. "For the last time, that was my father's decision! I had nothing to do with it."

"Right. Yet somehow, you end up with the family fortune, and I'm left here with nothing but a goddamn celery farm and nothing to show for it."

"What do you want from me? My hands were tied. And I would have paid you, had you done the job you were hired to do. Jesus, Herschel, you killed my son! You were supposed to kill the girl!"

"I told you, it was an accident. He fell. Now, I'm gonna kindly ask that you step off my property."

Herschel's arms come around and reveal the long object he was carrying behind his back. A double-barreled shotgun. Herschel aims it at Bradley, which looks a lot more ominous than Bradley's handgun.

"Now don't go doin' something stupid there."

"You killed my son!" Bradley screams, and I see glistening on his cheeks. He's crying. "I should just kill you both right now!"

Herschel lets out a heartless chuckle. "You think that's bad? How about letting your own kin rot to her death with no money to support her? You think losing your son is bad compared to that? Sonny-boy lost his mother! I lost my wife! You at least have another son, and grandchildren!"

"It's not my fault she died, Herschel!"

"You left her to die like a dog in the street, you piece of shit! She'd bore the son of a family heir, who got jack squat of the fortune! The least your father could've done was let her live in comfort, even if he wanted to forget his own daughter and grandson existed!"

Sonny cries out, blubbering and whimpering. Bradley gestures toward Sonny with his gun.

"Shut him up!" Bradley shouts. "Get rid of him! He's making me nervous!"

"What you say to me you can say in front of my Sonny-boy, too." Herschel sneers at Bradley, and then nods at Sonny.

"You got an allowance from us, every month. Thousands of dollars, I don't know why you're complaining about that."

"Thousands of dollars? That's chump change compared to what the Gailbraith family is worth. You cheated all of us because you wanted nothing to do with us."

I don't know what to do besides keep recording. This could go very badly, or I could get out of this easily. Maybe they'll all shoot each other and I'll never have to worry about Sonny coming after me.

"That's why I was paying you so much to get rid of Liz, to make up for it! Why did you have to kill my son? Why?" Bradley wails. "You were supposed to kill her! That whore!"

That snaps me back as if he slapped me. *Whore.* He's a murderer!

I was never after his son's money. I just liked the fancy restaurants and the fun trips and good sex. That's all. I wasn't even planning on spending the rest of my life with him. And it looks like my instincts were spot on about not wanting to join this family. The more I learn about these two families, the closer aligned they seem to be in not only morals, but lack of sanity and reason.

Bradley waves his gun between the two of them. Neither Herschel nor Sonny duck or even flinch.

Herschel takes a step backward and gestures to his son to get behind him. Bradley is a loose cannon right now. I've never seen this side of him before. The side that hired this man to abduct his son and his girlfriend on their engagement picnic, at the very spot he picked out. After shunning his sister and nephew all these years. Jolene never went missing. They knew exactly where she was—they just wanted nothing to do with her. Then they had her declared dead and no one cared when she actually died.

Herschel centers the shotgun on his target.

"You and your ilk never cared about people like me. You didn't even care about your sister enough to take care of her."

"Shut up. You didn't know her at all."

"I knew her better than you. I was married to her. I heard the stories of the way you people treated her."

"She was an embarrassment to our family. And *you*? You and your son were a mistake we should've erased a long time ago."

"Fuck you!"

The tone in Herschel's voice and the steps he takes closer to Bradley with his shotgun ready make me think it's about to happen.

My pulse races and I shut my eyes for a moment, trying to pretend this is just a dream. I look around, but it's too dark. So much darkness that my soul can't quite escape from it, like a piece of me will be trapped here on this celery farm for eternity. Maybe a piece of Jared is tucked away here too. Both of our souls connecting, shining through a small glimmer among the horror of what happened here.

Is this where Jared really died? Or did they kill him here and toss his body off that cliff in the forest? I wonder if I'll ever know.

Or perhaps they took him there, bound and gagged, just like I was on the stained mattress, then killed him and tossed him into the woods. I suppose anything in the surrealness of this is possible. I'm sitting here filming my dead boyfriend's father basically confessing to setting up the entire kidnapping. What sort of world does this occur in? Not one I want to live in anymore.

"You and your entire family," Herschel says, "*our* family, owes me. The amount of money your son was set to inherit is plenty to go around. I didn't even ask for what is rightfully mine and Sonny's fair share, and you should be grateful for that!"

"Grateful? Are you serious? You killed my son! You're a demon from hell!"

Bradley takes a step forward, and the gun in his hand is much steadier than it had been moments ago. I take a chance and step out onto the porch to get a better angle. One foot in, one foot out.

"I suggest you take a step back there, before you make a mistake and get yourself killed."

Sonny whimpers from behind him. The dog trots over to them, barking softly and panting.

"Stay behind me, Sonny boy."

"Don't do anything stupid, Herschel."

"You either, Brad. I know you're dumber than your daddy, but I don't think you wanna die tonight, do you?"

Looking from Herschel to Bradley, my hands are sweating so much the phone slips, but I don't drop it. I have this steely feeling this is about to end in a bloody shootout.

"You won't kill me, Herschel."

"The hell I won't." Herschel doesn't move.

"You want too much from me." Bradley's arm stops shaking, and he takes a step closer.

"But I don't need anything from you."

I jump back and nearly drop the phone at the loud firing of a gun.

THIRTY-EIGHT

I peek out the door. Herschel is on the ground. Sonny is running into the darkness of the woods, the dog at his heels.

My phone is still in my hand, though now slack at my side. It jolts up as though my hand has a mind of its own, returning to filming. I hope I caught the shooting.

Bradley trots after Sonny, and then I hear him curse at the trees. He probably lost sight of him already.

Does he know someone else is here? Chet's shiny car I'm sure looks too out of place down the road. But it's not like there's a municipal parking lot nearby.

The sound of a gunshot bursts through the night, and I cover my ears.

And drop the phone.

It clatters to the porch. Just a mere blip of a sound after the gun he fired. But Bradley turns around and looks at the porch. And me.

I duck, snatching up my phone, and move backward over the threshold and inside the kitchen. Bradley aims his gun, and I stop moving. But I'm thinking about the gun in the back of my waistband. The gun he can't see from his angle.

"Let's not drag this out, all right? I'm not going to hurt you."

Says the man who just killed the man he'd hired to kill *me*.

Bradley is getting closer to the porch. I can hear his feet crunching in the grass. I keep still. Quiet. My eyes barely blink as I peek around the door, watching his every move as best I can.

"You weren't supposed to see that," Bradley continues. "I'll pay whatever you want to keep quiet."

I'm sure you will, Bradley.

"It's what we should've done in the first place," he says in a lower voice.

Bradley takes another step. His shoulders heave and he's looking at the ground. I press myself against the wall. Out of sight from the door's opening, out of the line of moonlight. He aims the gun at the door. My heart pounds and my breath comes in short, quick gasps.

He has a glimmer of that look Jared had, a violent darkness surrounding his eyes. This is just like that, only multiplied by a thousand. I've never had anyone look at me quite like that before, and I know within my soul, this man is going to kill me.

My bowels loosen and my jaw clenches. I keep still as I try to scope out where to go, how to escape from this new hell forming around me.

I don't want to get too far from the door and wind up trapped in this house again. But there must be another door somewhere—where are all those secret doors that Sonny slinks in and out through?

"They killed my son! It's because of *you* that Jared is dead!"

It's everyone else's fault but his own, apparently. He spits on the last word. He coughs and spits again. I can see the anger firing off his eyes, bright sparks flying outward that are really drops of sweat. Or tears.

And then he shoots.

I duck and crouch, then run through the kitchen. Splintering sounds of the bullet hitting something on the porch that thankfully isn't me.

Bradley screams Jared's name in a primal way that sends a shudder down my spine. Any second now he'll burst through the door. I grip the gun and steady myself as I look for a place to hide. He's still screaming that it's my fault his son is dead. But none of this was my fault. Everything I've done since I was kidnapped has been a perfectly valid reaction to how I was wronged.

I jump into the pantry and press myself against the wall. The dumbwaiter would tuck me away, but I'm not getting inside that death-vator again. I can run out once he starts looking for me.

Bradley's feet stomp through the first floor. Maybe he won't even come inside the pantry. Maybe he left the keys in his car, and I can take off in the Mercedes. Go straight to see Ed and show him the video.

To check to see if the recording came out clearly, I pull out my phone and start playing the video. I can see both Bradley and Herschel, Sonny behind him, even in the moonlight. I skip ahead to see where the picture gets jumbled and bumpy when I nearly dropped the phone.

The door to the pantry creaks open.

I tuck my phone away and hold up my gun, aiming it at Bradley. I can barely make out his silhouette in the dim moonlight streaming in and keep my arms steady, resting my aim on what should be the middle of his chest.

"Don't move!" I shout.

His arms seem to lower, just an inch or two, but he's still holding his gun.

I take a step closer with my teeth bared. "Drop it!"

He stops moving but doesn't drop his gun. I cock mine back to show him I'm serious.

"I really should just kill you, Bradley."

He shakes his head. I aim the gun higher and take a step closer to him. It seems to scare him enough to finally drop his gun.

"Keep your hands where I can see them!"

His arms move upward, but then he hesitates.

He hangs his head and his shoulder silhouette shakes. I take a deep breath and the barest step closer to him.

"I hope you'll shed some light on this for me. Especially since I have a gun aimed at you and can call Detective Rawlings with a voice command on my phone."

"And tell him what?" He glares at me and shrugs. "That you came up here snooping around doing God knows what? That's called breaking and entering, Elizabeth."

"I didn't shoot anybody."

"Your word against mine. And I think my word carries more clout with the police department than yours does."

I take a minuscule step closer to him and tighten my grip on the gun.

"I'm game to find out whether that's true. Because I have the entire thing on video. You said they were supposed to kill me. Not Jared. What the hell does that mean, Bradley?"

He shuffles but doesn't lower his hands. I keep the gun aimed at him. I don't know how long I can hold him off. He's like a wild dog.

I shake my head. "You set up my kidnapping. Just to get me out of Jared's life. You sick son of a bitch. Did you set up your sister's kidnapping, too?"

Bradley takes a step forward. The distance between us is getting smaller. Scarier.

"Put your hands up where I can see them." I gesture with my gun toward his hands. He obeys, albeit slowly.

"We paid Herschel to keep her away from our family. After she died, he wanted more money. I should've shot him then."

Bradley's voice cracks on the last word.

"We just...wanted what was best for our son."

"Which included killing his girlfriend. That makes a lot of sense."

"We thought..." he pauses, coughs, and takes a deep breath. "About offering you money. But Katharine said you would've gone straight to Jared about it, and that we would've lost our son. He threatened to run away with you if we didn't give him our blessing."

My eyes well up with fresh tears. Bradley seems to make a slight movement, but his hands are still in my sight. I could just shoot him, and take off for parts unknown, like I was planning to before. But that doesn't seem like the right thing to do now. Was it ever?

It's my soul that's on trial here. My integrity to keep intact. I came up here to find a way to prove they kidnapped me and put them in jail. Keep Sonny from coming after me. And now I have this to contend with. This knowledge I didn't want. Truths coming into light that I almost wish had stayed in the dark.

Bradley takes a step closer. I raise my gun higher, aiming at his head.

"Stay still, Bradley."

He takes another step and I almost fire. My hand tilts to the left and Bradley flinches.

"I told you to stay still."

"I don't know what else to do, Liz." His voice is wet with tears. "I can't stop wondering how the hell I got here."

He starts to cry. Soon the sixty-year-old man is bawling like a baby.

Sirens sound in the distance. Could be an ambulance or cops on their way. Somebody could've called the police after hearing the gunshots.

Bradley groans. "I just want my son back!"

His voice cracks toward the end, and I can hear him slobbering with tears and a choking sound comes out. The sound of sirens grows louder, like a club-style steady beat complete with the flashing lights.

As much as I'd love to shoot Bradley Galbraith in the face right now, what I want is justice. I want to see the Galbraiths behind bars.

I lower my gun.

Then he lunges for me. I leap out of his reach and tuck into a ball, rolling away. He falls to the floor, and I run out through the door.

The sound of sirens is magnified as the blue and red flashing lights stream up the driveway toward the house and tires crunch on the gravel.

I tuck Andi's gun into my waistband and cover it with the smock of the burkini. I raise my arms above my head and face the police.

CHAPTER

THIRTY-NINE

THE POLICE CAR pulling up the driveway isn't a typical squad car. It's one of those dark, unmarked SUVs they use to catch speed demons on the road.

And the person stepping out of the car isn't a plainclothes cop—it's Ed Rawlings.

"Liz!" He lowers his weapon. "I got your text. What the hell are you doing here?"

"It's...not what it looks like," I say, even though it's probably exactly what it looks like. I'm dressed in black from head to toe wearing leather gloves. I'm certainly not here to sell Girl Scout Cookies.

"I-I came up here to..." I trail off. "Look for my ring." That sounds so lame. "And...find evidence to prove what they did."

Ed tilts his head as he looks at me. Don't I look suspicious enough with my outfit and being here, at this farmhouse where I was held captive? He'll probably arrest me anyway when he searches me and finds the stolen gun. I *am* trespassing.

"You shouldn't have done that, Liz. And there was no

need to. The sheriff just confessed to aiding the Johnsons in covering up your kidnapping, and now I'm here to arrest Herschel and Sonny."

I point at Herschel's body on the ground. "Bradley Galbraith shot him. And Sonny ran into the woods."

Ed rushes over to Herschel and radios for backup. He leans down and presses his fingers to his neck. Ed speaks into his radio, stating one of the suspects has run into the woods, and asks for more backup.

"I have it on video, along with Bradley confessing to setting this whole thing up."

"Where's Bradley?" he asks me.

I make a slight turn and nod at the house. "He's inside."

"Step back, Liz."

He moves closer to the porch. I move aside, keeping my arms stiff at my sides.

"Bradley Galbraith? This is Detective Rawlings. Have you had time to decide whether you knew Herschel Johnson before the abduction of Elizabeth Martel and your son?"

Bradley must be sweating bullets. It's probably killing him knowing his money can't save him now.

Ed takes a step forward. "I'm going to open this door. And I want you to come out with your hands up!"

He keeps his gun aimed at the door. I can hear sirens in the background, getting louder.

"Backup is almost here," Ed whispers to me.

Seconds later, several sets of flashing blue and red lights surround us as squad cars pull up the driveway. Ed directs them to pull up beside his car, and when the men and women in blue rush out, he gestures for them to surround the house.

"We've got you surrounded Bradley," Ed shouts. "Come out with your hands up—there's no other way out."

Ed inches toward the door and pulls it open. The other

cops keep their guns aimed at the entrance. Bradley doesn't come out.

"Come out with your hands up, or we're coming in after you!"

Still nothing from inside. No movement. Ed gestures at two of the cops and they huddle. I keep my eyes on the door. It's hard to see inside—

The sound of a single gunshot bursts from the house.

Ed and his backup trot over to the door, their guns aimed and ready. One cop shines their flashlight inside. I rush up behind them and peer in to see.

Bradley shot himself in the head. The cop with the flashlight rushes over and presses his fingers to Bradley's neck.

"He's dead," the cop says.

CHAPTER

FORTY

IT'S AN UNSEASONABLY warm day in November when I head outside. I'm meeting Ed at the precinct—he said he has a few things to talk about and didn't want to meet at the café. I hope he's not about to arrest me for trespassing at the farmhouse.

I run into Lenny on the front steps, smoking his morning cigarette. He tells me that the building is apparently going co-op soon.

"I can't afford to buy," he says with a short laugh. "How 'bout you? Think you'll be moving out?"

"I'm not sure. Maybe."

Jared always liked my apartment. He said it was comfy and cozy, which means small, but I could tell he was comfortable. I wonder if he would've helped me buy the apartment. Since he was going to relinquish his inheritance, we probably would've lived here together.

Courteney thinks I'll eventually start dating again, but I'm not interested in finding a new boyfriend, let alone getting married one day. I never wanted to get married before this whole ordeal anyway. Why would I want to now? She says I'm being too pessimistic, but she has no idea what it's like to have lost someone like this or go through the hell I just went through with the Galbraith family.

They arrested Katharine, her bodyguard, and one of the lawyers from the firm. The video I shot at the farm helped with the conviction. I was worried about Jared's brother Preston, but thankfully he wasn't complicit in any way. He had an alibi for every situation and was absolved of all wrong-doing, aside from having to deal with his parents having arranged for their youngest son's girlfriend to be kidnapped and murdered.

My parents apologized for not believing me about the kidnapping but are still insisting I fabricated the closet ordeal when I was fifteen. Courteney claims she doesn't remember it, keeping a rift between us, but it was nice to be vindicated over the kidnapping ordeal.

I confessed to Andi about stealing her gun. She was pretty upset and gave me a stern lecture about how much trouble she'd be in if I had used it on anyone. She softened a bit when I told her everything and showed her the video with Bradley's admission.

When I get to the precinct, Ed comes out to meet me.

"Liz, thanks for coming in. We found your ring."

"Where was it?"

"On the body of a woman we found near the farm. I believe it's the same woman you'd seen in the basement. You had suspected they hid her before we searched the house, and I think you were right. The medical examiner could tell from the rigor mortis, that the body had been moved."

I nod as my stomach churns.

"At first the coroner assumed it was her ring, but then we examined the inscription. J + E, just like you described."

"Who was she?"

"Jolene Galbraith, Bradley's sister. She's been missing for

over twenty years. She came up in the Missing Person database. You were right about the connection."

"How did she die?"

"She'd been diagnosed with pancreatic cancer just a few months ago, but the cause of death was a gunshot wound. We're not sure if it was self-inflicted."

I like to think Jolene found her own way of escaping the crazy family she was stuck with. Took her life into her own hands, literally. But I have a feeling Herschel shot her. Since I was her replacement for their "farm wife".

I try to contain my shudder as Ed hands me a sealed envelope. I open it, and my ring is inside with a little blue tag tied to it. I put it in my purse.

"I bet it's worth a lot," Ed says. "Jared had good taste."

I smile. He looks me in the eye.

"Thank you."

We stand there awkwardly for a few seconds, while he looks at me with an expectant smile.

I clear my throat and ask, "Did you find Sonny Johnson?"

"No, not yet. But we have an APB out on him, wanted lists and a warrant. We'll find him eventually."

That doesn't exactly sound comforting. I'm not sure how resourceful Sonny is, if he'll be able to find out where I live or even get down to the Boston area, but just knowing he's still out there is going to keep me up at night.

I need to get out of this state. Out of New England.

"What happens next?" I ask.

"You'll have to check with the lawyers on that. But I do know Katharine Galbraith has been asking to see you. Do you feel up for it?"

My pulse races. Do I want to see Katharine?

Part of me does. Part of me wants to see her in those shackles, cowering under my stare. But part of me wants to just put it all behind me.

"I'm not sure." I breathe deeply. "Do you think it's a good idea?"

"Up to you, Liz. If you're worried about safety, she'll be in cuffs and there will be guards nearby. You don't have to worry in that respect."

I nod.

"But if you simply don't feel comfortable, you don't have to."

"Okay."

I look off to the side and feel Ed's eyes on me. There's definitely a little something between us, but I don't know if this is going to go anywhere. He's got to be at least fifteen years older than me and married to his job.

Besides, I'm not ready to see anyone yet. Maybe I never will be.

I give him a tight-lipped smile. "Thank you, Ed. For everything. I think I will pay a visit to Katharine."

He arranges for someone to escort me to the holding center, and although I can feel the detective's eyes on me as I walk away, I don't look back.

THE POLICE ESCORT takes me to the visiting area, and I'm picturing the sort of stuff I've seen in movies, a Plexiglass partition and grimy telephones to speak into. But they show me to a room that looks like a high school cafeteria, with tables and benches lined against walls.

Katharine is already sitting at a table in the corner, wearing an orange jumpsuit that looks terrible on her. Part of me gets a sick little pleasure knowing she won't be wearing Louis Vuitton for a long, long time.

Two guards flank her table, and I walk toward her, feeling almost as intimidated as I used to when walking into the Galbraith mansion.

"Hello, Elizabeth," she drawls. "It's lovely to have you visit me. So sorry I can't offer you tea and crumpets."

I sit down opposite her at the table and keep my hands on top of it. Katharine does the same, although her hands are in cuffs. Restrained, just like I'd been in the farmhouse.

"I heard you wanted to see me."

"Your friend Detective Rawlings has a soft spot for you,

but I'm sure you're aware of that by now. I suspect a lot of men get that way around you."

"Why did you want to see me, Katharine?"

"My, my, are you direct, dear Liz! Gone is the timid little mouse I met for the first time two years ago." She smirks at me.

I roll my eyes at her. "Being kidnapped and restrained against your will can change a person."

Katharine chuckles. She throws her head back and her entire body shakes. I shift in my seat. I wonder if she was related to Sonny, and not just through her husband.

"I wanted to take one last look at you," she says. "I wanted to see what my youngest son was giving up his inheritance for. Gave up his *life* for."

My eyes narrow. "Gave up his life? It's because of you that he was killed."

Her head snaps upright. "It's because of *you*. You were supposed to be killed, not Jared. I suspect you flirted with the Johnsons so you could escape. And that's why they decided to kill Jared, so they could keep you as a sex slave."

My eyes widen and my mouth drops open. "That's ridiculous. I never flirted with those two, that's disgusting."

"Please, I know your type. You flirt without even realizing it, women like you. I saw how you got your hooks into my son. I saw what you did to him. He was a perfect gentleman, ready to become one of the finest men in the world. But then he met you. And you brought out a seedy side of him that tempted him into giving up everything that mattered to him."

"You don't know what you're talking about. Jared loved me. And clearly more than the money since he was relinquishing his inheritance."

"Right, Liz. Keep telling yourself that. Lust isn't love, my dear. And Jared knew we were never going to cut him off, he was calling our bluff with that financial statement you saw."

"I know you never liked me, Katharine. I never cared because I knew it only mattered what Jared thought. But I had no idea you hated me so much that you'd have me abducted. Same thing you did to Jared's aunt."

"Jolene was an embarrassment to the family. She was a drunk, and addicted to painkillers. Every party we had she got wasted and embarrassed us all. At one wedding she got on the dance floor and pulled up her skirt, and she wasn't wearing underwear! We wanted nothing to do with her. Any inheritance she received would be flushed away in drugs and alcohol, so we did what we thought was best for the family."

Katharine merely blinks, and the barest corner of her mouth turns up in a crooked smile. It's the only reaction I see from her. It makes me wonder, who was the true mastermind behind this whole thing. Bradley, or Katharine?

I feel sick to my stomach and just want to go home. "Can I leave now?"

"Why Liz, I'm the one in prison—I hardly think *you're* being detained."

And then she smiles at me, in that horror movie manner where someone smiles maniacally just before they're about to kill you. It sends chills down my spine and through the rest of my body. I stand up and head toward the door. I can still feel her eyes on me, boring into the back of my head.

Just before I reach the door, I turn back and glance her way.

"Keep looking over your shoulder, Liz," she drawls. "You never know who's coming up behind you...they never did find Sonny Johnson, now, did they? He's still at large."

Her words cover me like a sheet of icy sleet splashed up from a driver hitting a puddle and soaking me. And then she begins to laugh. The maniacal cackle grates into my ears just like Sonny's laughter. Now I have two horrible sounds to hear in the back of my mind for the rest of my life.

I rush out through the door, my heart pounding.

FORTY-TWO

KATHARINE'S WORDS scared the hell out of me. Is she going to hire someone to finish the job? I could tell Ed, but he'll probably want to put me in the Witness Protection Program or something, and I can only imagine how much that would suck. They'll put me in a midwestern state nowhere near a major city, with nothing but pan pizzas, salad bars, and a multiplex. I'd rather relocate myself, preferably somewhere warm, with lots of food and culture.

Maybe I should start packing some things into my travel bag and check the websites for deals out of the country. Amsterdam. Morocco. Some place where they'll never look for me, and I can be invisible. Live the life of a renegade, a nomad.

I walk past a bar that looks pretty lively. It's on the corner where the road forks. I stop and look inside. There's a tall, nice-looking man with dark hair standing near the bay window that overlooks the street. He reminds me a bit of Jared. He sees me and smiles, and waves at me to come in. The corner of my mouth goes up in a half-smile. I'm more interested in the thought of having a drink than meeting the guy in the window, though. I stand at the fork, looking from the bar to the road.

A piece of me died along with Jared and left an open cave inside of me that I fear will never be filled. I can either try to fill that cave by drinking, or by replacing him with another man. Should I do the healthy thing and move on to a new relationship? Or should I do the healthy thing by not going in, and not having a drink?

My skirt blows in the mild breeze that softens the sun's heat. It's a beautiful day. The inside of the bar looks so inviting, as if I can just dive right in.

But I turn away from the bar. There's a little forlorn look on the tall guy's face, but it doesn't faze me. The Florence Nightingale effect must be wearing off.

I glance to my right and see one of the rare travel agencies that are still around and feel a hint of butterflies in my stomach. The good kind. I take a few steps closer to the window and see pictures of Brazil, Montreal, Paris, and Tokyo. My heart starts to pound.

If there's one thing that hasn't changed, it's my urge to travel, visit as many places as possible, and find the city I want to truly live in.

Running away sounds like a better option, at least for now. I can go wherever I want. I can be somewhere that holds no memories of Jared. No memories of this life at all. Make a fresh start, somewhere far away. I could change my name, my hair color, and lie about my age.

And Sonny will never find me.

Maybe now is my chance to visit all the places I want to see. Delve into a nomadic life of travel, never staying in the same place long enough to develop roots. If I have ties to no one, I can't get hurt, right?

My phone vibrates—I've got a new voicemail. I didn't even hear it ring. I look at the screen and see I have a missed call from Accord Hotels. My heart skips a beat as I put the phone to my ear to hear the message.

"Hi, Liz? It's Amy Stuart, with Accord Hotels. We're interested in hiring you for the Business Travel Manager position. There are a couple more people for you to meet for second interviews, but it's more of a formality. Please call me when you get this, and we'll go over the details."

They want to hire me? After I completely blew that interview? I can't believe it. I call her back and she picks up on the first ring.

"Amy? Hi, it's Liz Martel. I just got your message."

"Liz, hi! There is just one thing I forgot to mention in the voicemail. They want to know if you're willing to relocate. The position changed a bit from what we originally posted on the job board."

"Relocate? To where?"

"San Diego. That's where our largest hotel in the chain is located, and you'll get the training done out there. And there is still of course travel involved, you'll just be headquartered in California. There will be a bonus for relocating out of state and an increase in pay due to the cost of living out there. They'll also pay for your rent for the first month and all moving expenses. Are you still interested in the position?"

San Diego? I've heard it's beautiful. And it's about as far away from Boston as I can get while remaining in the United States.

My heart is pounding while I take a deep breath, close my eyes, and tell myself whatever I blurt out right now will be my decision.

"Yes."

I thank Amy and she says she'll get back to me with dates for my formality interviews. We hang up, and I feel a fresh set of tears brimming underneath my eyelids, but I hold them back. This is one of those scary moments, like the first time I rode a roller coaster. Or when I stood on the edge of the cliff in the woods in Maine wearing Jolene's old wedding dress.

Only this time, the jump I'm planning to take is so much better.

Katharine's voice drifts into my head. *Keep looking over your shoulder — you never know who's coming up behind you.*

A chill passes through, and the back of my neck prickles. I turn around, half-expecting Sonny or a hitman to grab me—and the street behind me isn't empty, but no one is coming up behind to attack me.

Not now, at least.

No matter what path I take, Jared's ghost will always be stalking me, hovering over my shoulder for the rest of my life. I can move somewhere far from here, but he'll still be there.

San Diego is far enough away for me to not be worried for a while. Maybe I'll have to keep moving. And keep looking over my shoulder. But at least I'll be traveling.

It's what I've always wanted to do.

About the Author

Jenna Moquin grew up on the outskirts of Boston, and attended Massachusetts College of Liberal Arts where she studied creative writing and literature. Her short stories and poetry have appeared in *The Literary Hatchet, Asylum Ink, Heater, 34 Orchard, PARABNORMAL Magazine,* and *Wicked Sick*. In 2016, she released a collection of dark tales, *Safe: New and Selected Stories*. In 2021, she compiled a charity anthology featuring 1980s-themed horror stories by members of the New England Horror Writers. She is a proud aunt to 6 nieces and nephews, and currently resides in Las Vegas with her Devil's Ivy plants while working on her latest story.

www.jennamoquin.com

 x.com/JennaMoquin

 instagram.com/jennamoquin

 amazon.com/stores/Jenna-Moquin/author

facebook.com/JennaMoquinAuthor

ACKNOWLEDGMENTS

Many thanks to the wonderful folks at Liquid Mind Publishing for their hard work and dedication. Much love and gratitude to my good friend and critique partner Lily, and the great minds at the Porter Square Writers Group. Greg, Shannon, Kenneth, Ken M, Sara, Beth, Jodi, Maura and Miguel, this book became better with every workshop.

Most of all I want to thank my best friend Sara, who not only believed in me but showed me how possible it is to achieve your dreams if you just keep trying.

Made in the USA
Middletown, DE
17 March 2024

51649556R00163